THE SISTERS WHO WERE PROMISED

KAYLA COSENTINO

For Shanna, Nikolina, and Michael—
No matter where life takes us, we will always find our way back to
each other. This story is for you.

PROLOGUE

ALL THAT WAS LEFT was for the sisters to ascend. The fourth sister had been born. The elementals had been completed. Fire. Water. Air. Earth. But when the Oracle laid eyes on the fourth babe, only two hours old, she saw the prophecy—the future of these young sisters. *Four shall emerge, but only one will rise.* The mother shook her head viciously, blonde locks swaying as she clutched the pink-faced babe to her breast. Tears began to spill out of her crystal eyes as she looked at her husband. The man's knuckles had gone white as he clutched them at his side.

"There has to be another way," the father demanded, stepping toward the Oracle.

She shook her head. "They will all die if not separated." She gave no room for argument. "They must never be together again."

"But they were our blessings. Their power would restore the kingdom to greatness once again," he said, "You said it yourself."

The Oracle's gaze drifted to the babe once again, meeting her emerald eyes. "It changed."

Rage began to bubble up from the father, but he reigned it in. The Oracle could not be disobeyed. Their ancestors had learned that the hard way nearly a century ago.

The mother silently sobbed as she held her newborn babe to her chest. "Bring my girls to me. One last time. Just so they can meet their sister."

He went to move, but the Oracle raised a shriveled hand, "Do not. From this moment forward, they must not come into contact."

In another part of the castle, the room where the heirs to the kingdom of Linnosa often spent their time was quiet and comfortable. Walls of white stone, rows of books, and a plush carpeted floor evoked comfort, accented by a myriad of toys that were strewn about meant for all kinds of play.

A fire burned in a large hearth at the back of the room, illuminating the room in a haze of warmth. Everything appeared normal that night as the young princesses waited to hear about their mother and new sister. Only the occasional roll of thunder off in the distance broke the illusion of safety for the little girls within.

The three sisters sat on the fluffy white rug, playing with their magic as they waited for their new sister. Energy was high as the girls giggled and fire, water, and air weaved in between them. The oldest, only nine years old with ruby red hair and eyes of pure gold, flicked her fingers, and two crowns of flames adorned her sisters' heads. They burned as bright as real flame, but neither heat nor burns reached the tiny heads. In response, the youngest of the three, at four years old, sent a whoosh of air through her other sister's blue-black hair, ruffling it into her face. Her silver head tipped back in laughter as her sister sent an answering handful of water into her face.

The door of the room slammed open, the golden doorknob denting the ornate wallpaper. The oldest sister hopped to her feet, a wall of flames appearing, shielding her sisters behind her. Their father staggered in, red-faced and panting. "Girls get dressed. You are all going on a trip."

The youngest clapped her hands. "Where are we going, Daddy?"

He refused to look at her as he responded, "Don't worry about it, Aella." He then addressed the oldest, "Get them ready, Cyra."

Two guards in navy and gold came through the door, flanking their father. Cyra's flames continued to burn bright as her golden stare pinned her father. "Where is the baby? Where is Mommy?"

At the mention of their mother, the middle sister's sapphire eyes filled with tears. "I want Mommy now!"

Cyra walked through her flames to clutch her sister. "I've got you, Rhe." Rheanna pushed her blue-black locks out of her face, lone strands clutching her tear-stained cheeks. Her small hand trembled as it pulled the still-smiling Aella behind their older sister. Their father ripped his hand through his dark hair as he sighed. "Please. Do not fight me right now, Cyra." Something in the exhaustion of his voice, his plea, made Cyra drop the wall of fire.

Their father knelt in front of his daughter as if he would embrace her but instead snapped iron cuffs around her small wrists. She jerked back, crying out. Her father shook his head and breathed, "I'm sorry."

Cyra flared her arms as wetness flowed freely down her cheeks as the cuffs stifled her magic. She attempted to conjure flame, but the iron seared her wrists. "Take it off. Daddy, please. Take it off." As if the two younger sisters fed off Cyra's fear, they began to cry and run toward their older sister.

"Grab the other two," their father commanded.

The two soldiers hesitated as the young girls attempted to wield their water and air.

"That is a direct order from your king," his voice boomed, springing the two soldiers into action, each grabbing a squirming girl. Their magic lashed out by splashing and whipping the men, but they held true.

"Let go of them!" Cyra pleaded through sobs. The king placed his hands on his oldest daughter's shoulders and shook her violently.

"Look at me." Her gaze flicked up to meet her father's ocean-blue eyes to find they were frozen and cold, something she had never witnessed before. "You have to be strong now. You are not weak. You are not broken. Do not act like it."

One of the younger girls whimpered, but Cyra did not break eye contact with her father. "Until we meet again," he murmured as he turned on his heel to leave the room. "Prepare them for their journeys."

Silent tears marked Cyra's freckled cheeks as the soldiers placed Rheanna and Aella beside her, their small arms wrapping around her. The girls held each other until they were ripped apart for the first and last time.

CHAPTER 1

THE SEARING HEAT SETTLED within the Eye of the Storm Inn as customers came in and out, mostly travelers who had to stop in to try and cool off from the southern climate. Eye of the Storm was the only inn within fifty miles along the trail to the capital, Reddel of Linnosa in the West. The trek to Reddel was a grueling one, but many fled to its borders as it promised freedom and safety. There was only one path as a large body of water sat in the middle of the continent. Nowhere was truly safe as magical creatures from ancient prophecies emerged, born from the darkness that only deepened after magic was lost a century ago.

One of the creatures was working busily, going from table to table to serve the travelers, a smile fixed upon her tan face. Sweat beaded along her back, slipping down her brown worn dress. She wiped her clammy palms along her apron as she twirled away from a table full of particularly irritating men whose gazes pinned on her breasts then on her backside as she made her way to the bar.

"Yer better cover yerself up, Cyra. Yer don't want those men following yer," Ron said, concern flaring in his brown eyes. No matter how many times she assured him she could handle herself, he felt the need to assert himself when it came to her safety. She often wondered if her father would have been the same, overprotective and caring as she grew into her woman's form. At twenty-three, she surely had filled out, and the men seemed to notice, but Cyra had always been captivating regardless of her curves.

Despite Ron's warnings, she simply smiled at him, her dimples on full display. "Don't you worry about me now. If anything, you should worry about me stripping instead of covering up."

She winked at him as Ron stuttered, "Nah don't be getting any ideas. The heat is no excuse to not be covered. Look at the other ladies in here." He gestured his arm around the inn to emphasize his point.

Cyra followed his movement, and she had to admit she was the least dressed woman within the inn, but just looking at their long sleeves and covered chests made Cyra melt. Two measly straps of fabric held up her old, no-frills dress, which offered just enough coverage to barely meet the modest standards of Linnosa, where fashion was restrictive and concealing. Ladies did not dress as Cyra did, but she learned a long time ago that she was no lady.

She shook her head at the old man, but a smile laid upon her full lips as she sashayed away, swaying her hips from side to side when a conversation captured her attention. Two travelers, wraps concealing their faces, only the sunburned tops of their cheeks and eyes visible, sat in the far corner of the inn, hunched close to one another.

A female voice spoke quickly. "Gallant was attacked again by a monster they say."

The man huffed. "And of course the royals have done nothing. Just like when Rouland was sacked last week."

Gallant and Rouland were small southern cities that bordered the Black Lake. Cyra had heard whispered rumors of the monster attacks at the border cities and the unrest it caused within the capital, Reddel, and in turn, with the royal family.

"What can they do? Be honest with yourself," the woman chastised.

The man slammed his fists against the wooden table, causing Cyra to flinch as she pretended to clean the table next to theirs. "Add more guards. Use those princesses of theirs and their magic."

Cyra's cheeks grew red at the mention of the princesses.

"The only one that has been seen in over ten years is the youngest, Princess Petra, and she is only fourteen years old. You suggest sending a child against a monster?"

"That child has a better chance than me or any royal guard against one of those things."

Unable to listen any longer, Cyra moved away, taking the used dishes into the kitchen. Her thoughts were solely on Petra, the little sister she never met. She wondered what the girl's life was like without a whole family. It was strange to think that her sister was a stranger even though they were bound by blood and lineage.

Cyra no longer grieved the loss of her parents, but her sisters were something she could never let go of, a gaping hole in her heart and soul. As a child, her thoughts often drifted to the possibilities of why her parents cast them all aside, and on top of it all, why they separated her and her beloved sisters. Looking back on it, it seemed so cruel and unjustified.

Pushing those thoughts of abandonment aside, Cyra bottled her emotions, hearing the sounds of another table leaving, and waded through messy floors, catcalls and uneaten food.

She continued to shuffle around the inn, taking orders and stares late into the night and early morning the next day. When the remainder of the patrons went to bed for the night, Ron and Cyra found themselves plopped in front of the bar, each with a bottle of ale in their hands.

"I'm gettin' too old for this work,"' Ron said as he took a gulp.

"C'mon. You are as young as they come," Cyra responded with a wink.

"I'm serious, Cy. I ain't sure how much longer I can keep it goin'. I need y'all to be prepared."

Cyra's heart tightened at what he was suggesting, but she nodded her head, unable to speak about the possibility of losing the man who cared for her these past fourteen years.

"Time for bed. Give the lil one a kiss for me," Ron declared as he stood up noisily, a wrinkled hand going to his back.

Cyra downed her ale, the bitter taste filling her mouth, and grunted in agreement. She made her way through the rest of the Inn and past the small kitchen, where the smell of grilled, charred meat, simmering day-stew, potted meat, molding bread, and more clung thickly in the air. A small wooden door toward the back of the kitchen led down to a basement that had been converted into a home. The room itself wasn't much. It was small, square, with rough, splintery timbers above her head that rattled with dust when someone walked above. The floor was stone and smooth, helping to cool the room against the dessert heat.

Ron was convinced this was the safest place for her, especially since it had a lock and was separate from all the other rooms. Fourteen years ago, when Ron was entrusted with her, he was shocked but quickly adapted, trying to give her everything he could, the best life he could. He morphed the shabby, cob-webbed filled basement into something livable, adding a bed he made himself. Together, over the years, they slowly added more to the room, which was now painted a pale pink color, housing an assortment of wooden furniture.

Up against the wall in the center of the room on a bed full of an array of blankets lay a small figure. Her long strawberry blonde hair fanned around her, curling at the ends. A pink pillow smushed against her small, freckled face, which was consumed by sleep. Cyra drifted toward the dresser, changed into a light nightgown, and pulled her red hair into a ponytail as she splashed her face with water from the basin.

Once she was clean, she silently slipped into the sheets, pulling her daughter's sleeping form toward her as she kissed her plump cheek.

"Mommy," she muttered as she snuggled into Cyra's chest, her hair shifting to reveal a pointed ear.

"Sleep tight, Hollin," Cyra whispered, dragging her fingers along the small of her daughter's back.

CHAPTER 2

TENDRILS OF WHITE SNOW caressed the North's frozen
ground as the early rising sun sent hues of pink and purple
across the sky. The air was still besides the flurries that gave
no heed year-round as another creature of prophecies readied
herself for the day. Her pale hands worked quickly as she braided
her thick sheet of blue-black hair over her shoulder. She strapped
her polar bear fur cape over her navy dress as she dove into the
freezing air. The thick braid bounced against her chest as she
walked to the school, a small smile on her rosy lips. Despite the
cold, Rheanna had no complaints. Her job as the small town of
Dalmer's school teacher kept her mind busy and her heart full.
At only twenty years of age, she moved up quickly within the
community, loved and trusted by all. This village had become
the closest thing she had to a family. She, in turn, loved and
trusted the community just as much. She knew every nook and
cranny of the village inside and out, having spent years playing
and engaging with childhood curiousness with her best friend,
Maude.

While it wasn't fantastical like the castle she was meant to
grow up in, it was simple and pleasant, which was more than
enough for the woman she had become. There were far more

blue skies and beautiful clouds than overcast horizons, and even the snow and cold that almost constantly fell became regular to her. Long, wide streets, old buildings that were made to keep out the wind and frost, and thriving businesses built on trade to bring in outside goods from lower farmlands and far-off cities gave Rheanna everything that she wanted here and more.

Plus, the people. Hardy, good, honest people. The kind who wouldn't double talk to her face and behind her back. Who kept their word, and who helped one another. The sort of people who made life worth living and a delight to be with. Though...some people were more worth it and more delightful than others...

A thought that made Rheanna smile to herself.

The sound of wood chopping turned her smile into a full-on grin, and she picked up her pace until she saw Ivan. His dark brow furrowed as he brought the axe down on the block of wood. He wore nothing but black slacks and a gray, loose long-sleeve. Sensing Rheanna's presence, he looked up, his chocolate brown eyes filling with warmth.

"There's my girl!" he proclaimed, casting the axe aside as he wrapped his large arms around her, ruffling the top of her hair.

"Not like you saw me last night at dinner." She laughed as she leaned into him, inhaling his scent of wood and cinnamon.

"Every time I see you is special." He chuckled as he stepped back from her. She swayed closer as if she was a magnet following his movements but quickly pulled herself upright.

"You sure know how to flatter a girl." Rheanna giggled while silently chiding herself at her obvious giddiness. She had been stuck in Ivan's enthrallment for as long as she could remember. He was not only handsome, but also kind and hardworking. Once she even overheard his mother, Mrs. Bushnell contemplating their potential marriage with other women within the community.

"I am just lucky to have you to practice on." He winked, his dopey smile making Rheanna weak in the knees.

"Aren't you lucky." Rheanna shook her head and added, "I'll see you after school."

He responded by giving her a quick salute and getting back to work. Ivan was the oldest child of Mr. & Mrs. Bushnell, the family that had protected Rheanna for the past fourteen years. They had one other child, a seventeen-year-old girl who Rheanna saw as her sister. Maude Bushnell was as tall as her brother with a mane of wild curls and dark, soulful eyes. The girls were opposites of each other, Rheanna with her soft nature and Maude with her loud, demanding presence, but they balanced each other out, kept a sort of equilibrium as Mrs. Bushnell would say.

"Miss Rheanna! Miss Rheanna!" yelled a small voice from behind her. Her lips tugged upward one again as she turned to see the tiny boy, nearly lost by all the snow around him.

"Hello Benjamin." Rheanna reached out and scooped the boy up into her arms. Their large fur cloaks made him awkward to carry, but she could not bear to watch the boy struggle through the snow.

"You won't believe what Mema told me," he started, then continued quickly, "That the polar bears have skin so thick that they don't freeze in the water."

Rheanna chuckled and nodded. "Yes. They have a thing called 'blubber' that keeps them nice and warm."

"Well, I wish I had blubber," Benjamin sighed in reply.

"Me too, buddy." She placed him down on the steps in front of the school.

She looked up toward the building above her and sighed at the sight. The building itself was the most impressive in all of Dalmer. While it was imposing in a way, it was still welcoming, with it being as pale as the snow. Dark timber braced on each side to frame it properly. The peaked roof did little to keep its profile low, though Rheanna knew it was designed primarily to wick away the snow from accumulating atop of it that could potentially destroy the building from within.

Turning the doorknob of the large, thick, wooden door, she stepped inside the building. Inside was a hallway with a hardwood floor and a long carpet of various colors made of animal hides that led to five separate classrooms. A door for the headmaster sat in the front of the building and another for a small lunch hall that served as a supply room. It was warm thanks to the thick outer walls, but each of the classrooms was separated by a thin wooden wall that barely contained the noise of the others.

Benjamin happily bounced around, racing ahead as Rheanna followed him to the first door on the right, which held their classroom for the four- to six-year-olds. Once more, she turned the knob and entered. It was small, but Rheanna managed to bring the classroom alive. Paintings and art projects from the students covered the dark wood walls, and above the large fireplace in the front of the room was a rainbow, hand-painted by Rheanna and Maude.

Rheanna began to build the fire as more children filtered into the room, taking seats at the two round tables on either side of the room. Each seat had a mini mural of various scenes of nature painted on the back and crayons, pencils, and erasers were placed in the middle of each table. The students mingled and giggled as their teacher lit the lanterns placed around the room.

The cold midday air seeped through the wood panels of the classroom despite the warmth of the fire, but the occupants of the room did not seem to mind. Cups of hot cocoa graced each of their hands, and fur shawls draped over their shoulders. Rheanna smiled absentmindedly at her best friend, Maude, as she sipped on the rich drink. She frequently visited her friend while the students took lunch.

"The fact that there are only three boys around our age in this town and one of them is my brother is absolutely criminal," Maude huffed into her cocoa.

"Aaron and Reid aren't to your liking, then?" teased Rheanna.

Maude's curly head shook vigorously as her chocolate eyes narrowed to slits. "This isn't a joking matter."

Rheanna understood Maude's plight as she often wondered what it would be like to be around more men. Maybe she would already have had her first kiss if that were the case, but they lived in a remote town with few people and even fewer boys. She was still holding out that Maude's older brother, Ivan would be the one to kiss her though. Her mind began to swim with the beginnings of one of her fantasies when Maude waved a hand in front of her face.

"Stars help me, Rhe. Are you even listening?"

"I'm sorry. What were you saying?"

Sighing heavily, Maude continued, "You know I have already kissed both Reid and Aaron, and well, it was extremely underwhelming. Not the kind of romance and sparks we have read about. I want that." She put down her mug during her rant, crossing her arms and staring fiercely at the fire.

"You're only seventeen and have already been kissed. I'm three years older than you and still lacking in that department." Rheanna rolled her ocean eyes.

Her friend patted her arm empathetically. "In your defense, I took the boys for myself. I mean, you still have Ivan."

It seemed to be well-known to everyone but Ivan himself that Rheanna was infatuated with him. Maude had long become accustomed to her friend's longing glances, despite them never truly discussing it.

Rheanna fidgeted with her cup, tracing her finger around the rim, before opening her mouth to change the subject. "Have you decided what you will pursue after you are done with your studies?"

Maude's dark eyes studied her for a moment. "I was thinking I would become a teacher, like you. I quite enjoy their little faces."

"Are you sure? Have you thought about going to higher studies in the capital? You could be something more," Rheanna questioned, her own longing to leave this town, spilling out. She had always thought about traveling to the capital and continuing her education, but she was forbidden from leaving Dalmer. Maude was not.

One dark eyebrow arched, contemplating. "There would be more men there."

Rheanna let out a long sigh, shaking her head. "That is not the reason you should go."

Maude's laugh filled the room as she playfully pushed her friend's shoulder. "I know, I know, but it doesn't matter. I will not be leaving without you."

Overwhelming sadness suddenly washed over Rheanna. It was bad enough she couldn't leave; she didn't want to be the reason Maude couldn't either. Her mind drifted to her sisters momentarily, only a whisper of thought, before her students began to pour into the room. The sounds of their giggles filled the room as the lunch chaperone, Keena, made her way over to Rheanna, a sour look on her aged face.

The short woman stopped abruptly, face red and chest heaving. "They are so badly behaved. Benjamin kept biting his friends while Nadia and Fallon put snow into the pants of other students. You need to speak to their parents. It's abhorrent."

Maude hid her smile behind a hand and gracefully made her way to the door, waving before she went back to her own studies. Rheanna took a deep breath and began to placate the angry old woman.

CHAPTER 3

THE CREATURE CROUCHED LOW in the murky water, and her breath caught in her throat as she stalked her prey. The unsuspecting man pulled at his mule, the poor animal sinking into the swamp floor as it fought against the mud of the swamp. The water sloshed around them noisily, making their getaway all that more pathetic.

Aella did not know much about the man besides the fact that she was paid to kill him. He must have done something to piss someone off—most likely someone of power since they could afford her services. She cocked her head to the side as the man cursed under his breath, frustration rolling off him in waves as he tugged on the animal again. It protested and stomped its feet as it struggled to back away.

"You useless bloody piece of shit," the man started as his fist began to rise to strike the animal.

Aella struck first. She sprung from behind her hiding spot in the trees, twin daggers in her clenched fists. One blade went flying, cutting the lead connecting the mule to her target, then burying deep into the moss of the tree behind them. The mule did not need any further invitation and burst through the water, full of adrenaline from his sudden freedom.

The man spun toward her and drew his rusty, dulled sword from his belt as he stumbled back and stammered in surprise. Stringy, matted brown hair clung to his thinning pate, and as he looked upon her, he nearly dropped his sword to the marsh, stepping back in shock and fright.

"Please...just let me go... I haven't done anything wrong," he pleaded.

As a predator with prey, Aella's head tilted to the side, and she circled him. Her shoulder-length, silver hair sparkled like the moon as the early morning light reflected off it.

"Do you know who I am?" she purred, her voice a vicious song.

The man audibly gulped, his sword shaking as he attempted to keep her in front of him, but he quickly nodded his head.

"Then you know that no begging will bring you mercy."

She launched herself upon him, her small dagger singing against the man's unsteady sword. She swung her right leg out, colliding with his ankles and bringing him to his knees. A grin bloomed across her face as her blade slid across his throat. His body hit the swamp floor as she wiped her blade across her dark pants and ripped the other blade free of the tree. She placed both into the sheaths at either thigh and grimaced at the murky water that had soaked into her boots. It would take forever to dry them out now.

Despite the overwhelming tiredness that suddenly overcame her, she moved through the swamp with stealth, not wanting to be seen leaving. Whoever hired her to kill this man wanted to keep it quiet, and she simply did what she was told so she could get paid—she never asked questions. She didn't want to know why she was sent or who she was killing. The only thing she was concerned about was how and where. She was created for this.

A monster. That is what they called her. Aella never denied it because she was. There was barely anything human left in her; even her appearance set people on edge. Her striking violet eyes and titanium sheet of hair made her different, made her stand out, but what made her a predator was her power. She could choke the life out of someone with nothing but a clench of her fist, something she rarely did, though.

As Aella continued to travel back toward the Guild, she ducked beneath boughs of ivy and weeping willow branches and made sure to stay clear of brackish water. She thought about how she could have used her magic and strangled the breath from his throat before he even noticed her presence, but the thought brought a chill with it. The use of her power brought forth dark and terrible flashes of memory, ones that she had long ago chosen to repress. She was perfectly capable of utilizing her other skills to do the killing.

The sun was high in the sky as Aella strutted into the Guild. The dark and dingy building smelled of mildew, the walls slicked with bright green moss. Male voices muttered as she made her way to the dispatcher. Their menacing gazes followed her, but she jutted her chin out, not bothering to acknowledge any of them. They were well aware she was the best assassin within the Guild and that every client fought for her services. This made her a target. The fact that she was a woman insulted them even further.

Aella sent silent prayers to the goddesses as she made her way through the Guild, but just as she thought she was safe, the reason for her pleas stepped around a darkened corner. His blue eyes narrowed, and a smirk curled on his thin lips. "What assignment did Lin give you if you are back so soon?"

Her violet eyes cut to him as she froze mid-stride with disdain evident on her face. Lionel, like most of the men in the Guild, resented her for the reputation she had as a female assassin, but his resentment went deeper. He felt cheated when the previous owner of the Guild and Aella's personal tormentor passed the Guild to his son, Karif Lin, instead of Lionel, his right-hand man.

"I'm just that good. Maybe in your old age, you have grown slow." Aella smiled, but it didn't reach her eyes.

His head tilted, and he matched her predatory stance. Despite her being the best, he had still been in the game longer. He knew how to play. "We could always settle who is the best."

Aella stepped towards him. "Let's do it."

Lionel's smile exposed a row of shark-like teeth. He had them sharpened so that he could rip the throats out of his marks, his signature.

Aella ever-so-slightly adjusted into her attack position, readying for a fight when the clearing of a throat stole both of their attentions.

"While I would love to watch Aella kick your ass, Lionel, the Dispatcher needs to see her immediately," said Ripley, one of the personal guards to the Dispatcher—the owner of the Guild. He stood at the top of the stairs Aella was about to climb before Lionel interrupted her.

Lionel bared his teeth but stepped back, unwilling to challenge Ripley and in turn challenge Karif. Aella's smirk returned to her mouth as she made her way to the guard, who also happened to be one of the only people she could call a friend.

The rickety, old steps moaned under her weight, echoing the murmurs of distaste from her colleagues. She followed Ripley until they made it to the Dispatcher's door. Already stationed, a bulky guard with building muscles leaned against the frame. Ripley turned to take his place at the other side while opening the door for Aella and throwing her one of his famous smirks.

The room was unlike the rest of the Guild. Where moss and mildew clung to the stone and everything felt oddly moist and rotten, this room was clean and dry. A testament to the power of the owner of the room. The low ceiling was meant to deter overhead strikes from weapons longer than a dagger, and the wove floor mats protected the wood beneath.

A gleaming metal desk sat in the middle of the room, lit only by the flames of a candle but radiating out to the rest of the room as if lit from a hearth. Papers, pens, and various weapons littered atop the iron desk, while the walls beside it were covered in maps of not just Linnosa but also kingdoms far away.

Behind the desk sat an unnervingly beautiful man. His features were leagues above any other within the Guild, with only Aella challenging him. Pale grey eyes filled with mirth met Aella's gaze, while supple lips curled into a sneering smirk, and the candlelight danced upon his high cheeks. His dark palm collided with the smooth metal beneath him, scattering papers, missives, and a few coppers to the floor when he spoke harshly.

"It's about damn time."

CHAPTER 4

IN THE CAPITAL OF Linnosa, a creature sat curled up on the plush window seat with her golden-brown hair cascading in loose waves around her shoulders as she gazed out at the stars twinkling in the night sky. The day had been long, filled with lessons and etiquette training, but now, in the quiet of the evening and privacy of her rooms, Petra felt a sense of peace.

Her rooms were much as the palace was: Grand and richly decorated. The doors and windows were gilded in gold, with finer silver inscribed in an ancient alphabet that Petra could only slightly understand. The light green of the walls paired nicely with the opulent trimming of the furniture, which was equally rich and foiled with even more gold.

The room itself was large, with books littering every surface from the floor to tables and chairs to the bed itself. Even Petra's dresser was stuffed with them, most of which were dog-eared, bookmarked, or written with her thoughts in the margins. Of course, there was a method to the madness that only Petra knew. Any other person would have found the maze of literature maddening.

She liked it that way, though. It was her sanctuary. The books were, in a way, her friends. It wasn't uncommon for her to read a few pages of one and move onto another.

But it was more than the books that made it her sanctuary. Soft vines of deep green with wide leaves the size of her palms grew along the walls while white flowers blossomed between them. The earthy smell of life and plants filled the room and gave a natural perfume that was leagues better than the fake oils and tinctures she normally was made to wear. Nothing—at least to her—smelled better than a combination of wildflowers and a good book.

Her mother's gentle footsteps echoed in the silence as she entered the room, the rustle of her elegant gown brushing against the floor. Petra turned to see Queen Sienna standing in the doorway, her beauty radiant as always, though tonight there was a certain heaviness in her eyes.

"There you are, my little star," her mother said softly with a smile tugging at the corners of her lips as she walked over to Petra. In her hands, she held a worn leather-bound book.

Petra's eyes lit up at the sight. "Is that a new book for me?" she asked, her voice filled with excitement.

Sienna chuckled softly, but the sound didn't quite reach her crystal blue eyes. She sat beside Petra on the window seat, placing the book on her daughter's lap. Her hand lingered for a moment, smoothing a stray curl away from Petra's face. "Not new, my love, but one that has been dear to me for many years."

Petra's fingers traced the worn cover, her curiosity piqued. "What's it about?"

Her mother's gaze drifted out the window, soft candlelight casting an unearthly golden hue upon her pale blonde hair. For a moment, she seemed lost in thought, her face clouded with unspoken feeling. "It's a story about fate," she said quietly. "About how no matter how much we try to control our path, there are things—forces larger than us—that we cannot escape."

Petra's brow furrowed slightly. "Fate?" Her thoughts traveled to the Oracle who aided the royals' decisions with her knowledge of the future. "But even the Oracle says we can change our path."

Sienna's lips curved into a small, bittersweet smile. "Sometimes, yes. We make choices every day that shape our lives. But there are some things, some events, that are written long before we are born. Things we cannot change, no matter how much we want to."

Petra blinked, her emerald eyes searching her mother's face. "Is that...a good thing or a bad thing?"

Her mother let out a soft sigh. "Neither," she replied, her voice gentle but tinged with sadness. "It's simply...life. Fate isn't good or bad. It's just the way of the world. We all have a destiny, Petra, and no matter how hard we try to avoid it, it finds us."

Petra tilted her head, trying to grasp the meaning behind her mother's words. "If it's our life, shouldn't we be able to control it?"

Sienna's crystal eyes softened as she reached out to cup Petra's cheek, her thumb gently brushing over her skin. "Because some things are bigger than us, my love. There are forces we cannot see, events set in motion long before we even know to look for them. You will come to understand this in time."

Petra leaned into her mother's touch, but a flicker of concern sparked in her chest. "So, you believe in fate, Mother?"

Her mother nodded slowly, her gaze distant. "I do. I didn't always, but over the years, I've come to accept it." She hesitated, as if deciding whether to say more, and when she continued, her voice was quieter. "There are things I wish I could change, choices I wish I could undo. Sometimes, we must accept that we are not in control."

Petra frowned, her heart tightening. "What would you change?"

Sienna's eyes darkened for a moment, her expression unreadable. She didn't answer right away, and when she finally spoke, her voice was filled with a sorrow that Petra had never heard before. "There are things I fear I will be unable to protect you from. But no matter how much I may try to prevent them, I know they are part of a greater plan. One that even I cannot stop."

Petra's heart ached at the sadness in her mother's voice. She couldn't understand it fully, but the weight of her mother's words left an impression deep in her chest. "Why do I feel like something bad is going to happen?"

Sienna managed a soft, reassuring smile, though the sadness remained in her eyes. "Not all things that are destined are bad, my love. But they are inevitable. What matters most is how we face them. That is the one thing we do control—our courage in the face of what we cannot change."

Petra nodded, trying to take in her mother's wisdom, though the thought of not being able to change her future left her feeling uneasy. "So...we just have to accept it?"

"Not just accept it," Sienna replied gently, her hand resting over Petra's. "Embrace it. Understand that even the hardest moments have meaning. Fate may guide us, but it's our hearts that lead us through."

Petra looked down at the book in her lap as the weight of her mother's words sank into her.

Her mother followed her gaze, eyes settling on the novel. "It's a story about a man and woman who try to change their fate, but in the end, they realize that everything they fought against brought them closer to who they were meant to be. They couldn't escape what was written for them, but they found love and strength within it."

Petra smiled faintly, tracing the worn edges of the cover. "I think I'd like that story."

Sienna kissed the top of Petra's head, her hand lingering for a moment longer than usual. "It's a lesson we all have to learn, my darling. That no matter what, our fate will find us. But we can still live fully, still love deeply, even knowing what's to come."

Petra felt the strange heaviness in her chest once again as she looked up at her mother. "I love you, Mother," she said softly.

"I love you too, my love. Always."

They sat in silence for a moment with the soft rustle of pages filling the room as they began to read together. But even as the comforting sound of her mother's voice filled the space, Petra couldn't shake the feeling that something was lingering beneath the surface; something that made her mother's words about fate leave goosebumps across her flesh.

The next evening, Petra found herself dancing in her room, just finishing the story of star-crossed lovers her mother had given her the night prior. Her heart was full of love and wonder. As the girl danced, she hummed and twirled her skirts of her exquisite gown of a deep navy, the bodice pulled tight around her waist then puffed out around her. Her golden-brown hair was braided at the top of her head with a crown of wildflowers weaved throughout.

A knock sounded on the door, and shortly after, a deep voice called, "Princess, it's time for dinner!"

The princess groaned, but responded, "Just a moment!"

"Come on, Petra. You are already late."

The sound of desperation in the guard's voice made Petra's lips twitch up to a smile. She spun around one last time as she slipped on a pair of satin slippers then made her way to the bedroom door. Flinging it open, she was face-to-face with her favorite guard-in-training, Luca. His mouth turned upward in a half-smile, one dimple pronounced. Without thinking twice, Petra stretched onto her tiptoes and pressed a swift kiss to the smile. Luca stiffened, but his blue eyes twinkled in delight.

"Not here," he said gently, placing a hand on her arm. She nodded while looping her arm through his as he escorted her to the private dining hall, where she would eat with her parents. Luca was sixteen years old, two years older than Petra, but training to become a part of her personal guard. She had begged her father to let him into the guard a year ago when they met, claiming he had so much promise. He worked in the kitchen then, which made it nearly impossible for them to ever be alone. All Petra had to do was flash her pleading eyes and whine a bit, and her father quickly caved.

They walked in silence down the long corridors filled with portraits of long dead ancestors and draping curtains, but Petra could not help but let her gaze wander to peer up at Luca. His blond curly hair fell right above his ocean-blue eyes, his handsome face chiseled, but still reminiscent of adolescence. His tall and lanky presence gave her a feeling of comfort even before he began training. Petra was not allowed outside of the castle grounds, so her contact with people, especially her own age, was limited. Most of the staff avoided her as if she was contagious besides the guards, her personal maid, and Luca. The Oracle trained her, but the thought of the old, wrinkled woman brought chills down her spine. She tried to spend as little time as possible with her.

They stopped in front of the archway to the private dining hall. Luca bowed as he directed Petra to her seat and took his stance behind her, against the wall. The dining hall's vaulted ceiling rose high, streaming with silky banners that fluttered from an unseen breeze. The smell of rich food wafted through the room, and small windows at the very top of the ceiling allowed fresh air to sweep down.

Her father and mother were already sitting down, food piled onto their plate. They both looked as regal as ever, but her mother was extraordinarily beautiful with her small features and sharp jaw.

"You need to arrive on time. Practice etiquette," her mother said, shaking her head, the golden crown infused with navy jewels upon her head not moving an inch.

Her father grunted his agreement. "Your mother is right. You are getting too old for this behavior. You are a princess."

Petra's emerald gaze met her father's golden-brown one as she said, "Well, I was reading. It is important for a princess to be educated, is it not?"

His lips twitched, but before he could respond, her mother interjected, "Please, Petra. Just try for me."

Petra didn't argue; she never argued. A deep sadness weighed in her mother's eyes; one that always lay there, just beneath the surface which made it impossible for Petra to fight with her.

"Of course, Mother." She dipped her head in submission as she began to spoon various foods onto her plate. Chicken, mashed potatoes, and biscuits that made her stomach growl in anticipation.

"I just finished that novel you gave me, Mother," Petra said absentmindedly as she served herself asparagus. "It was so romantic and love—"

Her mother released a startled gasp, her chair scraping as she went to push her seat back. Petra's head snapped up to see blood dripping from her father's eyes, and his body started to convulse a moment later. Strangled sounds escaped her mother as blood and foam began to flow from her as well. Petra screamed, running to her mother, but the guards were there in an instant, calling for healers. She could do nothing as her parents seized, eyes full of blood. Her mother fell from her chair, and the crown toppled out of her golden hair, head bouncing as it hit the white tile. A strangled cry released from Petra as a familiar strength wrapped around her. She began to kick and fight, wanting to hold her mother. The place where the marble floor collided with her slippered foot shuddered and started to crack. Her father stopped moving.

Tears fell, blurring her vision as she sobbed, finally going limp in Luca's arms as her mother lay still on the floor in a puddle of her own blood and vomit. Someone shouted at Luca to take her out, but she cried, "No. Let me see them. Please, let me see them."

She looked up at Luca; his face had gone white with fear, but he held her tight.

"Get her out of here. Now!"

Luca shook his head as he dragged her back out of the dining hall and into the corridor. Petra fought, kicking her feet out and digging her nails into the navy of his guard uniform. Cracks continued to spiderweb out from beneath her feet as her power surged. He struggled to open her bedroom door and keep hold of her, but somehow, he managed to do it, and he locked them both inside. He released her and she fell to her knees, screaming until her throat was raw. She sagged onto the ground, fists clenched into her dress as she heaved, nothing but bile coming up due to her empty stomach.

"I... What can I... Do you need..." Luca stuttered as he raked his hands through his blond curls.

Petra sat up quickly on her knees, forgetting he was still there. "Get out."

"But—"

"I said get out!" she screamed as she slammed her palms toward him, vines shooting from the ground, wrapping around his limbs, around the door handle, and promptly shoving him out of her room.

With him gone, she fell silent. She was alone. Truly alone. No family left. No one left. She began to shake then, wrapping her arms tightly around her knees and rocking back and forth. Her mother was gone. Her father was gone. It felt as if someone had ripped into her chest, taking her heart with them, yet she was still alive. She could feel the thing beating inside her chest. She wished it would stop. As her tears dried and her rocking slowed, she fell asleep to the sound of her own heart beating, alone, on the floor.

CHAPTER 5

"M OMMY! MOMMY! MOMMY!" HOLLIN shouted as she bounced on the bed, right next to Cyra's face. "Grandpa Ronnie says get up!"

Cyra moaned but rolled over to grab Hollin, tickling her and sending her into a fit of giggles. "Can't Mommy sleep for a little bit longer."

"No...Grandpa Ronnie...told...me," the little girl attempted to get out around giggles.

"Well, let's get ourselves ready for the day, my little Holli-bean." Cyra lifted herself from the bed, tossing the little girl into the air before placing her gently on the ground.

Cyra and Hollin began to dress, both in garments that were closer to rags than cloth by now, but Hollin acted as if she were a princess, spinning her skirts and humming the way only a four-year-old could.

"Now, which scarf would you like to wear today?" Cyra asked while displaying a variety of different head scarves. They were each made of spare fabric Cyra came across and rolled together to create a thick band.

"Roses! Roses! Roses!" Hollin hollered as she pointed excitedly at a scarf with tiny red roses and a white background.

"Roses it is, then."

Cyra threaded the scarf beneath her daughter's strawberry hair, covering the points of her ears, and tying it at a knot on the top of her head.

"Can I have a fishy braid today?" Hollin's emerald eyes sparkled with excitement as Cyra nodded and brought her over to the bed. She began to string the girl's hair in and out, resulting in a fishtail braid that reached the middle of her small back.

"Thank you!" Hollin sang as she skipped toward the mirror.

Scooping the stray hairs into her hand, Cyra fixed her ponytail and gave it a quick pull. Satisfied with herself, she took her daughter's hand and made her way upstairs to make breakfast.

"I'm sure she'll be up any minute," Ron's voice drifted down the hall. Cyra paused at the sharpness of his tone, pulling Hollin behind her. She went to ask her mother why they stopped, but Cyra placed a finger to her lips. The little girl nodded her head in understanding, and Cyra pointed back down the stairs, mouthing, "Hide."

Her strawberry-blonde braid was a blur as she hastily tucked herself beneath their makeshift bed. Once she was assured her daughter was hidden, she wiped her palms on her dress, adjusted her bust, took a deep breath, then walked out into the main portion of the Inn.

There in the room stood several armored men who looked far and above the usual clientele that usually came. The Inn itself wasn't anything special, having been placed on the road and mostly designed as a simple rest stop. Compared to most taverns, alehouses, and the like found in larger cities, this one was a bit cheap: thick wood walls with several open spots for the wind to blow into, a thatched roof made of reeds, dried grasses, and twine, and a stone floor that needed to be constantly swept, covered in thin rugs.

"Hello! Are y'all looking for a room?" Cyra smiled brightly at the men in navy and gold. Her stomach tightened in panic and dread as she took in the six royal guards of the Voelbel family. "Not often we get visitors from the capital itself."

As she spoke, the guards stopped and looked at her from beneath their helmets—or at least the ones who wore helmets did. For a moment, it was silent as they stared and gauged her, with two in the back—a man with jowls and pimples, and another with a twisted nose and a scar—talked to one another before tapping the first guard in the front, showing a letter, and then as one, they turned in her direction.

"Princess Cyra Noelle Voelbel, you are required at the castle of Queen Sienna Linwood Voelbel and King Edgar Voelbel," the guard in the front with blond hair stated.

Cyra's knees buckled at the mention of her parents and royal title. She grasped onto the dark wood of the bar to keep herself upright as Ron shuffled to her side, reaching his hand out to brush hers. Her parents had cast her aside all those years ago, had cast all of them aside, and now they wanted her back. After fourteen years? Something had to be wrong.

"I have a life here. I cannot just leave," Cyra responded confidently.

"I'm sorry, but Princess, it is an order," the blond soldier said, but he didn't sound sorry at all. Cyra felt her magic pulse around her but kept it at bay; fighting them would not end well. She couldn't let them find out about Hollin. Her daughter was all that mattered.

"Ya know, I greatly rely on Cyra here. Are ya sure she can't stay for a few days?" Ron countered gently. His brown eyes flickered between the soldiers.

"No, sir. This is official royal business. She is needed immediately."

Ron went to say something else, but Cyra interjected. "Very well," she sighed. "May I have some time to say goodbye and get my affairs in order?"

"An hour is all we can give."

Cyra did not respond but instead turned to Ron, beckoning him to follow her down into her room. Once they were safely behind the shut door, she called out for Hollin, who easily shimmied out from the bed.

"What's wrong?" she asked, her head tilting to the side.

"Mommy has to go on a trip," Cyra said softly as she pulled her daughter toward her.

"But I am going to be five soon," Hollin whimpered. "You can't miss my birthday."

Cyra placed her hands on Hollin's freckled cheeks and stared into her emerald eyes. "I know, baby. I will be back, I promise. Grandpa Ronnie will watch over you."

Ron grunted in agreement, placing his wrinkled hand on Cyra's shoulder in support. "I gotcha, lil' bean."

Tears slipped down Hollin's cheeks, her small hand wrapping around her mother's like a plea. Cyra dragged her thumb across the small hand as she stood up and began to pack some of her essentials. A few old dresses, undergarments, sleep things, a brush. More than anything she wanted to bring Hollin. When she was finished, she kissed the girl on the forehead and whispered, "I love you more than all the stars in the sky. When you miss me, look to the stars and know I am looking at them and thinking of you."

"To the stars," Hollin echoed, another tear escaping her vivid eyes. Cyra wrapped her daughter in her arms one last time. "Now hide, baby."

Hollin turned toward the bed, her freckled face tear stained and crawled beneath. Once she was hidden, Cyra turned to Ron. "No one can know she is my daughter. We have to protect her from it all, Ron," she whispered.

He bowed his head in response. Cyra threw her arms around him as a silent sob choked her throat. His thin arms encompassed her as he sighed.

"Yer have my word."

"Thank you for all these years. I owe you my life."

"Yer owe me nothin'. Survive for us. Survive for yer family."

Cyra pulled away from Ron as her heart filled. She clutched his scruffy cheeks in her palms and smiled sadly. "Anything for you."

Reluctantly Cyra turned toward the stairs, her hands shaking as she wiped them down her dress. She took one last look around her home, at the people she loved, before she made her way up the stairs.

CHAPTER 6

T HE SCHOOL DAY PROGRESSED as normal, children laughing and learning, a few tantrums, and the kind words of a teacher who consoled them. By the end of the day, Rheanna was exhausted and ready to spend some time far away from her students. Once they were all picked up, she made her way back to the Bushnell's cottage. Everything in Dalmer was relatively close since the evergreens took up a good portion of it, only a few businesses and cottages sprinkled throughout. The town rarely received a respite from the harshness of the North's weather.

Black strands that had escaped Rheanna's braid knotted in front of her as the cold air thrashed violently. She pulled her cloak closer as she made the last few steps to their home. It was a quaint cabin that matched the rest of the small town in design. Several floors, a peaked roof, and a large yard meant for a garden when the warmer months hit, but the snow seemed never-ending. It was on the outskirts of town, though not too far to be lost in the timberlands. A large enough plot of land that denoted the family's stance in the town's social hierarchy, it was perfect for her and the rest of the Bushnell family.

Large icicles hung from the black tiled roof, with powdery snow lining around the maroon shutters. Shutters that shielded the glass windows from being damaged by the frequent ice storms and frost that followed.

Rheanna's head tilted in intrigue as she noticed the multiple tracks in the fresh snow, many more than the normal foot traffic to the Bushnell's. If it wasn't hers or the other Bushnells doing their daily chores, it was delivery boys bringing bought goods and services or Ivan bringing in firewood for the kitchen and fireplaces.

Ignoring it for now, Rheanna shrugged and entered the main foyer, kicking off slush and ice from her boots, hanging her coat, and stretching after a long day of schooling. The warmth of a fire lit within the hearth welcomed her. As she began to shrug off her outer layers, she heard a throat being cleared behind her.

Turning, Rheanna looked up, and her jaw fell open. Her heart leapt into her throat, choking on a surprised squeak as she saw the navy and gold metal armor of her family's royal guard.

Six men in full armor stood in the middle of the cabin, dripping slush off their cold armor and onto the floor, with nary a man among them wearing proper furs or cloaks. It was somewhat comical for her to see that they shivered and looked out of place in the dwelling, but she hardly had the time to focus on the humor as Mr. and Mrs. Bushnell stood next to them with an anxious demeanor.

"Princess Rheanna Mae Voelbel, you are summoned to the court of Queen Sienna Linwood Voelbel and King Edgar Voelbel," said the guard who stood at the front.

"I want to come," Maude interjected. Rheanna spun toward her, not even noticing that her best friend had also been in the room.

"I don't know if—" Mrs. Bushnell began to say, but the royal guard cut her off.

"Whoever wishes to accompany Princess Rheanna is welcome as long as we move quickly."

Rheanna finally reacted, stumbling over her words, "But... I... What? Well, what has happened?"

"All of your questions will be answered once we get to the castle," the same guard spoke again and gestured towards the door.

Mr. Bushnell stepped forward. "Let me fetch my son, Ivan. He will be accompanying you. We were entrusted with Rheanna's care and will continue to look after her."

The guard nodded, and everyone stared at Rheanna. Her heart pounded, but not out of fear. She would see her parents again. Her next words slipped out quickly. "And what of my sisters?"

"They have all been summoned as well."

Rheanna did not hesitate a moment more and quickly passed Maude to get to their shared bedroom. It was a small space with two twin beds with matching wool blankets and white cotton sheets. One wooden dresser sat by the door with lopsided drawers from years of use. The only other piece of furniture was the side table between the two beds, covered in drips of wax from candles left lit too long.

She packed her things in a knapsack as Maude questioned, "Are you happy to return, *Princess*?" The last word came out mockingly, but she ignored the remark.

"Of course," Rheanna responded. "I have never even met my littlest sister." The idea of seeing Cyra and Aella after so many years filled her with so much joy, she struggled to keep the grin off her face. Cyra, her protector, and Aella, the little troublemaker. She was a bit puzzled about why she was being summoned seemingly out of nowhere but couldn't imagine it was anything bad. Nothing that reunited her family could be bad.

Maude opened her mouth to say something when Mrs. Bushnell bustled in. "Let me help you, sweetie. It'll be a long trip, and you'll need a summer dress for when you hit the West. I can modify one of your others and—"

"Mom, please relax. She is going to the castle where she's a princess. I'm sure they will have plenty of pretty things for her." Maude rolled her eyes.

"Well, yes, but you can never be too prepared."

"You should be helping me pack as I'm the one who actually needs it."

Mrs. Bushnell hesitated but then said, "You will not be going with her."

"Are you kidding me? Ivan gets to go!" Maude's arms folded over her chest as she pouted.

"Yes, and he is twenty-three. You are only seventeen. Your father and I have decided. No point in arguing." Mrs. Bushnell grabbed one of Rheanna's dresses from the closest and left the room with no further words.

"I'm sorry," Rheanna broke the silence and shrugged at her friend.

"I never get to have any of the fun. Why do you get to be a princess?" She sighed and flopped down on their shared bed, her curly locks fanning around her head.

"Well, I haven't been one for a while. I don't think I even remember how."

"Can't be that difficult. Just stand around and look pretty, which is something that comes naturally to you." The girl winked at Rheanna, and they both fell into a fit of giggles.

"Enough of that, you goons," Ivan said sarcastically as he strutted into the room. "Let's say our goodbyes and head out." His arms circled around his sister and tugged on the end of her curls.

"Asshole," she muttered with a smile as she pushed him away. Rheanna and Maude's embrace was filled with tears as the former whispered, "I love you."

"Love you more."

Leaving Maude behind—or any of the Bushnells—was the last thing that she wanted to do. For years, Maude had been what she considered her closest friend. She adored Ivan, of course, and was glad he was coming along to protect her. But Maude had been there since she first arrived so many years ago and had been with her through all the trials and tribulations of growing up.

Maude had replaced the gaping hole her sisters and family left. She remembered Aella and Cyra, but those memories faded every day. Maude was the one to console while she cried and support her as she grew up and became a teacher. At only seventeen, Maude was Rheanna's most trusted confidant.

Yet, she was still excited. Of course, for traveling and seeing the world that she was forbidden and sheltered from for so long. The chance to be alone with Ivan for once, as well. Her sisters, her parents, and even the thought of the capital brought a smile to her lips. She had been dreaming of this moment for fourteen years. Nothing would sour her mood.

"You'll send for us, won't you, dear? If you need us?" Mrs. Bushnell's warm brown eyes moistened as she kissed her ward's forehead.

"Of course. Thank you for everything," Rheanna responded.

"You'll always have a home with us." Mr. Bushnell placed a hand on her shoulder, patting it gently.

Tears began to well in her eyes as she thought about how this could be the last time she saw this cabin. Her chest tightened as she thought of her students. Who would teach them now? A sort of panic seized her as she realized she did not get to say farewell to her class.

Rheanna grabbed Maude's hands. "Let my class know I love them." Her voice came out hoarse. Maude squeezed her hands once and nodded.

Ivan embraced both of his parents, his father saying, "Protect her."

"With my life." He winked at Rheanna.

Her heart fluttered at the meaning of what he said, her cheeks growing pink. She knew he would not need to defend her with his life especially once she was back at the castle, but the fact that he would made her giddy.

"It is time to leave, Princess," one of the guards said.

Rheanna and Ivan locked arms, following them out into the cold air. She took one last look at the cabin and then began her journey home.

CHAPTER 7

K ARIF LIN WAS NOT a man most people would want to keep waiting, but Aella had never been one to care. His arrogance and cruelty were all an act to hide his true weakness: his humanity. In this business, there was no room for it, but Karif had inherited the Guild from his father, Creaton. A man whose name still brought a twinge of fear to Aella.

"Oh, Lin. What's the fuss about? Did you miss me?" She winked as she plopped into the worn chair in front of Karif's desk.

"You have royal visitors," he responded through his teeth.

Any humor on Aella's face fled at those words. She sat up straighter in the chair, and her violet eyes scanned the room as if the so-called visitors would pop out from behind a piece of furniture.

"I took the liberty of leading them to our sitting room where they have been constantly demanding the presence of Princess Aella Leigh Voelbel. You can imagine how shocked I was to learn we harbored a princess."

Aella scoffed. Karif was well aware of her status as his father was the one who was entrusted with her care so long ago. She may have spent her first four years as a princess, but she hardly remembered it. The trauma of the past fourteen years outweighed any previous life.

"Can't I just kill them?"

"Don't be stupid, Aella. This is your opportunity to get out of this life." Karif's eyes softened. Aella was aware he felt some sort of protectiveness over her, but she was not about to be paraded around as a princess after the royals threw her away like trash. They didn't even bother to make sure she was safe. One visit would have exposed what Creaton did not just to her, but to his own son as well.

"Send them away. I'm not interested."

"They won't leave without seeing you, and they are setting the rest of the Guild on edge. Unless you want them all to know about your royal status, you need to entertain your company."

Aella rolled her eyes and sighed. "Fine."

Without another word, she stood and made her way from the room out into the deteriorating hallway. The Guild's base of operations held hardly any decorations. Built into an old, forgotten fortress that was slowly sinking into the mire, it made for a good place to conduct business. The hallways and myriad of rooms were like a labyrinth.

Perfect for the assassins here. Once a person memorized how the layout truly was, a skilled assassin could lead pursuers through these halls around and around and around again until they got lost and disoriented. Not that people ever did challenge the Guild in this way. No one had the skill or courage. Hence, it was the perfect place to come back to after missions.

Ripley's curious gaze found her, but she promptly ignored him. She kept her eyes straight ahead with the creaking floorboards announcing every step she took.

Soon, she made it to the door of the sitting room and saw four royal guards standing in the center of the room. It almost sent Aella into hysterics.

'The sitting room' was a place where business was conducted with those outside of the Guild, but the reality was, it was a thickly decorated room where Guild members brought their prostitutes and other 'relaxing' agents. All around were moldy couches covered in leather and overly stuffed, and lounging surfaces meant for bodies to pile atop, coupled with various tables and more.

The thought of the fluids that stained every inch of this room made Aella cringe and her skin crawl. She honestly hated it here. Other than the illicit sex, none of the furniture matched; it was all gaudy and made up of yellows, reds, and greens. The chipped and bubbling layers of mismatched paint revealed how many times the walls had been painted and repainted. The guards were really the only 'pretty' thing in here, comparatively.

The guards stood stoically in their golden armor, the royal crest at the center of the chest plate: fire, water, earth, and air, all displayed in each section of the X. Aella's eyes lingered on the four elements. At the sight of the air symbol, her chest tightened, but she managed to pull her gaze away.

"Princess Aella Leigh Voelbel, you have been summoned to the castle of Queen Sienna Linwood Voelbel and King Edgar Voelbel," the oldest-looking guard spoke, his eyes glued to the left side of her face where two jagged scars sliced across her cheek. The first and slightly longer cut reached from her temple to just before her nose, narrowly missing her eye. The second ran parallel to the first. She received it about seven years ago as punishment from Creaton.

"Weakness is not an option," he spat at her, his body visibly shaking from barely restrained rage.

"But...I...I...can't. He's my...my friend," eleven-year-old Aella managed to get out, a dagger clutched in her tiny hand.

"He is nothing. Not even vermin. He will die eventually, anyway." The older man held the boy by his throat. His watery blue eyes glistened as he struggled to breathe and pulled at the hand that blocked his airway. This boy had become Aella's friend, a poor orphan boy who had no one just like her.

When Aella did not act, Creaton hissed, "Do it, or I will."

She knew he was teaching her a lesson. She was not allowed to have any friends because friends meant weakness, but she could not get her trembling hand to act. Creaton sighed, and a sickening crunch filled the air as her friend's neck broke. His body fell limply to the ground as Creaton turned on her. She scrambled backward, hitting the wall.

"Remember this." His hand cupped her cheek for a moment, almost tender, but then pain erupted across her face as he dug his sharp nails into her flesh and pulled in one swift motion.

Karif, five years older than her, was able to get her a healing potion, unknown how to her, but it did not heal the two deepest wounds. She had not had a friend since.

The guard cleared his throat, which promptly brought Aella back to reality.

"I am not a princess."

"It does not matter what you claim. You are to be taken back to the castle," he answered smoothly.

"And who is going to make me?" A dangerous gleam filled Aella's violet eyes as she tilted her head. "If I am a princess, as you say, you wouldn't dare try to manhandle me."

"We would never hurt you, but we were ordered to bring you back to the castle by any means necessary," the guard spoke carefully.

"As if you could hurt me." Aella laughed at the guard's expression. He knew what she was, who she was. He was most likely horrified that such a creature could be one of his precious princesses.

"Please, Princess."

At the pathetically pleading sound of his voice, a sort of curiosity settled over Aella as she mulled it over in her mind. On the one hand, she didn't want to go. Her parents threw her away like trash so long ago, tossing her from their lofty heights to dote upon their newest and youngest daughter, who was probably nothing more than some pretentious pet who got whatever she wished with large doe eyes. All the while, Aella had to grapple with the fact that she was unwanted and handed off to a monster who turned her into one as well.

But she sort of did want to see her royal family. Not out of love for her parents, of course. She was both curious as to why they summoned her now, out of any other time they could have. Were they disgusted with how she ended up? Were they perturbed by the stories told of her prowess? What of her sisters? Were they summoned as well after being tossed aside and forgotten? If so, what were they like?

All she had inherited from the royal family was pain. It would be interesting to show her parents how ruthless she turned out to be in the end and how their daughter was now transformed into something harder and sharper. Something very un-princess like.

"Fine. I'll go," Aella finally said, crossing her arms over her bust before staring at the guard with a glint of malice and mischief twinkling in her eyes. "But not with you."

She didn't wait for their response. Instead, she spun on her heels as they called out to her and ran straight into the hall, knowing they couldn't chase her without being attacked.

This'll be fun, she thought.

CHAPTER 8

P ETRA SAT NESTLED ON her reading chair, an olive-green recliner that had seen better times, as she read an epic romance about a girl being whisked away by a prince. She hadn't left her room since her parent's death a little over a week ago. Instead, she consumed book after book and imagined herself away, wishing someone would rescue her.

"Princess," a soft masculine voice called as two knocks at her door followed. Petra didn't even bother to lift her head, glaring at the words on the page.

"The Oracle wishes to speak with you."

That piqued Petra's interest, so she placed the novel face down to keep her spot and opened the door to see Luca and the Oracle standing beside him.

"Hello, child," the Oracle said, bowing her greying head as she greeted her and entered the room just as Petra ushered her in and slammed the door behind her.

Petra stared at the wizened woman, still uncertain how to act or talk to her. It was funny to her how, even now, she didn't know how to properly engage with the woman after all these years. She was old, stooped, and crooked with age, and as long as Petra had known her, she had always looked this way.

The Oracle wasn't like any of the other staff in the castle. Most of them were either nameless or faceless unless she directly dealt with them, such as Luca. Most of the guards, the kitchen staff, and her maids, and were often a blur of differences that came and went. Yet her parents—when they were alive—showed deference to the Oracle when she was around.

Petra's gaze flicked to Luca, but only for a second before quickly looking away. As much as she wanted to look at him, talk to him, and cry into his arms, she had not quickly forgotten nor forgiven him for how he dragged her from her parents as they died in front of her. How does one forgive such an act? One day, she might be able to figure it out when her emotions weren't in as much turmoil.

Petra faced the Oracle with her hands clasped before her, waiting for the woman to speak.

"I have been handling the Kingdom's affairs," the Oracle said.

"Great. Is there something you need?" One of Petra's eyebrows shot up.

"There is something you need to know about the line of succession." The woman's voice sounded like gravel as her black eyes bore into Petra.

"I am the next in line. I am aware."

"You are not."

Petra stopped breathing, and her heart jumped in her chest as she took in the seriousness of the woman's heavily lined face. "What do you mean? Mother had no siblings. I have no siblings. Who else could possibly take the throne?"

The Oracle clucked her tongue. "You are fourth in line, little one. Your eldest sister will take the Kingdom."

Petra laughed bitterly, her emerald eyes lifting to the sky as her hands dragged down her face. Her eldest sister? Fourth in line? Surely, her parents would have told her about any siblings. They couldn't have hidden this from her. Her gaze drifted to Luca, the ever-diligent guard, stationed by the door, but his eyes were already pinned on her, wide, with a look of guilt she was quite familiar with these days.

"You have three older sisters, Cyra, Rheanna, and Aella. All sent away the day you were born," the Oracle continued.

Petra stared in stunned silence, her eyes glazing over for a moment as she thought about the childhood she could have had versus the one she had to endure.

The soft music of the orchestra filled Petra's ears, her feet kicking as she sat on her tiny throne, aching to dance. Even her mother and father drifted along the dance floor, mingling and dancing with one another. The young princess went to stand up, unable to keep still any longer, when a weight pressed down on her shoulders, forcing her to sit back down. She looked up to find the Oracle, hobbled and bent over her, black eyes disapproving.

"You must behave like a princess. Be still," she commanded.

Petra's eyes narrowed. "The other children get to dance and play."

"The other children are not princesses."

She let out a heaved breath but slumped against the back of the chair until Bianca Solo, the daughter of one of her parent's advisors, came up to her and bowed. Petra's posture immediately straightened, and she attempted to give her most royal smile.

The girl's face contoured into a sneer. "Do you think you are too good to play with the rest of us?"

Petra blinked rapidly, taken aback. "I..."

"Or maybe you are just daft, and your parents don't want to be embarrassed," Bianca said.

Before Petra could defend herself, the girl turned and scurried away, her blonde curls bobbing as she giggled with her friends. They all began to cast glances at her, and Petra turned to look for the Oracle. The old woman stood just behind her but did not interfere or say a word. Later that night, Petra cried herself to sleep, feeling the depth of her loneliness for the first time.

Petra snapped back into reality, and the little color she had drained from her face, and stammered, "How? Why?"

"Because I said so. It was what was best at the time, but that does not matter right now. One of them is here now, and the other two should not be far behind."

Petra's mind raced as she tried to process all the information. She couldn't help the way she looked at Luca, despite her anger at him. He gave her an encouraging smile, but he had kept the knowledge of her sisters from her as well. He had kept her from another part of her family. Her eyes snapped to the ground. Her stomach churned, and her heart did a leap at the thought of meeting her sisters. "Well, I will greet her then."

"Once you are properly dressed. It would not do any good for the castle staff to see you gallivanting around in your nightgown." The Oracle's gaze roamed over the pale blue of the dress Petra had worn for three days already.

Without another word, Petra was across the room, and Luca stepped out the door. Diving into her bureau, she slid on the first and easiest dress she saw, light pink with white rosebuds woven into the lace. She smoothed out her golden-brown tresses and asked the Oracle, "Where is she?"

"Come with me." The woman offered Petra a withered arm, which she took eagerly. Not only was she no longer the heir to the throne she had dreaded for all these years, but now, she had sisters. Despite her excitement and nerves, the feeling of betrayal from Luca and her parents drove deep into her stomach. Why hadn't they told her the truth?

The Oracle guided her down the gilded hallways, down the stairs, and toward the front castle entrance. They paused at the receiving room, the golden doors looming over them before pushing inside the ornate room. A large teal chandelier hung as the centerpiece of the room with a matching grand piano in the right corner. A plush white rug accented the yellow flower-patterned couches. Sitting on the bigger of the two was a woman with raven black hair and piercing crystal eyes, just like the late Queen Sienna. Petra wrenched herself from the Oracle, her eyes growing large as she stared at one of her sisters for the first time.

The woman's gaze shot to her face, her blue eyes growing large as she said, "I...little sister?"

"My name is Petra. And you?" Petra asked while analyzing every detail of the mysterious woman who was supposed to be her sister. Her hair fell over her shoulder in a thick braid, and as they stepped closer to one another, Petra could see the sheen of blue it gave off under the light. She wore a light blue dress, which was dirty at the hem from travel.

"Rheanna. I can't believe I am meeting you. I have dreamed of this moment for so long. Only Cyra and Aella being here could make it any better," Rheanna rambled on, her pale cheeks blooming with nervousness. Her hand flew to her mouth as she chewed on a fingernail.

"It is nice to meet you, Rheanna. Honestly, though, I am quite confused. I was unaware I had sisters." Petra played with her hands, finding it difficult to meet the gaze that mirrored her mother's. She swallowed the lump in her throat as the memories of her mother's unseeing and blood-filled gaze haunted her.

"Where are Mother and Father?" Rheanna asked.

Petra's heart froze at her sister's words. It became hard to breathe, and small gasps of air escaped as she struggled to control her grief. Green vines began to sprout from the tile as her magic reacted to the sudden burst of emotion, and Petra found herself incapable of responding.

"Petra," a gentle voice whispered as Rheanna wrapped her arms around her little sister's shoulders, "it's alright. Everything will be alright." Rheanna ran her fingers down Petra's waves as she attempted to soothe her.

"Enough of all the hysterics, child. You are a princess," the Oracle quipped. Her nails dug into Petra's upper arm as she shook her slightly.

"Leave her alone," Rheanna shot back with a venom coating her words.

The Oracle's black eyes bore into Rheanna's, but she released Petra and said nothing else. Petra felt Rheanna shiver with her arms still wrapped protectively around her. Rheanna pulled her to the couch as she continued to console her.

When Petra was able to breathe evenly again, she said in a trembling voice, "They were killed."

"Oh goddess," Rheanna managed to mumble. Her eyes began to fill with tears as she took in Petra's shattered and grief-stricken face. "I am so sorry." The pain Petra had been dealing with for days on her own was now clear on her sister's face. Her dark eyebrows pulled together, and a wrinkle formed between them.

"I'm not alone." Petra leaned further into her embrace as sobs wracked her body.

"No. Never again." Rheanna rubbed circles into her back.

After a few long minutes, Petra pulled away from her older sister and looked at the Oracle, who stood by the door. The old woman's black eyes bore into the girls, and Petra could swear there was a bit of hatred behind that stare. She knew that the Oracle had been their trusted advisor for years, so she tried to shake it off.

"Why were my sisters sent away?" Petra questioned in a hoarse voice, throat raw from crying.

"We will discuss it when the other two return," the Oracle said stiffly.

Petra and Rheanna exchanged a quick glance before Rheanna said, "Tell me everything about your life. We have fourteen years to make up for."

"Come. I'll show you my rooms!" Petra stood quickly, joy blossoming over her face, erasing the sadness that filled it only moments ago. She tugged on her sister's pale hand as she started toward the door.

"Don't go too far. The others should be here shortly," the Oracle called after the girls, but they were already running down the hall.

Petra watched as her sister took in the grandeur of the palace. Though she was used to its beauty, she could see the look of amazement that blossomed across Rheanna's face.

"It is even more beautiful than I remember."

Rheanna halted in front of a portrait of Petra and the King and Queen. Her hand reached out as if to stroke her mother's cheek but fell against her skirts. Petra looked between her parents and Rheanna and could make out small similarities. Rheanna had the crystal blue eyes of their mother; even the shape, slightly upturned at the ends, matched perfectly. Her delicate frame was a mirror to their mother's, and her nose seemed to be the smaller version of their father's. Petra could imagine that she and Rheanna shared features despite their varying shades of hair and eyes.

"How old were you?" Petra asked softly.

Rheanna turned, bringing her eyes to her sister. "I was six. Our older sister, Cyra was nine, and Aella was four."

Pain clenched her chest as the reality of it all hit her. They were little children who were ripped from their parents, from their home. Petra was fourteen and had barely survived the loss. How did three little girls cope?

"I'm sorry." Petra's hand clasped her older sister's once again.

"You have nothing to be sorry for." Rheanna smiled sadly then said, "Now, show me your rooms!"

Rheanna followed her sister, a light smile pulling at her lips as she was dragged through the vaguely familiar gilded halls. They stopped in front of the room where vines and flowers grew wildly around the door frame, as if they sprouted from the gold itself.

"These are my rooms!" Petra exclaimed as she threw the doors open.

An overwhelming floral aroma assaulted them, and every inch of the room was covered in greenery or books. The room resembled an overgrown forest floor with furniture simply placed within it.

"Well, you certainly have some interesting choices in decorations," Rheanna laughed as she drank it all in.

"It usually isn't as bad in here, but it can be hard to control my powers when my emotions are so strong. Mama used to have a landscaper come and trim it up." Petra's face fell at the last sentence.

"It is truly beautiful! Why don't you show me where I will be staying?"

"Didn't you have rooms when you lived here?" Petra asked.

"Cyra, Aella, and I shared a room. We couldn't bear to be apart for more than five minutes let alone sleep separately," she answered wistfully.

Petra nodded, but her expression seemed even sadder than before. How would it have been if she had grown up with them? Would she have slept bundled in the warmth of her sisters?

"I can have the staff set you up —"

Luca stepped into the room, cutting Petra off.

"No need, Princess. I will escort you both to Princess Rheanna's chambers. They have already been prepared." He said this softly, as if afraid he would scare Petra off.

"If you must, Sir Luca." Petra suddenly seemed closed off, her pretty face going blank in reaction to the boy.

"Thank you, Sir Luca." Rheanna's face shined with gratitude, despite her eyes flicking back and forth between the teenagers. Petra tried not to squirm under her sister's scrutiny.

"Just Luca is fine, Princess Rheanna," he responded.

Rheanna nodded as Petra moved forward to link their arms once again. She pulled her sister away, though Rheanna's blue gaze followed Luca, her brows furrowing.

CHAPTER 9

R EDDEL COULD BOTH BE heard and smelled far before it was seen. Set in a deep mountainous ridge, the sounds of the city drifted up along the plains like a musical cacophony full of life and excitement.

Cyra and her escorts eventually made their way to the city itself, where the sounds of screeching children, arguing merchants, wheels on cobblestones, and a murmur of talking, laughing, fighting, arguing, and more brought a smile to Cyra's full lips. It had been ages since she saw the city, and she could picture the vibrant capital streets full of the smells that came with all that noise. Baking bread, sweet honey, heady perfumes, and oils from around the world as traders far and wide came with local, mundane, and exotic goods to swap, sell, buy, and more.

For a moment, she closed her eyes, remembering how it was when she was little. The nostalgia seemed to dull comparatively, but it was something that she held onto since she was nine years old. It was also strange how she had given up ever being a royal again or ever being with her parents, yet now all she wanted was to be in her mother's embrace and for her father to retell stories of battles while her sisters were cuddled next to her.

Was it odd that she felt so conflicted? She hated how she, Aella, and Rheanna were just tossed aside. Clamped in irons and pushed out of the castle and their lives for circumstances still left unknown. She grew and had many of her firsts—first womanly bleeding, first kiss, first love, first date, first carnal encounter, first alcohol, first birth, and more—without her parents or sisters around. The only one to raise her was a man she was entrusted to who treated her more like a daughter than her own parents did and knew nothing about growing girls.

Yet, there was happiness before it all changed. Nights reading by the fire, eating rich foods, stories, hugs, kisses, and learning how to be a princess and one day, the Queen. Was it wrong of her to want that again after so long and maybe put what had happened behind her?

Maybe. She was no longer a child but a fully grown woman with her own life to lead and a daughter of her own to protect. Hollin was so young and didn't know anything of Cyra's past, and she was uncertain if she wanted to involve her in such. How does one even mention it to parents who were never there? Hollin was her priority above everything else, and given her pointed ears, her fae heritage was impossible to hide.

Linnosa was not a progressive kingdom. Especially ever since the magic disappeared years ago. The other species—such as the pixies and nymphs who needed magic to survive—fell ill, died, or fled the continent to other lands that still pulsed with it. The fae followed them shortly afterward since their magic was stifled in Linnosa.

Due to this, humans who dwelled here began to resent the other species and even turned on magic in general. Hollin's father was one of the few who dared to venture into Linnosa and was Cyra's first and only love despite how she appeared to other men and flirted about to get her way.

Would her parents have even approved of their daughter falling in love with a fae? She wouldn't know or entertain the thought of them finding out. Though she didn't have time to finish that thought as a guard's brusque voice broke her concentration.

"We will be entering the city soon, Princess," one of the guards, Will said, "For your protection, put on the hood of your cloak."

Without question, Cyra tugged the cloak on. She doubted anyone would remember the fiery-haired princess who used to explore the streets, but the royal guards were enough to garner attention.

The afternoon sun blazed high in the sky, warming the streets below and enhancing the smells of spice and bread, as well as bringing with it a billowing breeze that blew through the streets and wove itself through tightly packed buildings. The sound of the horses' hooves clopping the streets was rhythmic and dull, and it lulled Cyra into a trance as she stared at the various shops, peddlers, and people. Some buildings stood open with their goods on display—blacksmiths hammering metal, farmers hawking meat and cabbage—while others remained closed, enticing buyers inside. Clothiers and cobblers offered their wares, while alehouses and taverns promised food, booze, and coital love—for the right price.

Few people glanced their way. Who wanted to gain the ire and attention of the royal guards? Most instead kept to their tasks, with their attention on their own little world.

Travel had been rough for Cyra, and she readjusted herself and rubbed her burning, aching thighs as she sat upon her horse. The rawness of the saddle dug into the flesh of her legs. However, as she did, a small object hit her in the chest, hurting enough to cause her to cry in pain and almost knocking her off her horse.

The song of steel rang out as the guards unsheathed their swords. The clink of metal echoed out their mistrust of all around them as they homed in on a young boy who came to a halting stop in front of the party and froze, cowering beneath them.

A sword from one of the guards pointed beneath his chin, digging into the soft flesh of his jawline as he stumbled back, a thin line reddening on his skin. His large brown eyes frantically darted from one figure to another, and Cyra stared down at him, meeting him with her golden gaze.

"I am so sorry ma'am. We were just playin'," he managed to choke out.

Cyra glanced down to see a red ball beneath the horse and quickly said, "Stand down" to the guard, whose sword instantly lowered. Her gaze shifted back to the young boy, and she smiled. "No harm done, little one."

The silence of the street finally dawned on her as she realized her hood had fallen during the altercation. She felt their stares on her skin as a whisper broke out.

Princess Cyra is back.

"Let's get going," Cyra urged the guards as the whispers became shouts. The boy staggered out of the way as the horses picked up speed and began to gallop. A sudden tug on the edge of Cyra's cloak almost made her topple to the ground once again, but instead, fire burst around her in a protective bubble out of instinct.

The man who attempted to grab her winced in pain as the fire licked his hand, and he hissed, "You are the Unworthy."

Before Cyra could even think of a response, he yanked her off the horse's back. She tumbled, landing headfirst on the dirt path without enough time to orient herself. Fire lashed out around her, head dizzy from the fall as she attempted to stand. A flash of silver dashed forward, and a spray of blood coated Cyra's horse and dress as a small figure quickly slit the man's throat.

"Hi, sis," a woman with shoulder-length silver hair and violet eyes winked at her.

"Aella," she breathed.

Aella smirked and hopped onto the back of Cyra's horse, reaching out to pull her sister up. "We need to get to the castle, or I'm going to have to kill more of your people."

Despite the surprise on all the guard's faces, they heeded Aella's advice, and Cyra quickly mounted. Chaos erupted as they began to move. Citizens clamored to get a look at the princesses or to hurl insults at them. Shouts of "The Unworthy" and "Our Queen" filled the square, but no one made a move to harm them. It seemed Aella's show of force was enough to keep them from any physical assault.

Once they were secure, Aella jumped off the horse with Cyra quickly following. Her mouth hung open as she took in the tiny but deadly human that was her baby sister. All 5'5 of her stood honed with edges and sharpness. She was no longer the soft-cheeked toddler Cyra remembered.

"Have I rendered you speechless?" Aella asked, one pale eyebrow shooting up.

"Aella." Cyra rushed forward with her arms outstretched to embrace her estranged sister, but Aella quickly stepped back. "I never thought I'd see you again."

"Princess Aella," one of the guards called, interrupting before Aella could reply. "Where is your escort?"

"Probably on their way to the castle." Aella cocked her head.

"They were meant for your protection on your journey," the guard stammered in surprise.

"They were unneeded."

Cyra watched as Aella's eyes narrowed on the guard who spoke to her, a predator latching onto its prey.

"Well, she's here and safe, so no harm done," she interjected quickly, her tan hand grasping Aella's toned forearm.

Her sister stiffened at the touch but didn't make a move to pull away, so Cyra gently began to guide her toward the brass gates of the castle as people moved out of their way. Groans echoed in the distance as machinery twirled and cracked, pulling up the great steel gate to bring the portcullis up and let the sisters within.

Cyra stared up at the castle, letting her mind wander back to before once again. The castle was the same as she had left it: large and imposing. Made of light stones and accented with golden windows and shutters that caught the rays of the sun and shone its richness down to the city below. The black roof and trim contrasted with the whiteness, and the tallest peak disappeared among fluffy clouds. Hard to imagine that this castle had stood for hundreds of years and was once smaller, though that was just in fairytales. For her, it had always been like this and would always be.

An array of greenery and wildflowers climbed the rocks and across the courtyard with thick, fat bees buzzing contently among the flowers. Birds fluttered around them, kicking up into the sky in a shower of downy feathers as they frightfully scattered at the horses.

Cyra didn't recall the foliage being this dense when she was a little girl, which she imagined had to do with her youngest sister. The three elder sisters each had an elemental power, so it made sense that their youngest sister did as well.

The thought of meeting that youngest one—the one they kept—was an ache that she didn't know how to decipher. Her parents abandoned her, even if they called her back now, but the youngest girl was innocent of those decisions. No matter how she felt, she did long to see them again.

Several steps before the threshold of the castle, Aella froze and turned to her sister.

"Did they tell you yet?" she asked, her purple eyes hard as they bore into Cyra's golden ones.

"Tell me what?" Cyra's brows furrowed.

Aella rolled her eyes and sighed, exasperated, "The King and Queen are dead."

The words hit Cyra like a blow, knocking the breath out of her chest as she clenched her hand over her heart, balling the brown fabric of her dress. It suddenly all made sense. Why else would they all be called back to the castle? Any hopes of being held by her mother or forgiving her father disappeared. Cyra must have staggered because Aella was fiercely gripping her forearms now, her face twitching with emotions, but Cyra couldn't discern them.

"How?" Cyra croaked, tears making her eyes liquid gold.

"Poison."

Cyra recoiled at the thought of someone assassinating their parents. They were loved by the citizens of Linnosa as far as she was aware. Maybe another kingdom or realm? Or were there issues she was unaware of behind the scenes? Her thoughts wandered to the idea of someone on the council who wanted to claim power for themselves, but that would mean she and her sisters were all in danger as well.

"We need to get to the others," Cyra said as she composed herself, wiping the runaway tears that streamed down her cheeks.

Aella nodded curtly, and they both turned and took their first steps into their castle.

A tall, dark man in brown trousers and a loose off-white shirt stood among a group of soldiers, conversing about whatever it is men talk about. His curly black hair struck a nerve of familiarity in Cyra. As if he felt her gaze on him, his head turned toward her, revealing depthless brown eyes and a shadow of stubble across a wide jaw. His full lips parted as he took her in. The sudden realization of who he was smacked into her as he began to barrel toward her. Before she knew it, a woodsy scent of cedar and spice encased her, and she was swept into his arms, her feet lifting off the ground.

"I can't believe it's you!" he gushed, putting her down and ruffling her hair with a large hand.

Cyra stared dumbfounded at her first crush and childhood playmate, Ivan Bushnell. Never had she thought she would see him again. Her words usually never failed her, especially with men, but she was utterly speechless.

"Not excited to see me?" Aella interjected, breaking the trance Cyra seemed to be under.

Ivan's dark eyes flickered to Aella, quickly assessing the small girl. "Oh, Aella. Do you even remember me?"

"Honestly? No," she deadpanned.

Cyra felt a surge of gratefulness at her sister, and the short respite she gave her to compose herself.

"Aella was always the silly one," Ivan laughed.

Instead of responding, Aella crossed her arms, causing the muscles in her arm to bulge, and stared at him.

"She definitely has a sense of humor for sure," Cyra laughed awkwardly.

"So, she does speak." Ivan's dark brow quirked.

"Clearly." Aella rolled her eyes.

Before the interaction could grow even more awkward, Will, one of the guards who escorted Cyra, interrupted them. "I can take you to Princess Petra and Princess Rheanna."

"Rheanna is here already?" Cyra asked, eyes going wide and heart beating faster at the revelation.

"I accompanied her on the journey, Cy. She has been living with my family for the past fourteen years," Ivan offered.

A sort of bitterness flickered in Cyra as she thought about Rheanna living with the Bushnells. How different her life would have been if she was the one sent with them. Maybe Hollin would be Ivan's, and they would be married, but Cyra shook those nasty thoughts away. She should just be grateful her sister was well cared for.

"Thank you for keeping her safe," Cyra responded.

"Always," nodded Ivan.

Will gestured down the hall. "If you may, Princesses."

CHAPTER 10

A ELLA COULD NOT STAND one more moment of Cyra and her puppy-dog eyes, so she was glad when the guard dragged them away. She was not planning on even interacting with any of her sisters, but when she saw Cyra get attacked and realized how incapable the guards were, she couldn't stop herself. It was clear something more was going on in the capital. First, their parents were murdered, and now, people in the streets went after Cyra, who was once their beloved princess. She'd heard whispers of a rebel group stirring trouble but found it hard to believe. It seemed it was all more complicated than she thought.

The halls of the castle were just as gaudy as Aella had imagined. It made her sick to think about the privilege the royals had, but not once did they think to look in on their four-year-old daughter. The sound of laughter grew louder as they approached an open door. Inside was a lean, black-haired woman and a smaller, brown-haired and freckled girl. They both looked up as Cyra and Aella entered the room.

The woman with black hair, who Aella instantly identified as Rheanna, gasped in excitement and ran toward them. Her long slender arms wrapped around their necks, pulling them too close for comfort. Aella stiffened and pushed herself away from the embrace. She quickly became resentful of the amount of touching she already had to endure since meeting her sisters.

Rheanna's deep blue eyes studied both of her sisters, tears pouring down her porcelain cheeks as she gestured toward the younger girl who walked forward.

"This is Petra, our baby sister." Rheanna smiled softly, placing her hand on her arm.

Aella watched as Cyra's eyes widened momentarily while taking in the young girl as she moved forward to wrap her arms around her.

"I have dreamed of this moment for so long, Petra. I am so incredibly happy to meet you." Cyra's words seemed to soothe Petra as she leaned into her touch.

Aella stood back and gave her sisters a tight-lipped smile that resembled more of a grimace, her hands folding to cover her chest. Despite the clear differences in hair and eye color, her sisters all looked shockingly similar. Rheanna was the most like Aella, with her high cheekbones and sharp jaw, while Petra resembled Cyra, both with round faces and a thick smattering of freckles across their faces. The three older sisters shared the same slender, ballpoint nose, but Petra's was a bit wider and upturned. Rheanna was the lightest in complexion as if she had never come into contact with the sun. Aella suddenly wondered whether she looked the most like their mother or father but quickly discarded the thought. It didn't matter which one of those gene donors resembled her more. She just had to make it through this little reunion, and really, she could leave at any moment. She knew she could have easily evaded the guards and this whole ordeal, but she let her curiosity get the better of her. It better be worth it.

"If I had known you existed, I imagine I would have as well," Petra responded as she pulled back to look at all her sisters. Cyra and Rheanna exchanged shocked glances at the news.

"They didn't even bother to tell you about us?" Aella's tone came out disgusted.

"I think they knew I wouldn't stop until I met you all. I can be extremely stubborn," Petra said, but tears began to fill her eyes. "I can't imagine they would do anything to hurt us intentionally."

"So instead, they erased every trace of their three daughters? Pathetic," Aella spit out. She would not be so forgiving.

"I can't believe it," Cyra whispered. "I remember the day we were separated; Petra's birth. Father seemed so cold, so angry. At the time, I thought it was at me, but..."

"They must have had a good reason," Rheanna interjected.

Before Aella could snap back with a retort, a gravelly voice joined the conversation.

"They did."

Aella's eyes darkened and narrowed as she saw an old, haggard woman walk in. Instantly, she took a dislike to her, sensing something about the woman that made her squirm internally, even if she didn't understand why.

There was something unnatural about the way she moved, and she didn't like how she studied each of her sisters with her beady, black eyes. In her line of work, deception was a tool that was used to unease and unseat opponents. More than once, Aella had to appear weak to get a target off balance, and she knew an actor when she saw one. The old woman was ancient and perhaps wise, but she was hiding something.

And Aella hated when secrets were kept from her.

Her skin hung off her like leather flaps, slipping along her bones as if she had no muscle, and her back crooked and hunched over as she shuffled into the room. Long, silvery hair hung in straggly strands along her back, and she carried with her a walking cane to hold herself upright.

"What do you have to do with all of this?" Aella asked, her arms crossed.

"I am the one who told your parents to send you away," the Oracle replied calmly.

Fury burned just beneath her skin, itching to get out, but Rheanna's hand laid soothingly on her bicep as if she could sense her anger. She had always been the more sensitive sister, the most caring of them, even at a young age.

"Why did you do that?" Cyra bit out with spite. Aella felt a sort of camaraderie with her. They both had the same anger, but Aella wondered if it was due to the fire her older sister wielded rather than the situation.

"I saw a prophecy. Four shall emerge, but only one will rise." The Oracle's lifeless black eyes bore into them, and Aella had to repress a shiver.

"What does that mean?" Petra asked.

Possibilities already ran through Aella's mind, but the most obvious were pushed to the forefront.

"We all die except one."

Three heads snapped toward her at the words. They were all thinking the same thing; she had only said it out loud. She had never been superstitious, and this was not when that would change.

"That is how I foresaw it, but prophecies are tricky things," the Oracle agreed.

"So are oracles, I hear," Aella responded smoothly.

The Oracle did not even bat an eye at the comment, instead ignoring it. "Regardless, you are all unsafe, but it was time for you to be united once again."

"Because of our parents' deaths?" Cyra asked.

"Yes. Cyra, you are the rightful Queen of Linnosa. Any heirs you shall produce will be next in line as well."

Aella watched as Cyra wiggled uncomfortably at the news, then her attention shifted to Petra. She expected to see some sort of animosity from the young girl from the loss of her throne, but she seemed relieved if anything, so Aella followed up with her own question. "Will the kingdom accept her?"

"Why wouldn't they? She is still their princess." Rheanna's dark brows furrowed.

"That was fourteen years ago. They have a new beloved princess now." Aella's gaze shifted to a startled Petra.

"I...I...I don't want to be Queen. I mean, they raised me to take the throne, but I would never take Cyra's place. It is rightfully hers," Petra said quickly, emerald eyes wide. Rheanna moved closer to Petra as if to provide her comfort.

"I'm not even sure how I feel about this. I have a whole life waiting for me in the South," Cyra mumbled.

"It doesn't matter. You will take the throne," the Oracle said calmly.

"Cyra didn't receive the warmest welcome when entering the city," Aella finally confided. Cyra's gaze snapped to hers, golden eyes swirling with something she couldn't pinpoint.

"What do you mean?" Rheanna's voice filled with panic and worry for her older sister.

"It was nothing, Rhe. Don't worry about it." Cyra's soft smile visibly eased Rheanna.

"Cyra will take the throne," the Oracle repeated.

Aella rolled her eyes. "We get it."

A knock at the door interrupted their conversation, and a petite woman with jet-black straight hair that reached the nape of her back shuffled in. Aella felt her eyes roaming over her body and her beautiful, soft, heart-shaped face a little too long. The woman glanced toward her as well, but Aella snapped her gaze away, studying the tiled floor instead.

"Dinner is ready for you all in the private dining hall." Her voice was like bells and instantly sent shivers across Aella's skin.

"Thank you, Natalie. We will be there shortly," Petra responded politely.

Natalie curtsied, and her dark gaze settled on Aella again before she left. That woman was exactly what Aella needed to relax in this place. Her confident facade settled over her as she thought about the ways to get the pretty little maid in her bed.

CHAPTER 11

T HE CASTLE WAS SO overwhelming that Rheanna had to prevent herself from gaping in every new room or hallway she entered.

A lot of it she recognized from her early life, before she was sent away, though it felt like it was so long ago that it was more of a dream than a memory. Many things were much the same—elaborate paintings, decorations, tapestries, and more covering the walls. Yet some newer things such as furniture, books, or exotic trinkets from distant lands seemed so strange and new that it felt as though she was walking into the castle for the first time.

The private dining hall was as grand as the rest of the hall, just as she remembered it. Long tapestries hung in the rafters above while the distant windows in the vaulted ceiling created shafts of white light down atop the table to give it a natural glow. Though the carpeting was new and fresh, colored in the same dark blue hue as the royal guard.

Spread across the central large, gold-inlaid table were a variety of sumptuous dishes. A roasted hog with burnt, cracking skin, steamed atop a bed of fresh vegetables and fruit, while an apple hung in its mouth to greet any guests and tempt them into taking a portion of it. Biscuits, olives, cheeses, plates of pasta, pastries, and more encircled the roasted hog, each layered atop one another with napkins and forks at the ready to spear and tear and eat.

It was a banquet, and one that Rheanna hadn't partaken in or even seen in years. Food in Dalmer was plentiful thanks to trade and game when the snow would let up, but it was always well-preserved, salty, and hard unless boiled. Flour was preserved for bread, and butter was mostly used to sweeten meats and vegetables in the stewing pot rather than make cakes and muffins and the like. So, the sight of all the richness in front of her made Rheanna's mouth water a little bit in anticipation for the coming meal.

Five place settings were set up, and it made Rheanna question who else would be joining them. There was, of course, her, Cyra, Aella, and Petra; four sisters, four places. Who was the fifth?

Her question was soon answered when Ivan walked in and simply took the empty seat next to Petra without waiting for guidance from anyone else.

"And who are you, little one?" he asked, his dark brows rising.

"I am Petra, Princess of Linnosa," Petra answered shyly.

"Very nice to meet you, Princess," he smiled warmly.

Rheanna couldn't keep herself from studying him, their gazes locking and Ivan bowing his head of black hair. They all began to fill their plates besides Petra, who appeared extremely uncomfortable, leaving her plate empty. Before Rheanna could comment on it, Aella spoke. "Where have you two been all this time?"

Rheanna answered first. "I've been living in a small town called Dalmer with the Bushnells, Ivan and his family. I teach preschool."

The mention of her profession brought a pang of guilt in her chest causing her to think of her students and instantly missing them.

"I live in the South with Ron, who used to be the head of the royal guard. We own an inn," Cyra said.

"How quaint." Aella's voice came out bored, but Rheanna could sense the underlying harshness in it.

"What about you, Aella?" Petra's small voice asked.

"Well, I wasn't being a pampered princess or schoolteacher, that's for sure," her sister snapped.

"That's not fair," Cyra interjected.

"No. What's not fair is leaving a defenseless four-year-old with a cruel and evil man." Aella clenched her silverware tightly in each hand.

"I've heard about you," Ivan gasped. "Silver Death."

Cyra's mouth dropped open as she realized who Aella was while Rheanna and Petra looked at them all in confusion.

"Ah, my little nickname. Quite fitting, I suppose."

"You're the most notorious assassin in Linnosa," Cyra breathed.

"I would argue in a few different continents, actually," Ivan said, his eyes wide with wonder.

"Could you train me?" Rheanna questioned suddenly.

It was Aella's turn to be surprised. "Well, I suppose."

"I can't use my powers either," she whispered, but at her sisters' stares she continued, "I never learned how to manipulate ice before I went to the North. After everything, magic was no longer fun for me without you two."

Aella nodded in agreement. "I can use my powers but tend to stick to my other skills. What about you two?" She nodded toward Petra and Cyra.

"I have strong control over my Earth manipulation. The Oracle trained me, and I have a bit of experience with sword play, but I'm not the best at hand-to-hand," Petra informed them.

"I'm shocked they let your train in combat at all. Doesn't seem very princess-y," Aella scoffed.

"Father wanted me to be able to defend myself."

Aella's eyes rolled, and Cyra said, "I have pretty good fire skills due to my training before we left, but my combat skills definitely need some refining."

"Good thing you're in the presence of the most notorious assassin in Linnosa." Aella winked.

"I could probably learn a thing or two from you," Ivan added.

"The invitation of training only extends to family," Aella responded coolly.

Ivan's eyes narrowed, but Rheanna knew he just wanted to be included and wouldn't start a fight with Aella. Aella raised a cocky eyebrow as if daring him to though and a flash of anger crossed his features.

"Why don't we start tomorrow?" Rheanna asked quickly, attempting to interrupt whatever was happening between the two.

"Fine," was Aella's one word response.

"I think I'll head off to bed," Petra said, yawning. Her plate was empty, and Rheanna didn't see her take one bite. She would have to figure out what was going on with that.

"I think I shall as well." Rheanna excused herself and followed Petra out of the dining hall, toward their private quarters. Her room was only a few doors down from the younger girl's.

"You didn't eat anything," stated Rheanna.

There was a long pause of silence, and Petra's hands twisted once she finally spoke. "They died in there, and I watched it happen."

Rheanna's forehead wrinkled in worry. "Have you been able to eat at all?"

"A bit, but not in the dining hall."

"Then we will no longer eat there. We can take meals in our private quarters." Rheanna's hand wrapped around her sister's entangled ones. "You are no longer alone."

Tears pricked at the corner of Petra's emerald gaze. "Thank you."

After seeing Petra safely to her room, Rheanna made her way to her own. Thankfully, none of the guards or staff stopped to ask her anything or bother her, even though she heard talking from the hallway of the dining hall. A small part of her wanted to return to talk to Cyra and Aella, but another part told her that she'd have time later. She might have lost a lot of that time with her parents, but she felt confident that her sisters would be around.

Of that, she'd make sure of.

Her room was nearly as exquisite as her sister's but lacking in the clutter of wildflowers and vines covering every inch of the room. As was to be expected of luxury, Rheanna's room was gilded in gold with silver filigree and many precious works of art depicting snow, ice, and the northern lands as well as past Kings and Queens that were her ancestors lining the walls. There weren't any books littered across the ground like in Petra's, which Rheanna was glad for since it opened the space enough for her to easily move around. The furniture was ancient, carved from rich woods deep in the hearts of ancient forests back when magic was rampant across the land.

It was all soft and comfortable. In Dalmer, the furniture was often as stiff and unyielding as the people itself, mostly because it had to be treated to not let the moisture of the snow and ice in or else it would rot. Here, the cushions bent beneath her weight and were light enough that even she could easily move them around.

Even the bed—as large and dominant as it was—yielded to her mild strength. It was a canopy, one that Rheanna could only have dreamed of with silver curtains that shuttered around and kept the warmth of the room within. It was the centerpiece of the whole room, made with intricate carvings of waves along the headboard and navy sheets atop it.

In fact, everything in the room was evocative of the colors that defined her. Blues of every hue with silver highlights. At least when the gold didn't shine through.

Smiling, Rheanna made her way to her small backpack and quickly changed into a wool nightgown, which was far too thick for the temperate climate outside. Even at night and with the window open, it was far warmer than Dalmer would have been even in the mild months of the warmer seasons.

But it was all she had for now. The staff informed her earlier that they would have her and her sisters measured for tailored clothing in the morning. For now, she'd make do, though she wouldn't complain. It was hers, and that's all that mattered.

A knock at her door pulled her out of her thoughts as she went to answer. The overwhelming scent of wood mingled with cinnamon overwhelmed her, and she instantly felt relaxed.

"I need to speak with you," Ivan said as he pushed himself into the room.

"What's wrong?" Rheanna felt worry bubbling up, watching him pace the length of her room.

"I don't trust her?"

"Who?"

"Aella."

"That is ridiculous. She is my sister," Rheanna shook her head.

"And an assassin. You knew her fourteen years ago, Rhe." He paused to stare at her.

His words stung, but she defended her sister. "It sounds like she went through horrific things."

"Exactly. The last time you saw her she was a toddler."

"Stop it. I just got them back, and I will give them the benefit of the doubt." Rheanna's voice was hard as she glared at her lifelong friend.

Ivan looked shocked at her words. She typically listened and hung onto every word he said, but not when it came to her sisters. They were untouchable in her mind. Yet, Rheanna found herself wondering if he had a point. Aella had changed so much—had grown into someone fierce and cold. Would that kind of life leave her with loyalties intact?

"Fine, but don't say I didn't warn you."

"Out," she demanded, her finger flying toward the door.

Ivan shook his head in surprise but listened to her, nonetheless, leaving Rheanna angry and a bit wary.

Cyra drifted in a haze of exhaustion, her body sinking into the plush, unfamiliar bed in the castle. The weight of her return to the royal life pressed heavily on her, but her heart bore the greatest burden—aching for the little girl she had left behind. Sleep pulled at her until she found herself in a familiar, dreamlike landscape.

She was no longer in the cold, gilded halls of the castle. Instead, she stood in the unforgiving heat of the morning sun, back at the Eye of the Storm Inn. The air smelled of fresh bread, and the soft hum of a child's laughter filled the space around her. She felt light, free from the heaviness that had followed her since leaving Hollin behind.

"Mommy!" Hollin's voice called out, as bright and carefree as ever.

Cyra turned to see her daughter running through the doors of the inn, her strawberry-blonde hair catching in the sunlight. Hollin was spinning with her arms stretched out, twirling in a circle with wild abandon. The fishtail braid Cyra had so often woven bounced against her back, and her pointed ears were carefully hidden beneath a white head scarf.

"Hollin!" Cyra called, her voice thick with longing as she began to run toward her daughter.

Hollin stopped spinning and turned toward Cyra, her emerald eyes sparkling with joy. "Mommy, come play! Look, I made a flower crown for you!" She held up a crown made of small red roses.

Cyra's heart surged as she closed the distance between them. When she reached Hollin, she knelt to the girl's level, the ground soft beneath her knees. "Oh, Holli-bean," she whispered, pulling her daughter into her arms and holding her tight. The familiar scent of Hollin's hair—the smell of sunshine and wildflowers—washed over her, grounding her in the dreamlike haze.

"I miss you so much," Cyra whispered into Hollin's hair, her voice trembling with emotion.

Hollin pulled back slightly, her small hands reaching up to place the flower crown on Cyra's head. "I miss you too, Mommy," she said. "But you promised you'd come back."

"I will," Cyra promised, her throat tightening as she met Hollin's wide, trusting eyes. "I'll come back to you, Holli. I swear it."

They sat together in the golden light, the world around them peaceful and quiet. The sound of the wind rustling through the grass and the distant hum of birdsong filled the air, and for a brief moment, Cyra felt whole again.

Hollin giggled as she grabbed Cyra's hand and tugged her to stand. "Let's chase the butterflies!" she declared, pointing to a flurry of colorful wings dancing above the sandy ground.

Cyra let Hollin pull her along, their feet kicking up dust as they chased the butterflies together.

"Look, Mommy! I caught one!" Hollin shouted, her hand cupped carefully around something small and delicate.

Cyra knelt beside her again, smiling as Hollin slowly opened her hands to reveal a butterfly with wings as golden as the sun. It fluttered gently in her palms before taking flight again, disappearing into the sky.

Hollin's eyes followed the butterfly's path, and for a moment, she was quiet. Then she looked back at Cyra, her expression more serious, more thoughtful. "You won't forget, right?"

Cyra's breath caught in her throat. She knew this was just a dream, that Hollin wasn't really here, but the question still hit her like a punch to the chest. "Forget what, baby?"

Hollin tilted her freckled face. "To come back. To the stars, remember?"

"To the stars," Cyra whispered, the words slipping from her lips like a prayer. "I could never forget, Holli. Never."

Hollin wrapped her arms around Cyra's neck, pulling her close again, and Cyra held her tightly, pressing her cheek against her daughter's soft hair.

The sun began to dim, clouds casting a gray hue over the once bright landscape. Hollin's form started to dissolve in her arms, like sand slipping through her fingers.

"No..." Cyra whispered, her voice breaking as she tried to hold onto her daughter. "Not yet. Please, not yet."

But the dream was slipping away, and Hollin's voice echoed softly in the distance, "To the stars, Mommy. To the stars..."

Cyra woke with a start, and a sob tore up her throat. She was back in the empty room of the castle. Her chest ached, her arms felt hollow, and the bed beneath her suddenly seemed too large, too empty without Hollin beside her.

"To the stars," she whispered into the darkness, her voice barely audible.

But the stars felt so far away.

CHAPTER 12

PETRA HAD A FITFUL night full of nightmares. Nightmares that included the deaths of her parents. The sounds of her father as he gurgled on blood; the sounds of her mother hitting the ground and convulsing as she tried to speak. How one could ever forget such a horrific sight, she didn't know.

It wasn't as if she didn't know that death was a reality and that people could die in a plethora of horrible ways. Her stories that she loved were full of them. Villains who died at the end of a sword strike from the charming prince. Monsters vanquished. Minor bullies and more put in their place with a well-timed push from a damsel. Her stories were rife with examples of how death came.

Yet the reality of it was so much different. To watch someone you love die before your eyes was a horror she wouldn't wish on her worst enemy, not that she had any.

All Petra knew was that eating, sleeping, and even living had been difficult following her parents' death. The thought of her sisters being here now at least was a comfort. Even if she hadn't known of their existence.

She knew them less than a day, yet she could already feel the love from them. Especially when Rheanna showed up with a plate of pastries, fruit, and warm tea.

Cyra was welcoming as well with her hugs and soft touches, reminding her of their mother. However, it felt as if Aella didn't really have any desire to know her. If anything, she felt hostility from that sister.

She wondered what had happened to her that made her the way she was and turned her into a trained killer. No sooner had the thought crossed her mind than Aella barged into her room without knocking, dressed head-to-toe in form-fitting leather armor that protected her vitals and made her look ready for battle. Her daggers were strapped to her hips, and she sneered down at Petra, who still had the pastry crumbs from breakfast all over her face.

"Ready to train?"

Petra popped another buttery pastry into her mouth and nodded eagerly, jumping to her feet. Rheanna followed suit, but Aella raised a silver eyebrow.

"You cannot train in that." She gestured to their gowns, and Petra blushed deeply.

"Of course, I'll change into some pants," she muttered.

"I don't have any," Rheanna said a bit shyly. She had no need for pants in Dalmer.

"You can borrow some of mine," Aella offered.

Rheanna nodded and followed Aella out. Petra turned to her wardrobe and picked out a training outfit. She ended up with brown trousers, a white long-sleeve shirt, and dark brown combat boots. Lastly, she braided her hair and wrapped it around her head making a crown. Once she was ready, she headed into the gilded hall and met her sisters. She stifled a giggle at the sight of tall Rheanna in leather pants several inches too short for her. Rheanna glared at her for a moment, knowing exactly what was so funny, but then broke into a smile of her own. Cyra was in an outfit similar to Petra's yet hers was a little more worn and not as finely made. Her scarlet curls were bundled away in a bun on the top of her head.

"Lead the way, Petra," Aella said.

Petra brought them to the outdoor training ring that was specifically made for her and her powers. It used to be a part of the garden when she was little, but as she grew—as well as her abilities—the Oracle had this part cleared of decorations, bushes, rocks, flower beds, and more.

Though now it was still overgrown, just from her training alone. A large stone slab was buried into the dirt while heavy boulders from the mountains were laid around the slab at random intervals, with some boulders already having chunks blown out of them. Racks of weapons of all types—from swords to knives to even hammers—hung on a nearby wall and were maintained by the castle's smith. There were even wooden ones as well, made from a hard wood from the northern lands and designed for punishment. Several training dummies were also placed close by, with several broken, beaten, and blasted.

Thankfully, today was rather warm, with a light breeze. Petra trained in all sorts of weather before, but uncomfortable ones such as rain or sweltering heat made it hard for her to focus her attention and powers when she was trying not to slip and fall on the cracked stone floor.

The others didn't seem to mind the way that it looked, though. Cyra stared all around, Rheanna wandered to the weapons to fiddle her hands against various tools, and Aella looked blankly ahead with her arms crossed beneath her bust.

"Why don't we all give an example of our powers? So that we know what we're working with in that department," Cyra suggested, and since no one else moved, she moved toward the center of the ring.

Slowly, she lifted her arms, palms upturned at the sky as fire shot out of them. Her hands moved in front of her, and a wall of flames engulfed her. It licked at her skin, and Petra gasped in fear, but the heat didn't seem to affect or burn her. A grin spread across Cyra's face as she stood within the fire, looking as if she was a part of it herself. Her hair blended within the flames, and her eyes burned gold like a fiery goddess. Her arms fell to her side, and she laughed with her chest, bending over. "I haven't done that in a while."

Rheanna stepped forward next but said, "Prepare to be underwhelmed." She lifted one hand and concentrated hard, her brows knitting together. After a few seconds, a single pebble of water appeared. Her tongue poked out from the side of her mouth as she lifted her other hand and twisted it. The drop turned into a small stream about a foot high, sweat beading along Rheanna's forehead and her arms began to shake. The water splashed to the ground, and Rheanna slumped with a sigh escaping her.

"You did great," Cyra encouraged. "We'll have you commanding entire oceans in no time."

Rheanna smiled sadly and left the center, Petra now realizing it was her turn. She knew her magic was the most advanced out of her sisters, and a part of her wanted to show off and show that though she was young, she was powerful. She didn't even need her hands to manipulate her magic, but she knew they definitely added to the show. All she had to do was think, and the earth was hers to manipulate.

Petra stomped her left foot, splintering the stone of the ground and webbing out just in front of her sisters at the edge of the ring. An assortment of different colors of wildflowers shot out from each of the cracks: blue for Rheanna, white for Aella, and red for Cyra.

"Beautiful," Rheanna said as she bent to brush her fingers over the delicate flowers.

Petra twisted her body, and leafy vines wrapped around each of the surrounding pillars. The vines grew out from the ground around Petra, creating a thick canopy around her body, blocking her from view. She threw her hands out, and the vines exploded into a mirage of flowers, all streaming to her feet.

Next, she took on the boulders, lifting an especially large one and crushing it with the palm of her fist. The little particles turned into dust that got swept away into the oranges of the morning sky.

Petra turned to her sisters, not even a little bit winded, and bowed. Rheanna and Cyra fell into a fit of giggles, but Aella stood there stone-faced and arms still crossed.

"Your turn," Petra said.

"No," Aella replied.

"But—"

"I said no. I agreed to combat training, nothing else."

The giggling quickly ceased as they took in Aella's cold demeanor. Chills raced up Petra's back, and she wondered what had made her older sister so angry. She wondered if she would ever have a relationship with her or if it would always be strained and uncomfortable. Petra let go of that thought and decided she would do her best to make her feel safe here.

"Why don't we see what you've got, baby sister? You said you had some skill," Aella finally said, breaking the small stretch of silence after her refusal.

"I doubt I stand a chance against you, but let's do it!" Petra said excitedly as she went to grab a practice sword from the wall.

"No. Pick up a real weapon," Aella demanded. Petra hesitated but then chose her favorite sword, a small dainty thing with an amethyst at its hilt. Her father had given it to her on her thirteenth birthday.

They both took their stances and slowly circled one another, much as Petra was taught to do so. Though a slight bit of worry crossed her mind as she started to wonder if she was getting in over her head. After all, Petra had never actually fought off an assassin before: Just different guards and Luca, and it was always in her favor since no one wanted to hurt the princess.

Comparatively, Aella had killed...however many people in her life and was a feared assassin with a fearsome reputation that many people knew about. Even she, who was as sheltered as she was, had heard of the famed Silver Death.

Gulping, she tried to focus. That was what she was taught to do: empty her mind of everything except the fight. She eyed Aella, who stared at her with those frozen, icy eyes of hers, cold and uncaring. Petra held her weapon closer to her chest, keeping the pointy bit aimed at Aella.

Figuring it was best to go on the offensive to catch Aella off guard, Petra pressed her heel to the ground and dashed forward with a wide, arcing slash. Putting all her weight on her front foot, she recognized her mistake almost immediately after her arms were committed to the attack and she couldn't adjust.

Aella stood there with a bored expression, knocked her sword from her hand with a single parry, reached out, and grabbed Petra's collar before pulling her to the side to disorient her further, and then down to the cold, stone ground hard enough to knock her head against the floor and daze her momentarily.

She rolled onto her back, panting from the minor exertion as stars flicked in and out of the corner of her vision and stared up at the wicked smile of her sister, who mockingly pressed the front of her foot to Petra's side.

"What was your fatal mistake?" she asked.

"I didn't evenly distribute my weight," Petra panted out.

Aella moved off her sister, offering her hand to help pull her up as she said, "Exactly. Keep yourself grounded. It seems whoever was training you was going easy."

Petra felt defensive at that. "It was my fault. I know better."

"It was, but we'll work on it. I will be ruthless, unlike anyone you have fought with before. Can you handle it?"

"Yes." Petra stood.

"Then let's go again."

The sisters trained in combat all morning, taking turns one-on-one with Aella and then practicing with whichever of the other sisters was free. Their bodies were bruised and aching by mid-afternoon, but they were all happy and joking with one another. Even Aella had seemed to have softened up to them a bit. As they were walking back to their rooms to clean up, the Oracle stopped them.

"I need you all to clean up and have lunch promptly. You will be meeting with the royal council this afternoon."

"Isn't it a bit too soon for all this?" Cyra questioned nervously.

"They're extremely eager to meet with you all. There are currently no acting rulers of Linnosa, and it's essential that we get you crowned and on the throne quickly," the Oracle responded.

"Is it due to the unrest?" Aella asked. The Oracle glared at her as Petra asked, "There is unrest? What is happening?"

"Do not concern yourself with it now. It will be discussed at the meeting. Now, hurry along." The Oracle ushered them forward and hobbled away.

"She sure does like to boss us around," Rheanna muttered.

"She means well, I promise. She was mother and father's closest advisor," Petra defended hurriedly. While the Oracle could be a hag, she knew she could be trusted.

"I wouldn't depend on that," Aella chided.

"Well, let's just get this meeting over with then," Cyra said. Petra could hear the slight tremor in her voice. It must be hard for her to grow up nine years assuming she would be the Queen only to get ripped away from the responsibility of it for fourteen years and then thrown back into it again. Petra was a bit relieved she no longer carried the burden. Not only was she no longer the only heir, but she was now fourth in line. She never truly wanted it and did what she had to do out of duty.

"After we clean up, we can all take lunch in my rooms," Petra offered.

They all nodded in agreement and headed off to their separate destinations.

As Rheanna drifted down the hall, she caught sight of the blond-haired boy, Luca, slouched outside Petra's door. When he noticed her, he stood straight and said, "Good afternoon, Princess."

"Rheanna," she said with a small smile.

"Right, Rheanna, sorry," he stuttered.

She gestured down the hall. "Walk with me."

His blue eyes flickered to Petra's door and back, but he went to Rheanna as she began to walk.

"What happened between you and my sister?" she asked, her eyebrows almost touching her hairline.

He blushed deeply. "Oh, nothing."

Rheanna waved her hands and said, "Don't give me any of that. Be honest."

He sighed. "Well, we were dating before...well...before your parents died."

A few strands fell loose of her braid as she tilted her head to the side. "And?"

"I was ordered to take her away when everything was happening, and she blames me for not getting to say goodbye." His head hung low.

"They didn't give her time?" Rheanna questioned. How unfair it was to drag a girl away from the only family she had and not even lett her say goodbye. Rheanna at least always had the Bushnells to depend on.

"No. The Oracle demanded they be burned immediately," said Luca.

Rheanna stopped walking. "They didn't have an autopsy?"

"I'm not sure."

Rheanna continued walking but was silent for several moments. "Just give her time. She has been through a lot, but I can tell she loves you."

His blue eyes lit up. "You really think so?"

"I know so," she said with a smile.

CHAPTER 13

C YRA'S NERVES WERE ON fire as they all headed toward the war room. She had never been allowed inside it as a little girl, her parents claiming she was too young to be privy to such matters. She remembered how frustrated it made her as she was to be Queen after all. The small bit of food she managed to force down during lunch was now threatening to come back up as she stepped into the room.

It was as opulent as any other room in the castle but with a more stern air about it. While the main portions of the castle—even down to the servant quarters—were richly decorated and gave off an air of luxury, this room was more utilitarian and meant to evoke the power of the kingdom of Linnosa instead of the wealth.

Where fabrics would have hung upon the stone walls to keep in the warmth and not make everything look so drab instead hung maps of various places all throughout the world. Linnosa, the townships and provinces it commanded, and also of their allies such as Hefguard, and even maps of their stated enemies—the Fae Realm.

Weapons of all sorts of caliber and designs hung on the walls. Many of them were artifacts from powerful generals of the past, legendary soldiers who went above and beyond, and even past kings who commanded the realm. All were given a venerated part of the room's proceedings as a reward for those who did well in service to the Kingdom.

There was a glove the size of Petra in the far-right corner, indelled in thick ink, and decorated with leather and paints that nearly glowed. Even the table in the center of the room was far different from the one in the dining hall.

The one where they ate and took their meals was lightly varnished with gold, while the one here was made of a dark oak, varnished in multiple layers until it was darker still but glistened by the candlelight from the chandeliers overhead. Instead of gold, brass was inlaid around the legs.

Four seats were left empty at the head of the table. Four thrones that were of equal size and majesty with pillowy seats meant to comfort the sitter. Around the table were eight other people who were accompanied by their own private guards.

Unlike many in the castle, they were not happy and helpful-looking. Instead, they were stern and haughty in appearance, and their stares pierced the four sisters as they made their way in. Watching them in total silence as they walked to their seats and took them.

Once they were seated, a man in his mid to late forties sitting closest to Aella spoke. "It is a pleasure to meet you all. I'm Norton Hansfield, one of the representatives from the North." He smiled warmly, his dark features all lighting up as he introduced himself. Cyra instantly remembered him from when she was a girl. She looked around the table and realized with some relief that she recognized most of the people sitting at the table besides two of them, a younger girl not much older than herself with blonde hair and an old, haggard man who sat next to one another.

They continued to introduce themselves as Cyra evaluated each of them. The other North representative was a woman named Marine Glen with graying hair and bright blue eyes. The Southern representatives sat next to them, Lola and Nell Donovan, the only married couple within the council. On the other side sat the West members, Sidney Tapia and Levine Alaverz, and the East representatives, Jasper Talmadge and Bianca Solo. The last two, Cyra didn't recognize, causing her to automatically be suspicious of both of them.

"How did you two become representatives?" Cyra asked curiously, "I don't recall seeing you."

Talmadge grunted and said, "I took the position when my brother died just after you three were sent away as he had no heirs."

"My entire family was assassinated less than a year ago. I was the last option," Bianca said, her chin jutting in the air.

Cyra was inclined to pity the girl, but something about her spoke of arrogance and privilege which kept her from trusting her.

"Could it have been the same person who killed our parents?" Petra interjected.

"That is why we wanted to have this meeting," Norton said before Bianca could give her opinion. "Someone has been targeting the council members and their families for a while, and now it has reached the castle."

"There is unrest in the city as well. Cyra was attacked in the streets," Aella added.

Cyra thought back to the people who grabbed at her and the man specifically who called her "unworthy". It made her fear what they would do to Hollin, especially with her half-fae heritage. How was she supposed to be Queen? How was she supposed to bring her innocent child into this world?

"This was not reported," Talmadge declared. "Every threat needs to be reported immediately to the council."

"Well, we weren't exactly briefed on royal council business protocol." Aella rolled her eyes.

"Common sense, girl," the old man huffed.

"Who are you calling girl?" Aella's eyes blazed, her posture appearing relaxed, but stiffening as her hand slid casually to the dagger at her hip.

"Please understand Talmadge, we have not been in the capital or involved with any royal business in over fourteen years now," Cyra said, trying to diffuse the situation.

"Exactly why you are unfit to rule." His snappy reply caused everyone at the table to freeze but Aella, who was playing with one of her knives, spinning it so the tip dug into the flesh of the table.

"I would be careful in the manner you speak to your future queen," she hissed.

"And what will you do, Silver Death?" Bianca dared to sneer; her pretty face contorted with disgust.

Aella smiled widely. "I could help reunite you with your family if you so wish."

Bianca's face went red with anger, her petite fists in balls on the table as if she was about to leap over it and claw out Aella's eyes. This meeting was going downhill quickly, and Cyra had no clue what to do. Maybe she really was not made to be queen.

"Now, now. Let's all calm down," Marine Glenn soothed. "Princess Aella's history does not matter. She is one of the royals we are sworn to, and Princess Cyra is the rightful heir. No if, ands, or buts."

Cyra offered the auburn-haired woman a gracious smile and said, "I think it is more important that we figure out who is targeting us and why."

Sidney Tapia spoke up for the first time. "We have heard rumors about a group called 'The Cleansers' in the West."

"Do you have any intel on what they want?" Cyra asked.

"Levine and I have been hiring help to look into it. It seems that their goal is to purify the royal line in some way." Sidney glanced at Aella when speaking about the hired help, which made Cyra wonder if they outsourced assassins for this work.

"We aren't exactly sure what they want or what is motivating them, but they are definitely behind the unrest in the capital and most likely behind what happened to the King and Queen and Solo family," Levine added.

"It is not just the Cleansers that are the issue," Nell Donovan finally joined the conversation. "In the South, we are hearing reports of creatures stalking the night, killing livestock, taking children. The people are blaming the royals and council for this."

This made Cyra shiver. She heard rumors of monsters, but without seeing any herself, she found it hard to believe. Many travelers came into the Inn claiming to see impossible things. She and Ron had chalked it up to the rigor of travel getting to them, but to hear this be discussed in seriousness in the council made her nerves light up. Ron and Hollin were still in the South.

"All stories." Bianca laughed. "You are seriously going to let ghost stories worry you?"

Lola quickly came to the defense of her husband. "These are not just ghost stories, and even if they were, the people believe them, and that is all that matters."

"We have bodies piling up in the South. The reports do not lie. Their bodies are mutilated," Nell built upon their argument.

"Why don't we ask Princess Silver Death if her people have been in the South lately?" Bianca said with a snicker.

"Mind your mouth," Cyra snapped. "She is your princess. I will not allow you to speak to her like that."

Aella reached over Rheanna and patted her arm. "Don't worry, Cy. I know how to shut the little wench up."

"What did you just call me?" Bianca shoved from her seat, knocking it over.

Aella simply grinned at her while Rheanna sighed, her head falling into her hands, and Petra looked around alarmed between the two girls.

"This is getting out of hand," Norton stated.

Bianca nodded feverishly, "I agree sir and—"

Norton cut her off. "No, Bianca. You are completely out of line. Sit down, and keep your mouth shut, or we will have you escorted from this meeting."

"I think we are done for today anyway," Cyra declared, "We all need to calm down and remember our place." She stared pointedly at the angry young blonde from the East.

"We must discuss your coronation," Sidney said.

"At another time," Cyra stated with finality. She stood, with her sisters standing to flank her as they exited the room. They were all silent as they followed her into Petra's room, which had quickly become their safe place to convene.

The second the door was shut, Aella laughed and said, "Well, that was a load of shit."

"I have to agree with Aella. That was shit," Rheanna stated in such a serious manner that everyone burst out in giggles. "What?" she asked. "It really was."

"What are we going to do?" questioned Petra. "The East representatives seem to hate us."

"What do you know of them?" Cyra cocked her head at Petra.

"Father always said that Talmadge was a grump and wished his brother still held the seat, and Bianca has always been like that, even before the death of her family. She takes any chance to sneer or look down on me."

Cyra took this into consideration. The East clearly did not support her on the throne and completely distrusted Aella based on her history, but the rest of the council didn't speak out against them and all seemed eager to see Cyra crowned.

"They don't matter," Aella said before she had the chance to. "The rest of the council is with us. They can't even seem to stand Talmadge or Bianca."

"It didn't help that you continued to antagonize Bianca," Cyra said with a roll of her eyes.

"She was picking a fight she couldn't win." Aella plopped on the edge of Petra's bed with a wink.

"Either way, we can only truly trust one another," Cyra stated.

The girls all nodded in unison.

"Do you all believe the rumors of the creatures?" Petra whispered.

Aella grimaced. "Unfortunately, I can verify those rumors."

"What have you heard?" Rheanna asked.

"It is not just what I have heard but what I have seen as well. Spiders as large as those boulders Petra was crushing earlier, blood-thirsty wolves, and sirens who have lured men into the waters."

Rheanna looked as if she was going to be sick as she slumped next to Aella on the bed. Petra's green eyes were wide with child-like fear. Cyra felt the overwhelming urge to run back to Ron and Hollin but knew she could not. The only way she could truly keep them safe is by figuring out how to stop all of this.

"But magic has been lost in Linnosa for over a hundred years..." Rheanna trailed off.

"Until us," Cyra said.

"Exactly," confirmed Aella. "We brought magic back with us."

"But none of the citizens have magic again," Petra observed.

"It might have something to do with the prophecy," mused Cyra.

Cyra knew they had to do further investigation into the Oracle and her prophecies. She needed to know exactly what the old woman had seen. Even as a child, the Oracle set her on edge. There was something sinister in her gaze that always unsettled her.

Cyra voiced her thoughts out loud. "We need to look into the Oracle."

"I don't trust one word out of that old hag's mouth," Aella scoffed.

"Me neither," Rheanna agreed.

"Mother and Father always trusted her. She was a great advisor to them," Petra tried to defend weakly.

"She sent us all away," Aella replied blandly.

Petra shrugged her shoulders. "She thought she was protecting us, protecting the kingdom."

"It didn't do much since we are all here now. The prophecy will still come true if you believe her then."

"Do you really think that all but one of us will die?" Rheanna shivered.

Aella shook her head. "The old woman is a crook. If the rest of the kingdom doesn't have magic, what makes you think she is the exception?"

"*We* have magic," Petra argued.

Instead of answering, Aella sent her a glare, and Cyra said, "I need some rest after all of that, and I bet you all do too. We will talk again at dinner."

She hugged each sister, even the begrudging Aella, and headed toward her rooms. She thought of everyone she loved as she walked the halls. Of Hollin, Ron, her sisters. How was she going to protect all of them? Becoming queen was the first and only step she could see for securing all their safety. She must be crowned quickly because once she was, she would have access to everything and could control the decisions being made. She had failed her sisters once, and it would not happen again. Cyra would not fail Hollin, either. As a fae, she was in bigger danger than any of them, especially in the capital where the hatred for fae was deeper than anywhere else. She would be reunited with her daughter and would not lose her sisters ever again.

Cyra stared up at the gilded ceiling of her room as she drifted asleep and dreamed of the day her family would be one again.

CHAPTER 14

PETRA WATCHED AS AELLA sauntered into the guards' training yard like she owned the place, which technically, as a princess, she sort of did.

The space was similar to her private one in the garden in several ways. Though, whereas hers was a sanctuary in the inner portions of the castle's defenses, this place was more utilitarian and meant for work rather than designed to hone the skills of a single person.

It wasn't covered in vines, flowers, or broken chunks of rock. Instead, it was a larger courtyard with various mannequins and training dummies meant to train swords, shields, spears, bows, and even hand-to-hand combat among the guards. Various mats were strewn around the outer edges of the training yard where the soldiers and guards could take a break and catch their breath or administer quick repairs and adjustments to their armor and weapons. Weapons of various designs—all cheaply and quickly made by the blacksmith—lined up against the walls with several misplaced from careless rookies. Tables, a few iron braziers, and a board with roll calls, notes, and other messages stood out the most, with several doors leading off to either different parts of the castle or parts of the barracks.

The most noticeable difference? The fact that nothing here was gilded in gold. *There wasn't any use to have it out here*, Petra remembered her father saying.

At the time, it made sense.

All in all, it was still a place that Petra liked to amble toward once in a while when she was bored of luxury and wanted to see how the guards worked or to sneak off to watch Luca train. Now, even more, Petra found herself curious about what Aella was looking to do.

"Princesses, what do you need?" asked a blond guard named Mikah.

"I need to practice sparring with someone bigger than my sisters," said Aella, one hand on her hip.

The guards all shared uneasy glances, and Mikah backed up, unwillingly to spar with a princess. Petra felt bad for them and found herself subconsciously scanning the yard for Luca before she scolded herself.

"So, who's it going to be?" Aella asked.

"I'll do it." The voice came from behind, and they both turned to see Ivan leaning against the framed entrance. His dark hair was cropped as if he had gotten it freshly cut, and a glint lit up his dark eyes.

"I wasn't aware you were a guard," Aella teased with a smirk.

"No, but I know how to swing around a few weapons," Ivan said, raising a brow. "Come on, not telling me the princess is afraid of a challenge from a friend, right?"

She laughed in reply before she stared him down, judging him. "Are you very sure you want to try your luck?"

"Positive," Ivan said, his eyes lighting up to the growing challenge.

A devious smile formed on Aella's face. "Wonderful."

Petra silently prayed to the goddesses that Aella wouldn't kill or maim Ivan. The disdain between the two was palpable. The guards parted as they made their way to a training mat. All other actions and noise in the courtyard ceased as they took their fighting stances. The two of them looked almost comical next to each other with Ivan practically a foot taller than her.

Slowly, they circled one another, Ivan slightly hunched, his hands already up, while Aella had a more relaxed position with her hands at her side.

"Might as well give up already," she said, a devious look on her face.

Ivan smirked. "In your dreams."

Aella lashed out, her first connecting with his right cheek. His face snapped to the side, but he quickly regained focus. He went after her, diving for her waist. She jumped to the right. Instead of making contact with her, he grabbed at air. She smiled. He growled in frustration.

"Give up, pretty boy."

"Never."

He kicked out at her, which she easily evaded by using her leg to match his. That didn't slow him down as he swung out widely with his arm to clothesline her, attempting to use his superior height and weight to drag her down to the ground.

Aella easily dodged it, dropping down beneath his arm, circling to his front where he was unsteady, and then jabbed out with her fists , connecting with his chest several times before he could catch his breath.

Caught off guard, Ivan grunted, gritted his teeth, and staggered off-balance. Sensing his momentary weakness, Aella lowered down and kicked her foot out in a sweep to hook her foot to the back of his ankle and pulled.

Just as Ivan stepped back, he caught himself again, swinging his arms out wildly for balance. Undeterred, Aella rose, slamming the hard, meaty part of her palm against his nose in a loud, thick smack that echoed off the walls. The coppery smell of blood filled the air just as she struck him, and he fell flat on his behind and rolled to the side.

For a second, Petra thought the fight was over. Ivan went down without landing a hit back against her, but instead, he growled and recovered quickly as he staggered to his knees and wiped away the thin crimson line that streaked down his face.

"Had enough?" Aella said in vicious mockery.

Ivan shook his head and lunged at her with full force.

Aella expected it. She feigned right, and at the last moment spun behind him before he leapt and slammed her elbow down between his shoulders using the full force of her smaller weight to her advantage, hitting him with the ball of her elbow.

He cried out, falling to his knees as his shoulder jerked, and seeing that he was now vulnerable, Aella jumped onto his back. Her hands gripped the back of his neck, squeezing the pressure points to cut off both blood and airflow and in a moment, he swayed and fell to the ground, gasping for breath.

Instead of pushing him harder and being even crueler than she was, Aella pushed off him, pinned her foot to his slouched shoulder, and looked out around the rest of the courtyard to the awed, scared guards.

"Who's next?"

Again, the guards all backed up, shaking their heads.

Aella pretended to pout. "That's no fun."

The next few days followed without incident with the sisters training at least once a day, sometimes even more in both combat and magic. They became increasingly more comfortable with one another, but Aella still refrained from displaying even a breeze of her power. Petra wondered if she would ever show them. She wanted to ask her older sister why she refused to use it but decided it was better to leave it.

They were currently training below the night sky, the stars twinkling and the moon watching over them as Cyra and Rheanna took a respite, watching their two younger sisters duel. Despite Aella's refusal to use her power, she encouraged her sisters to, though Petra rarely did. Feeling incredibly sore and tired of coming out the loser, she decided to reach for her magic but kept it at bay until the right moment. Aella was advancing on her, backing her into a column, while Petra feigned exhaustion, merely blocking the blows instead of trying to make any of her own.

"Don't get lazy on me now, little sis," Aella said with a coy smile.

Petra winked, a grin spreading across her face as Aella took another step forward, but could not lift her foot, a vine wrapping around her ankle. Surprise lit up her face as she stumbled for a moment and went to use one of her daggers to slice her ankle free.

Before Petra could hesitate, she landed a blow into her sister's abdomen. The only sign of the punch bothering Aella was a singular grunt, and within a second, Aella had her younger sister against the column, the dagger used to sever the vine now against her throat.

The younger girl's chest heaved as she said, "HA! I got you!"

Aella shook her head, released the dagger, and rewarded her with a small smile. "That you did."

Feeling tired, but excited after their late-night training sessions, Petra was practically skipping down the hallway to her bedroom. Maybe Petra had only imagined the hatred and indifference she saw in her older sister, or maybe, Aella was just finally warming up to her. The hand-to-hand combat matches between the two youngest sisters were the most entertaining since Aella refused to go easy on her like Cyra did, and fighting Rheanna was similar to fighting a toddler. Her skills were by far the most under-developed, and that was putting it nicely.

Petra's thoughts and steps came to a halt when her gaze took in the familiar figure that leaned against her chamber's door.

Luca quickly straightened, his blue eyes widening as he said, "Please speak to me, Petra. I can't do this anymore."

"You dragged me away from my dying parents," she whispered. Her hands began to shake, so she squished them against her chest by crossing her arms. She was tired of dancing around the truth; if he wanted to confront her so badly, then she would no longer avoid it.

"I was trying to protect you," Luca begged. "I had to follow orders."

The anger Petra was so used to calling upon when it came to her former lover was now shifting into an overwhelming sadness. Tears threatened to spill, but she willed them in by squeezing her eyes shut.

"That was the last time I ever saw them." Their bodies were now burned as tradition in Linnosa when royalty died, but no one had even thought to give Petra a moment with them before doing so.

"I'm so sorry." His tousled blond head dropped, pinned to his white boots.

"I know," Petra said softly. "I just need some time."

Luca's head snapped back up as he nodded. "Whenever you need me, I will be here."

Petra offered him the smallest of smiles then moved around him to the door. Once she was through and the door was closed, she collapsed into a fit of sobs.

Everything was still so surreal. The one person she would normally lean on had betrayed her. Luca had only done what he was ordered to do, but she couldn't help the overwhelming panic that filled her chest since their murder while in his presence. Her parents had kept her so isolated to hide their secrets and prevent her from learning the truth about her sisters, even though it seemed as if everyone else in the kingdom knew about the three girls who came before her. But Petra would not let herself be consumed by resentment for them. She already had too many emotions to keep in check. They were dead and, therefore, unable to explain themselves. Petra refused to hate them.

With that resolution, Petra wiped her eyes and began her nightly routine. Once upon a time, an array of servants would be scurrying around her to aid her in this, but now she enjoyed being self-sufficient and craved her alone time. After seeing her sisters tend to their own needs, she felt inspired to do the same.

Petra soon found herself pacing around her flower-filled room in her nightgown and slippers. Even the fictional characters and their woes in her most current read were unable to ease her restlessness. Wrapping a satin robe around her waist, she headed toward the kitchens. She was hoping a warmed chocolate could soothe her. When she was young and couldn't sleep, she would crawl into bed between her mother and father. Just as she was about to turn down the hall, a voice made her jump in surprise.

"What are you doing up, little sister?"

Petra turned to see Aella standing in her bedroom's doorway, arms crossed. Even her night clothes looked fierce, a loose-fitting shirt and tight cottoned pants, both in black.

"I can't fall asleep." Petra hung her head, embarrassed to confess the truth of her nightmares.

"Maybe I'm not working you hard enough in training," Aella said with a slight smirk on her lips.

"I suppose not." Petra felt a loosening in her chest at the jest.

"Why don't you come to my rooms? I just asked the kitchens to send up some warmed chocolate." Aella gestured inside, and Petra's face instantly lit up.

"I would love that."

With warmed chocolates in their hands, the two youngest Voelbel sisters sat between a mountain of cream pillows atop Aella's lavender bed. Her rooms, as were all the sisters', mirrored Petra's except Petra's was filled with personal effects and a whirlwind of flowers. Each room varied in color to complement the girl's powers, resulting in Aella's being accented with soft purples.

"Nightmares?" questioned Aella, breaking the silence.

"Every time I close my eyes, I watch them die," Petra whispered, one tear escaping her emerald eyes.

"As you know, I am not the biggest fan of the King and Queen, but I am sorry that happened to you."

Petra looked up at Aella with surprise, fully expecting some snarky comment about their parents.

Aella rolled her violet eyes. "I may be seen as a monster, but I am capable of empathy, you know."

A laugh escaped Petra's throat as she said, "Could have fooled me."

"Hey!" Aella scoffed while tossing a pillow, hitting Petra square in the face and almost spilling the chocolate.

"Be careful! My drink!" Petra whined, a smile gracing her lips.

The girls continued sipping and discussing training techniques until Petra drifted off. Snuggled next to her sister in a mountain of pillows, Petra's dreams were devoid of nightmares for the first time since her parents' death.

CHAPTER 15

LIGHT KNOCKING CAUSED AELLA to shoot upright and out of the bed, startling the sleeping girl next to her.

"What's wrong?" Petra yawned as she rubbed the sleep from her eyes.

"Nothing," Aella said. "Just time for breakfast I assume."

Aella called for them to come in, and the pretty maid with jet-black hair walked in the room, juggling a tray of pastries and fruits. A hunger that was not aroused by the food but rather the one carrying it overcame her.

"Petra, why don't you go back to your rooms." Aella formed it as a suggestion, but it was clearly a command.

Petra nodded and said, "Thank you," before wrapping her arms around Aella. For a moment, she froze but then relaxed and hugged the girl back. Despite herself, Aella had grown quite protective and proud of Petra while training her sisters. No matter how hard Aella pushed, Petra pushed right back. She saw her own fight in her.

Petra left with the pretty maid following close behind her when Aella said, "You stay."

The woman turned around to face Aella, her almond eyes narrowing. "Can I help you, princess?"

"I would like your company while I eat."

One dark eyebrow shot up. "I hardly believe that is appropriate."

"Seeing that I am a princess, I think I can dictate what is and is not appropriate." Aella's eyes flicked to the chair across from where she sat at her small dining table, a silent command.

The woman bowed her head, hiding the roll of her eyes. "As you wish." She went to sit as Aella asked for her name.

"Natalie."

"I'm Aella."

"I'm aware."

Aella let out a sharp laugh. She liked the cockiness this woman had, especially considering her profession. She wasn't used to her confidence being matched.

"How long have you been employed within the castle?" Aella asked while biting into a strawberry.

"Longer than you've been a princess." A smirk spread across Natalie's perfect rose lips.

"I like you," Aella said bluntly. She was not the type to dance around things.

One of Natalie's dark eyebrows arched. "Oh, really?" She shifted forward, placing her elbows on the table that separated them, causing her cleavage to spill forward. Lazily, she plucked a grape and popped it into her mouth. Aella's gaze tracked every movement, and her restraint broke. Without a word, she stood and pulled Natalie out of the seat. Violet eyes looked up into dark ones for a moment before their lips crashed together.

Natalie's hands were frantic. Her fingers explored Aella's torso while Aella's tangled into her hair. Natalie's back hit a wall.

Their lips and hands did not stop their search. A burning need filled Aella's core. She needed more. She wanted to be consumed by this woman.

Natalie came to a sudden halt, her petite hands pressing against Aella's heaving chest.

"I need to get back. They'll start to ask questions if I'm gone too long."

"Come back tonight."

"Fine." Natalie's eyes sparkled, and her cheeks were flushed, which made Aella want to do everything within her power to keep her there. Slowly, Aella stepped away from Natalie, letting her slip from between her and the wall and out the door, sending a wink over her shoulder.

Aella managed to get dressed and compose herself, but she needed to do something with this energy that was buzzing in her. Natalie had set her on fire, and she needed to douse it. She decided she would poke around the castle and find out some information. Specifically, she wanted to learn more about the Cleansers. The idea of some group of citizens that want to rebel and the people who attacked Cyra outside the gate left her paranoid.

Two girls, one redhead and one brunette, who were barely older than her were giggling as they swept the hallway. Aella watched as they jested and decided they would be great informants. From her experience as an assassin, she knew the help, especially young girls, always knew what was going on.

"Hello." The sound of Aella's voice made the girls jump, and they stood straighter as they processed who was in front of them.

"Uh, Princess, how can we help you?" the red-haired one stuttered, her freckled face turning red as they both curtsied.

"Could I ask you some questions?"

They looked at each other nervously, the brunette girl towering over the other, but both nodded. The brunette said, "Of course, Princess."

"What do you two know about the group that calls themselves the Cleansers?"

Their eyes widened almost simultaneously, but they both moved in closer, and the redhead said in a hushed voice, "They have been popping up everywhere since the death of the King and Queen. A lot of us younger citizens only ever heard rumors of you princesses; you were kind of like a myth to us, but it was like the Cleansers knew you'd all be coming back."

"Why would this matter?" Aella's eyebrows rose.

"Well, they believe Petra is the rightful heir. She has always been referred to as the Beloved," the redhead added eagerly.

"Petra has always been our princess, and you are all new," the brunette said.

"Do you believe these Cleansers?" Aella's purple eyes narrowed to slits.

"Uh, no. Of course not," the brunette said quickly, shaking her head. "But it is all a lot to take in, and with all the unrest and rumors about the creatures that have been coming out of the Black Lake..."

"It has made us all nervous, especially with the rest of Linnosa being without magic," the redhead finished her friend's thought.

"Are you aware of anyone who works within the castle who could be involved?" Aella asked even though the chances of them telling her the truth were extremely thin.

They both shook their heads vigorously, and the redhead said, "We would never be involved in something like that."

"Are you aware of who I am?" Aella's voice dropped dangerously low.

"The princess," the brunette stated slowly.

"Have you heard of Silver Death?"

The girls' facial expressions turned into alarm as they stumbled back, creating distance between themselves and Aella.

"Come to me any time you hear anything about the Cleansers, and we won't have a problem." Aella smiled at them, delighted that her reputation stretched far across the kingdom.

"Of course," the redhead struggled to get out. The brunette said nothing, her face extremely pale causing her hazel eyes to stand out.

"What are your names?"

"Laney," the redhead stated quickly.

"Cora," the brunette stated.

"Nice to meet you Laney and Cora. I can sense a wonderful friendship between us three."

Aella turned on her heel, feeling accomplished with the little information she received. At least now she was aware of some their motives. These Cleansers had nothing against Cyra except the fact that they wanted Petra to be queen. The tensions have been high in the kingdom given the recent monster attacks. The citizens were on the brink of rebellion already, but the sisters coming back was the ammunition they needed.

CHAPTER 16

RHEANNA CRIED OUT AS she used every ounce of strength she had to manipulate her water into a sword, but it came crashing onto the cobblestones of the training arena. She stomped her foot, feeling like one of the preschool-aged children she used to teach.

"This is impossible." She turned toward her sisters, heaving. Loose strands of black hair framed her face where they came free from her braid.

"That mentality is what is making it impossible," Aella said, rolling her eyes.

"Not all of us can be killing machines," Rheanna snapped but then quickly continued in a softer tone, "I'm sorry. I'm just frustrated."

Aella laughed. "It's alright. I like to see a bit of attitude in you. Stop with all this submissive shit."

Rheanna hung her head, suddenly embarrassed by her own personality. All three of her sisters had strong, fierce personalities, and she felt left behind, in the background. She didn't know how to be like them.

"Let me help you." Cyra stepped toward the center of the arena, planting her feet firmly on the stone ground. "Our elements are the most similar in how they can be wielded."

Rheanna nodded and lifted her arms to mimic Cyra's stance.

"Think of your power as an extension of yourself. It's a part of you, like a limb. You don't need to control it but use it. Imagine what you want it to do in your mind." While explaining, Cyra's hands twisted, flames appearing and morphing into the shape of a blade. "Close your eyes if you need to. Just feel your magic."

Rheanna took a deep breath and closed her eyes. She pictured her power and morphed it into a blade similar to her sister's. In her mind's eye, she watched as it smoothed and sharpened into a glistening sword of water.

Someone clapped, causing Rheanna's eyes to snap open, but her concentration remained.

"You're doing it!" cheered Petra.

Surprise lit up Rheanna's face as she took in the shimmering blade exactly like the one she conjured in her mind only a few inches away from her.

"Try to grab it," Aella instructed, curiosity lining her tone.

Rheanna immediately did as her sister said and was shocked further when her hand wrapped around the solid hilt.

Cyra gasped. "I have never even done that."

"Impressive." Aella's one-word compliment sent joy and pride shooting through Rheanna.

"I want to try making weapons out of rock next!" Petra said excitedly, practically jumping up and down.

"I need to see if I can touch my flames." Cyra tilted her head, examining the blade of water in her sister's hand.

"You should be able to," Aella weighed in. "You keep your flames from burning us in training. I doubt they could harm you."

Rheanna released her magic, and the sword turned into liquid once again, splashing at her feet.

"That was amazing," Rheanna let out in a whisper. That was the first time she was able to truly use her magic besides soaking people with it.

"Think of all the things you can do," Aella mused. "You just need to know you are capable."

Rheanna shied away from the praise. "Well, Cyra helped."

"All I really did was show you how to focus, Rhe. That was all you." She smiled, a dimple forming on her freckled cheek.

A blush creeped op her neck from the attention and compliments. She was not used to all of this. Being the center of attention was always Maude's job growing up, but Rheanna felt that she quite liked the spotlight.

"I would like to see all of your powers," said a new, but familiar voice. Ivan, dark hair still wet from a recent shower, walked out onto the training ground. His bulging muscles strained against the simple white shirt he wore.

Any amusement that was on Aella's face vanished at his entrance. Rheanna stared longingly at him. They hadn't spoken in over a week after what he said about Aella.

"Sisters only," Aella purred. "No boys allowed."

Before Ivan could respond, Cyra said, "I'd like to show him a few of my tricks."

Aella scowled while a pit of jealousy formed in Rheanna's chest at the way her older sister looked at Ivan. And how he looked at her.

"Would you?" Ivan responded, his dark eyes sparking with mischief.

"Not here. I don't think it would be child-appropriate," Aella said with disgust.

"Hey! I'm not a child," whined Petra.

"It might be useful for Ivan to help us train," Rheanna added quietly.

Finally, his eyes met hers, and he smiled appreciatively. She could melt from that smile alone.

"He can do nothing I can't," Aella snapped.

"Learning to fight someone my size could help you," he countered.

"I have killed men two times your size."

"I bet," he grimaced. "I could help your sisters, though."

"If you must," Aella sighed. "But we are done for today."

"If that's all then I'm starving," complained Petra, giving them all a goofy grin and wave.

Rheanna started toward Ivan, mouth open to ask him to have lunch with her, foolishly thinking he was waiting for her, but instead, he locked arms with Cyra. Even after a grueling training session, her older sister was the picture of perfection. The action bloomed a faint hue of blush to her freckled cheeks, and the ruby curls that fell out of her messy bun delicately framed her round face. Rheanna promptly crossed her arms and stared in disbelief at their backs as they left.

Aella patted her back. "If it helps, I don't like or trust him."

"He said the same about you."

"He's smart, at least. I'll give him that."

"I'm used to not being recognized," Rheanna sighed.

Aella crossed her arms and said, "If you told Cyra how you felt you know she would immediately back off."

"They obviously like each other. I'm the one who needs to get over it."

Aella shrugged her shoulders and walked off, leaving Rheanna alone in the arena. It suited her fine with the way she was feeling. Petra was elated at her improvement in combat, and Cyra was thrilled with the attention from Ivan, while Rheanna was left alone.

Even in Dalmer where she was the responsible one and Maude did as she pleased, she was always overlooked. The Bushnells were good to her, true, but deep down, she knew their blood came first.

Maude also received all the attention of the boys in town while Rheanna lurked in the background. Even now, she lagged in so many ways compared to her sisters. With Cyra, it made sense; she was the oldest and most mature of the four. But Petra was the youngest and was leagues ahead of her in terms of magic—plus, she had that guard boy she fawned over. Aella was skilled and far above any of them when it came to training. Rheanna had also heard the rumors of her and one of the maids.

She debated leaving and just slinking off to her room to be alone and wallow in misery, but instead, sat crisscrossed against one of the pillars, using the coldness of the stone to punish herself as she stared up at the open sky above. Instead of feeling worse, the cold only made her nostalgic for Dalmer and simpler times.

Figuring she should at least practice, she played with droplets of her water magic, creating tiny daggers in her hands that looked like Aella's, minor figurines that she made dance and move, among other things. She was improving bit by bit, but was it enough?

Would she even be as noticeable or unique as any of her sisters? Aella said she was meek and submissive, and maybe she was. She was nothing but a shadow of a princess. That only enhanced her jealousy as she bitterly thought about how her sisters could attract people just by being themselves while she had to fight for attention.

A group of guards came running into the arena, their swords clanging against their armor. They marched up to Rheanna and shouted, "Emergency council meeting!"

Rheanna didn't hesitate for a moment before propelling her long legs out of their sitting position and letting the guards escort her toward the war room. As they made their way there, they ran into the other three sisters with Ivan following close behind.

"What's going on?" Rheanna asked.

"I have no idea," Cyra answered breathlessly.

The doors to the war room exploded open, and only four people were already inside; Bianca Solo, Norton Hansfield, Marine Glen, and Lola Donovan. They all looked as confused as the princesses, except for Lola. The South representative was covered in dirt, her hands and the front of her cream-colored dress stained in a dark hue that could only be blood. Her midnight curly hair was spilling and frizzing from the bun on the top of her head.

"Are you alright?" gasped Rheanna.

Tears welled in Lola's eyes as she whispered, "My husband is dead."

Rheanna's jaw dropped in shock. Another royal dead.

Cyra stopped at the entrance of the door, placing her hands on Ivan's chest and pushing him out of the room. "You are not permitted to be in here."

"But—" he began to challenge.

"No," Cyra said and then commanded the guards, "Guard the doors. Do not let anyone in this room."

Norton cleared his throat, his face grave. "It turns out the whispers of monsters are not simply rumors."

"Where is everyone else?" Aella asked before the discussion could go any further.

Bianca, looking as regal and polished as ever, said, "We have provinces to govern. We do not all reside in the safety of this castle and relax all day."

"We are not doing this today, Bianca. It's not the time," Norton silenced her and prevented Aella from any response she might spew.

"What do you mean about the monsters?" Petra interjected.

Lola squeezed her bloodshot eyes shut, tears falling freely, and dropped in her seat. "Neil and I were on our way home when we were attacked by a spider-like creature the size of a cow. Most of our guards were killed, and I barely got away. Neil, he...he sacrificed himself for me. Stayed behind so the remaining guards and I could flee." Her voice was hoarse and raw.

Bianca looked like she wanted to say something, but Cyra spoke before she could try. "So, it is confirmed. Monsters are back."

"But magic isn't," observed Aella. Her eyes narrowed; Rheanna could practically see the gears turning in her head.

"But you four all have magic. These sightings have been reported for the past decade, right after Petra was born," Marine said. The woman cracked her fingers, rubbing and pulling on her hands.

"And now that we are all together again, the reports have almost tripled," Cyra added.

"We are not prepared for this," Rheanna stated in a hushed voice. She shivered, thinking about what would come next and the fact that she felt so unprepared.

Bianca seemed to be having the same thought process because she said, "We need to find a way to bring back the magic. You four alone will not be able to fight them all."

The four sisters traded glances. They already knew the prophecy. *Four shall emerge, but only one will rise.* Rheanna did not think now was the time to let the council in, and apparently, neither did her sisters because no one said anything.

"She's right. We will need to add more guards to the lake. There needs to be soldiers stationed around the entirety of it so that any creatures that emerge can be swiftly taken care of," Norton agreed.

"We barely have enough soldiers as it is. Our army is spread too thin," Marine said.

"We might need to call a conscription," Bianca stated boldly.

"That would cause the citizens to revolt even more," Aella countered as she shook her head.

"We can't force them into a war!" cried Rheanna, turning toward Cyra with pleading eyes.

"I don't know if we have a choice," Cyra said. "It's either that, or they all die. If the monsters make it to the towns, they won't stand a chance without being armed and prepared."

"But we won't have nearly enough time to train them all," Aella said.

"We can't just do nothing though," Cyra responded, placing a hand against her temple and massaging.

"Why don't I travel to the Black Lake? I could investigate what's going on, and it should only take me less than four days for the whole trip," Aella suggested.

"You can't go by yourself! It's not safe," Petra cried, her hands slamming against the wood of the table as she went to stand. Rheanna didn't say anything, but she agreed with her little sister. Aella couldn't walk into that alone.

"I will go with her," said Cyra, chin held high.

Several council members gasped, but Marine was the one to voice her concern. "That is not a good idea." Her hand grasped over her heart.

"There's also the coronation to think about during all of this. It's prudent we get you crowned as soon as possible," Norton said.

"If we don't want to anger the rebels, why would we put her on the throne?" spat Bianca, her pretty face screwed into a disgusted expression.

"We need to appear strong. I propose we crown Cyra this upcoming weekend," Norton suggested, but something in his gaze seemed unsure as if he was not quite confident this was the right course of action.

"We need to do what we can to protect ourselves," Lola got out between sobs and then added, "How am I going to tell my children their father is dead?" Her hands clutched at her face.

"I am sorry we failed to protect your husband, but I swear I will do everything in my power to keep your children from harm," Cyra said gently, walking over to the hysterical woman and placing a hand on her shoulder.

Lola looked up at her Queen, her tear-soaked hand squeezing Cyra's, and whispered, "Thank you."

Cyra smiled encouragingly and then looked around the room, meeting each members' eyes as she said, "After Aella and I return from the journey, I will ascend the throne and take my rightful place as Queen."

"Without the agreement of everyone else on the council?" Bianca's eyes almost bulged from the anger she attempted to control, her palms slamming into the dark wood of the table they sat around.

"She has the consent of the three other heirs and a majority of the council. The rest can object to the idea when they arrive if they wish to do so," Marine said calmly, clearly confident that no one would.

Bianca didn't respond but pouted with her arms crossed in her chair. Rheanna knew her sister would do what was best for the kingdom, whether she agreed with the methods or not.

Looking at Cyra now, she could see that she would be a great leader.

"Let's begin preparations then. For now, I believe it would be best if we call back the other council members and that you all reside here," Cyra said.

Norton, Marine, and Bianca nodded, for once all in the agreement.

"Lola, we'll have your guards brief the rest of the soldiers so they can be aware," Norton added.

"I can take care of that for Lola," Marine said gently, then turned toward the crying woman. "You go clean up and rest, honey."

CHAPTER 17

T HE TWO SISTERS TRAVELED through Reddel in secrecy, avoiding any interaction with citizens and potential Cleansers. Only three guards and Ivan accompanied them to keep any attention minimal, and they were garbed in simple attire. They wanted to avoid being identified as much as possible, so instead of wearing royal armor, they dressed plainly for travel with riding pants and loose blouses. In a simple riding outfit, they attempted to dull Cyra's appearance, but it was almost impossible.

After all, that was how she was spotted when she first came in and was attacked. A princess and soon-to-be Queen with fiery red hair, flaming eyes, and unmatched beauty. No one in Linnosa matched that description. Aella had gotten away with slipping into the shadows unrecognized, but her appearance was just as striking and unique.

They only had three guards with them, chosen because of their average features. Aella complained she wanted to test their combat capabilities out, but Cyra had to argue that it would take far too much time.

So, the guards they had were whoever was willing to go and protect them. There was Mikah, a blond guard who looked young but swore he was skilled with shield and blade. Nahlil, a lanky man with dark skin and a sarcastic nature. He rode in the front atop a black horse and looked imposing as he served as the lookout, taking this mission and the duty of traveling with the princesses seriously. Then there was Ryder, the stoutest of the three with a wide face, wider shoulders, and a closely shaven head. He took the rear and had a crossbow strapped across his back.

Ivan held up the rear with Ryder, leaving both Aella and Cyra in the middle. Each of the princesses wore a simple linen cloak, the hoods lifted above their heads to hide both the red and silver of their countenance from any onlookers.

The path through Reddel was simple enough at the hour they left. Hardly anyone was in the streets, and eventually, they made it out without any incidents to stop them. Soon they made it out until only trees and wildlife surrounded them, following a simple black path that guided travelers around Linnosa and linked the four sectors of North, South, East, and West.

"Did you really have to bring your pet?" asked Aella. Her silver hair shined in the sun as it waved in the light breeze. She sat atop a taupe-colored horse.

Cyra looked particularly pretty in dark brown riding trousers and an off-white flowing blouse. Her curls were contained in a ponytail on the top of her head. She glanced back at Ivan, who was already scowling. She took a moment to respond, a slight frown on her lips. "He wanted to be here to protect me."

Aella scoffed. "I will protect you."

"You should both remember I am capable of protecting myself."

"I know." The younger sister stared forward in silence for a few moments, hesitating, before asking, "How much do you remember of us as kids?"

Cyra looked at her sister, golden eyes finding violet ones as a small smile formed on her lips. "I remember it all."

"Tell me about it."

Cyra's heart filled with joy at the request. As she told a story, Aella felt as if she were seeing it, almost remembering it herself.

The three girls sat at a small dining table in their shared rooms, their parents nowhere in sight. They rarely ate meals together as a family, but the girls were inseparable, even sleeping in the same bed together. Toys and books scattered the floor haphazardly. The ornate wallpaper of white and gold was marred in places by various drawings in crayon of stick figures and random objects. Servers danced around the mess, serving the girls one of their favorite meals of shepherd's pie with raspberry juice.

Once the adults left them, Aella and Cyra exchanged mischievous looks, glancing at Rheanna. "Come on," whined Cyra. "Play with us."

"We are princesses. Do not be gross," Rheanna said, primly picking up her silverware and taking a neat bite of her food.

The youngest and oldest sisters shared another glance, giggling, as they each placed their hands behind their backs and dipped their faces into their meals. They began to lap up their food, meat and mashed potatoes spilling over the edges.

Rheanna groaned, trying not to look at the two while consuming her meal. "You guys are monsters."

Aella lifted her head from her plate with food smashed up her nose. "Don't be so boring."

"I'd rather be boring than gross," said Rheanna, small arms crossing her chest.

"Just try it! It's fun, Rhe," exclaimed Cyra, her cheeks smothered in meat and vegetables.

The six-year-old looked down at her food, eyebrows shooting up. She didn't want to be left out, but the idea of shoving her face in her meal turned her stomach.

"Do it! Do it!" chanted Aella, slamming her fists into the table, shaking their plates and silverware.

Rolling her eyes, Rheanna slowly bent toward her plate, but before she could take a bite, someone pushed her head, smashing her face into the soft pie. She popped back up, rubbing the potatoes out of her eyes and glaring at the perpetrator. The silver-haired four-year-old was already darting back to her chair, a glint in her violet eyes.

"Aella!" A quiver entered Rheanna's voice, but before she could enter into hysterics, Cyra grabbed a fist full of her food and chucked it toward the youngest sister. The food hit Aella straight in the face, catching her off guard.

Rheanna busted out in laughter, with Cyra and Aella following quickly when Aella began coughing and then sneezing. Rheanna and Cyra both gagged as snot hung out her nose and into her mouth.

"What?" asked Aella.

"I can't—" Rheanna choked off with a dry heave, getting up from the table.

Cyra pushed a napkin toward Aella, avoiding looking at her. "Wipe your nose!"

Aella broke the memory Cyra shared with laughter. "We were pretty gross! I don't blame Rheanna."

Cyra smiled. "Hey, you were grosser. Always sneezing with those giant boogers at dinner. I could gag just thinking about it."

Nahlil turned to look back at them from his horse and said, "You lot sounded like fun." His dark eyes were alight with amusement.

"I remember when we were all young, Aella used to be quite the little prankster," added Ivan. She glanced back at him, expecting to see a scowl, but he seemed to be reminiscing as much as the sisters.

"You remember me as well?" asked Aella, hesitantly.

"Of course. I was always tagging along with you guys when you would let me. You girls were as thick as thieves."

Cyra nodded. "We had a no boys rule for most things."

"Especially when it came to your races. Aella always won, even then," Ivan said while chuckling.

Aella found herself grinning along with them, but she wished she could remember the memories for herself. Even Ivan could remember her, could remember her sisters. Instead, her childhood memories were clouded with darkness and pain when they should have been full of laughter and light.

"Should we race now?" Cyra said, her gold eyes twinkling.

Aella shook her head. "We have to keep riding so we have you back in time for your coronation. Plus, I'd just beat you anyway."

Cyra chuckled. "You're probably right, but it would be fun."

Mikah, the blond guard, joined the conversation then. "No offense, Princess, but would it really be that fun to lose?" His head was turned toward them, his grin flashing.

Aella laughed heartily while Cyra let out a sigh. "I could have been training for this very moment all these years for all you know."

"I'll race you once we make camp," challenged Nahlil.

Cyra smiled broadly. "You're on."

The group made their camp a little over halfway to the Black Lake. The little area they chose was simple enough for their needs; close to the woods in a small group of trees that made setting up tents, tethering horses, and gathering firewood much simpler. Branches and logs were everywhere on the ground, and the trees were young and thick enough to hold any lines attached to them. A clearing next to them that led off road made riding the horses so much easier if they needed to move or flee for any reason.

Mikah started a small fire to guide them as the darkening sky made it harder to see with every passing moment. There was at least another hour or two before it got truly dark, so Ryder—the ever-silent, brooding one of the group—went off to the field to hunt rabbits. He returned after a little while with three hares in hand to skin, cook, and eat for a simple stew for the night.

As they laid out their cots, Nahlil looked from his makeshift campsite towards Cyra and smirked.

"So, are we racing or what?" asked Nahlil, his dark eyebrows arched.

Cyra began to stand up when Ivan grabbed her wrist and pulled her back down. Aella's eyes narrowed on him.

"What?" asked Cyra, her face crunching together in annoyance.

"Sorry, it's just not safe for you to be running into the woods in the middle of the night," Ivan said, shrugging his shoulders, but Aella could swear there was a hint of jealousy in his tone. Regardless of that, she agreed with him. There was no way her sister would be racing in the dark. There were too many unknowns right now.

"Nahlil will protect me," Cyra said, shooting a grin at the man. He smiled back, pleased by the attention she was giving him.

"No." The word was demanding and possessive coming from Ivan.

Cyra went to object, but Aella said, "Let the race wait until morning where you don't risk tripping over a tree root and cracking your head open."

Ivan looked at her, his expression full of appreciation, but she ignored him. She did not side with him. She only wished to protect her sister.

"Alright. Such the responsible sister," said Cyra, begrudgingly biting into a bit of her rabbit.

"Don't worry. I'll still be capable of beating you in the morning," said Nahlil, ignoring the glare coming from Ivan.

"You should let her win," said Mikah. "She's about to be queen. What if she locks you in the dungeons?"

Nahlil smirked. "I might like that."

Aella rolled her eyes, but Cyra fell over in laughter. "Oh, now, you might make me want to lose!"

Ivan's discomfort and distaste deepened, his glare now falling on Cyra, who was oblivious. Aella met his eyes for a brief moment, daring him, before he looked away, his cheeks red.

CHAPTER 18

"SHOULD WE STILL TRAIN?" Petra asked as Rheanna entered her room to eat breakfast. Rheanna was dressed in a simple nightgown, still wearing the wool one she brought with her from Dalmer.

For a second, Rheanna blinked as if processing what was asked of her. The obvious effects of sleep were still upon her as her hair was a mess, and she looked as though she had a fitful, restless sleep the night before. Petra easily sympathized with her sister as her dreams were full of worry for their other two sisters as well.

Rheanna stumbled her way toward the table full of breakfast goods—sweet tarts, meats, and fresh fruits that made their mouths water. The servant only brought it moments ago with fresh tea and cream. Rheanna's bare feet barely missed any of the misplaced books on the floor as she shuffled to sit, grabbed a tart, and popped it into her mouth before waking up from the sugary baked good.

"They aren't here anyway. We might as well take a break," she said finally as she sat, already moving to grab an apple tart.

Petra picked her own tart and asked, "Do you think they are alright?"

"Of course. They have each other and the guards." Rheanna said the last word bitterly, remembering how eagerly Ivan volunteered to go with them. She wished she had asked to go in that moment as well.

"I guess so."

They ate in silence for the remainder of the meal until the Oracle stepped into the room, her pale skin and black robes contrasting heavily. "We shall have class today," she said to Petra, who nodded glumly. Since Petra was still school-aged, the Oracle acted as her private tutor whenever she had time.

"May I join?" asked Rheanna curiously, her head tilting to the side.

The Oracle scrutinized her with that black gaze before nodding. "Come now, girls."

The old woman waited for the sisters to dress out of their night clothes, as it wasn't proper for the princesses to walk around the castle barely dressed. Once they were properly fed and dressed, they followed the old woman down a long hallway toward the opposite end of the castle to a section that overlooked the gardens, training yards, and part of Reddel in the distance. This portion of the castle was much like the rest; white walls, plush carpeting, thick doors of ancient wood with carvings engraved on them to bring out the richness of the building. Long streaming banners hung overhead, and large windows at the end of the hallway allowed the light to illuminate the entire path.

Soon, they came to the school room, and upon entering Rheanna gasped at the beauty of it. It was far different from what she had in Dalmer, and she wished her students could learn in such splendor and majesty.

Comparatively, her classroom was dull. It was small with a hardwood floor, a simple hearth, and thick windows, and it always felt cold even when the fire was made and the children were allowed to run around for a break from learning. This classroom was large and commanding, almost as big as the dining hall itself. Substantial bookshelves that reached to the ceiling were full of books of all kinds, from every kingdom, age, and literary genre. The far wall away from the view of the garden had maps and diagrams from different scientific and philosophical disciplines norm to the curriculum—though the maps were of a different use from those in the war room.

An assortment of different experiments and tools filled out four rectangular tables, with glass beakers full of colorful liquids within and a small gas burner used to heat them when in need. There also sat papers full of numbers and other data. Several large diagrams depicting animals and birds hung overhead, fluttering in a gentle breeze from an open window, and a large fireplace sat wedged between several bookcases made up but not lit in case of nightly studies.

It was mesmerizing. In a corner, the marble floor housed a shaggy white rug with reading chairs and tables. The room could have fit Rheanna's entire class or even her entire school within it.

But as Rheanna watched Petra take her seat at the single desk made up for her in front of a chalkboard, the loneliness of it hit Rheanna in her heart. This girl didn't have the luxury of school friends to play with. For most of her life, she only had herself, her parents, the Oracle, and occasionally Luca for companionship. With her students at the school, they might not have had a tenth of what the room possessed, but they were happy and eager to come to class each day because it was where their friends were, and Rheanna did her best to make learning fun. How much fun could it have been to be here by oneself with the Oracle of all people as her only source of company?

Despite all the beautiful things that Petra had growing up, she had been alone for far too long, and seeing her sit by herself at the desk made Rheanna even more determined to make sure she never felt that loneliness again.

"We will discuss a bit about the history of the fae in this session," said the Oracle, pointing to a map of the Fae Realm. Rheanna sat in her seat, placing her chin in her palm and leaning forward, already interested.

"I've heard all the stories already," said Petra as she took a seat next to Rheanna at one of the wooden tables. The Oracle moved toward the front of it.

"Exactly. Stories. You have heard stories. It is time you learned the history." The Oracle lifted a book from the table, opening the first page and showing an illustration of a fae. "Fae are easily recognized by their pointed ears. They tend to be taller than humans as well."

"Aren't they faster than us? And stronger?" Petra questioned.

"Yes, about two times faster and stronger than us. Their senses are better, too. The most impressive of all is their magic range. They tend to mate based upon strength, making each generation stronger."

A chill ran down Rheanna's back. She had always been terrified of the fae as a child. The only thing that made her feel better was that they didn't roam Linnosa any longer. "What do you mean by mate?" she asked.

"Fae tend to have mates, which is a deep soul connection. It seems to be based on their power levels. They either have to accept or deny it, but denying it has consequences."

Rheanna liked the idea of having someone's soul tied to her so she wouldn't have to worry about Ivan or any other men. It would be easier.

"What kinds of consequences?" asked Petra.

The Oracle's gaze darkened. "No one really knows besides the fae, but I have heard of death."

Rheanna and Petra gasped in unison.

"Do they only mate between the fae or with other species as well?" asked Rheanna, twirling a stray piece of her dark hair.

The Oracle raised an eyebrow and Rheanna's cheeks reddened. "The mating bond is only between the same species," the Oracle answered.

"Oh."

"Now, let's get to the part that matters; their history in Linnosa." The Oracle cleared her throat before continuing, "Fae and humans, along with all the other magic-wielding species, lived within Linnosa in harmony for years until magic disappeared. These species became sick. The sickness affected them all differently, some almost died while others were pushed to madness and violence without their magic. Instead of understanding, the humans of Linnosa rioted, and the ruling King placed a ban on them all, casting them out. That is how the Fae Realm was started."

"The second they left Linnosa, their magic returned just as strong, and they were healed, but it didn't matter. They were already painted like monsters. In all honesty, the humans always resented the other species as their power was always stronger. Humans with magic are an anomaly, but every fae, nymph, and shifter are born with magic."

Rheanna had never heard about the fae like this. Instead, she heard the stories of the cities they destroyed and people they killed.

"But they are still dangerous, aren't they?" asked Petra, eyes wide.

"Anyone can be dangerous. Look at you and your sisters. Those powers are dangerous as well," the Oracle said, her voice grave.

"We would never hurt anyone," said Rheanna, defensively.

"You and Petra, perhaps. But what of Princess Aella? She is known as the Silver Death, after all. She has even killed since coming back to the castle," the Oracle retorted.

"That was different, though. Aella was protecting Cyra from people who wanted to hurt her. She didn't mean to hurt anyone," Rheanna protested.

"And you think the fae set out to hurt people?"

Both girls were silent, unable to answer that question. They looked at each other and then back at the Oracle.

"Is there anything else in particular you would like to discuss today?" the Oracle asked.

Before Petra could speak, Rheanna said, "How exactly do you see a prophecy?"

The Oracle stared blankly at Rheanna. "If you are going to be here today, do not disrupt our classes. They are for Petra's benefit, not yours."

Rheanna blushed. The idea of magic and fae had Rheanna wondering about how the Oracle could see prophecies. Was she magical as well?

"Wait, but I want to learn about you. About prophecies," said Petra, her emerald eyes widening.

"There is not much to know. I am the kingdom's Oracle and serve you by providing advice based on my intuition and prophecies," said the Oracle simply, but her right hand curled into a fist.

"There has to be more to it! How do you become an oracle?" asked Rheanna. This information could possibly help them figure out what to do about their prophecy.

The Oracle's expression turned stormy, wrinkly face growing colder. "Do not ask questions that do not concern you. I see you are both uninterested in learning anything else today, so forget about the rest of the lessons." The woman turned out of the room and disappeared through the doors.

The sisters looked at each other, confusion scrunching their brows. "Of course when we're actually interested in learning something, it's off limits," Petra sighed, running a hand through her brown waves.

"How strange," said Rheanna. "I don't remember any stories or myths about her. Not even from my time here."

"Me neither." Petra paused and shook her head. "Well at least we learned more about the fae. You seemed pretty interested." Her eyebrows raised suggestively.

Rheanna's face reddened. "It's not like that. I was merely curious."

Petra laughed. "No, I know. I'm curious myself. Part of me wishes to meet one."

"Petra! They're monsters!"

"Yeah, yeah, but it would be pretty cool, if they didn't kill us."

The older sister shook her head. "You're crazy."

"Perhaps, but the idea of soulmates seems so romantic."

Rheanna couldn't argue with the girl since she had the same thoughts only moments ago, but instead of agreeing, she shook her head.

A strange slurping sound woke Cyra. She rubbed her eyes and attempted to stretch her stiff back from the hard forest floor. The sunrise set a slight shadow across their camp as she squinted, looking for the sound of the noise. Her eyes widened in horror, and a scream climbed up her throat. A bird-like creature about the size of a child hunched over Nahlil, pecking into his throat and licking at his blood with a long, forked tongue. At the sound of her scream, the monster titled its head, and its cat-like yellow eyes dilated. A squawk filled the air as it started at her, brown wings splayed.

Cyra scrambled backward. Her hand went up right before it reached her. A wall of fire erupted, and it shrieked in anger. A few of its chest feathers got caught in the flames. Ivan shot from his cot and to her side, pulling her to a standing position as Aella and the others woke up. The wall stopped the creature for only a few moments before it flew over it and dove at the pair. Ivan pushed Cyra. She stumbled out of the way as the bird collided with Ivan. They both landed on the ground. Ivan shook with the force of trying to keep its beak from his neck.

Aella shot into action. Her dagger sank in between its feathers in its back, taking its attention off Ivan for a second. Cyra's flame shot for the bird, sending it off Ivan and away from Aella. The younger sister took the opportunity and jumped on it with both daggers out of their sheaths and hacked at its neck. Using his sword, Ryder waited for Aella to move and beheaded the creature. Its head rolled to the side, leaving a trail of black blood in its wake.

"Holy shit," said Mikah. He ran a hand through his blond hair, standing in front of his cot and staring at the creature.

"Thanks for the help," grunted Aella, wiping the blood off her daggers on her pant leg and putting them away.

"I have never seen anything like that." Mikah's gaze trailed to Nahlil's body. His brown eyes were open and unseeing, his dark skin already looking ashen with death.

Cyra shook her head. "None of us have." Silent tears ran down her cheeks as she stepped toward his body, kneeling down. She reached out a shaking hand, sweeping it over his face and closing his eyes. His head was nearly decapitated from where the creature dug into his neck. Cyra squeezed her eyes shut and looked away.

Aella laid a hand on her sister's shoulder and said, "I think we should go back to the castle."

"I agree." Ivan nodded, stepping closer to Cyra as he surveyed the forest around them.

Golden eyes snapped open, and she sprang to her feet. "Nahlil's death will not be in vain. We need answers. *Our* kingdom needs answers." The last sentence was directed toward Aella.

Aella opened her mouth to speak, but Ryder, talking for the first time, said, "The Queen is right. Nahlil deserves more."

Cyra's golden eyes met his gray ones, a storm seeming to build behind them, and nodded. Instead of arguing, Aella shook her head while Ivan huffed in annoyance.

"We must leave his body. We can't bring it with us." Ryder's gaze drifted to Nahlil.

Mikah nodded. "It'll only lead more of those monsters to us."

Swallowing back the bile that climbed up her throat from that thought, Cyra said, "We can use my blanket to wrap his body." She hated the idea of leaving Nahlil behind, of him not getting a proper sendoff like he deserved, but she knew the others were right.

Without a word, Ryder dropped down and started to dig a hole with his bare hands. A moment later Mikah fell in beside him, then Ivan, and then Aella. Each of them scooping out large chunks of earth as they reverently worked.

The future Queen looked towards Nahlil with tears streaming down her face. She went and wrapped him up gently, preserving his privacy and honor as much as she could.

After that, she dropped to the ground and worked in silence with everyone else. The first death of their party weighed heavily on her heart.

CHAPTER 19

ONCE THEY HAD FINISHED burying Nahlil's body, they began to pack up, but Cyra found herself lingering. She stood, her gaze stuck on the packed dirt before her. Her mind was filled with the weight of the upcoming coronation and the responsibilities that loomed before her. If she was unable to keep one soldier safe, how could she protect an entire kingdom?

A soft crunch of footsteps behind her broke the silence, and she turned to see Ivan approaching. His presence brought a strange mix of comfort and uncertainty—feelings she wasn't sure how to navigate.

"Cyra," Ivan greeted softly. "You look like you could use some company."

She offered a small, tired smile. "I suppose I could. There's so much on my mind."

Ivan came to stand beside her, his hands resting casually at his sides as he gazed at Nahlil's burial ground. "You couldn't have predicted this."

Cyra nodded, the weight of those words sinking into her chest. "But we should have known since we are getting closer to the lake. Nahlil's death was unnecessary."

"Then that was the responsibility of us," Ivan said firmly, his gaze shifting to her. "The ones here to protect you. Not yours."

"It's just...a lot to take in. The Cleansers, the monsters. It's like there's danger coming from every direction."

Ivan stepped closer, and his presence grounded her in a way she didn't expect. "You've got me. You don't have to carry all of this by yourself."

Cyra looked up at him, her golden eyes meeting his dark brown ones. For a moment, she saw the sincerity in his gaze—the way he looked at her, not as a queen or a figurehead, but as a person. Someone he cared for. Her heart tightened, and she let out a quiet breath.

"Ivan," she began softly, her voice almost hesitant, "this kingdom and my family are my main priority. I cannot let anything or anyone get in the way of that."

Ivan nodded, his expression thoughtful. "I understand. You're not a little girl promising to marry me anymore."

"Exactly," Cyra said, her brow furrowing. "I'm not the same person I was when we were children."

"That's true," Ivan admitted. "We have the chance to build something new now."

Cyra's heart skipped a beat at his words. There was a comfort in the familiarity of Ivan, but there was also the fear that they didn't truly know each other. Her mind drifted to Hollin.

"I've changed. My life has changed. There are things...things I can't even tell you about. I don't want to give you false hope."

Ivan's expression softened, and he reached out, gently taking her hand in his. "I know you've changed, Cyra. How could I expect a twenty-three-year-old woman be the same as an eight-year-old girl?"

Cyra's heart raced at his touch, and for a moment, she found herself wanting to believe him—to let herself fall into the safety of his words. But doubt still gnawed at her. "You don't know everything, Ivan. There are parts of my life that you can't understand."

"Then help me understand," Ivan said. "I don't care what's changed or what you've been through. I care about who you are now, Cyra. And I want to be part of your life, no matter what that looks like."

Cyra stared at him, her breath catching in her throat. Could she really trust him? Could she let herself open up to him when so much of her life was consumed by secrets?

She looked down at their intertwined hands, the warmth of his touch sending a shiver through her. Slowly, she nodded. "I can't promise you anything, but I would like to try."

He gently pulled her closer. "That's all I ask."

For the first time in what felt like weeks, Cyra allowed herself to relax, to lean into the comfort Ivan offered. She rested her head against his chest, listening to the steady beat of his heart as his arms wrapped around her.

The group traveled on, uneasiness hanging in the air. Ivan, Ryder, Mikah, and Aella formed a tight circle around Cyra on their horses as they grew closer to the lake, and tension grew higher. Aella noticed how her older sister would jump at every sound, her hands raising in preparation for a fight. Nahlil's death made everyone nervous, but the future queen the most.

As the second day of their journey drew to a close and the sun set, Ryder said, "We need to make camp."

Cyra tensed on her horse, hands gripping the reins. "We must take turns keeping watch."

"Of course, Princess," Mikah confirmed.

Aella nodded sharply. "I will take the first watch. I won't be able to sleep anyway."

"As will I," added Ryder.

The lightheartedness from the day before was gone as was the need for unnecessary conversation. They worked quickly to set up camp, deciding against a fire despite the chill the night brought, to prevent bringing any more attention to their group.

Aella and Ryder each sat against the base of a tree as they listened to the heavy breathing of their sleeping comrades. Aella's hands wrapped around her knees, pulling them to her chest, her violet eyes wide and alert, scanning the forest. Her attention frequently snapped to Cyra, who was sleeping beside Ivan. Despite herself and her feelings toward the man, she was a bit grateful he was on this trip for the comfort he could provide her sister.

"You are right not to trust him." Ryder's husky voice broke the silence, only loud enough for Aella to hear.

Aella glanced at Ivan, taking note of the deep, steady breaths that indicated sleep before she responded. "Why is that?"

Ryder paused, then answered, "Just a feeling."

She nodded, understanding what he meant. It was a gut feeling—that instinct that told you when danger was near. Something she had always relied on thanks to her training and years of abuse and torment at the hands of her handler. Ryder was an observer; someone who rarely spoke, but his actions were more than enough.

She had seen it all throughout the journey thus far. His eyes always analyzed knowingly at her, Cyra, Ivan, and the others, as well as the surrounding landscape. Aella knew that the quiet ones were always the ones who knew what was truly going on. The best assassins of the Guild were much like that, and in a way, Aella wished she was similar to them. Even if it was fun to tease, cajole, and piss off her opponents by mocking them, it was a whole other strength to know when to keep quiet.

Laying her head against the tree beside her, she listened to the soft breathing around her and the low cry of hunting owls. Without meaning to, she began to conjure images of the king and queen in her mind. Though she had no real memories of them—having been just barely a toddler before they shoved them in chains and kicked them out of the castle—she took notes of the portraits that hung within the castle walls and the way that Petra affectionately talked about them. These paintings featured the queen's golden hair and the king's blue eyes, which she imagined were similar to the ocean that stormed within Rheanna's. Each of their features held a fragment of her sisters and even herself, though she hated to admit it. She envisioned the way the queen might have tucked her and her sisters into bed and the king reading them a story.

With a growl, she banged her head against the tree and felt the bark scratch into her scalp, using the pain to forget the image and those feelings. What use was there in mourning the life she never had? Parents that were not hers? She needed to live in the real world now more than ever.

Aella turned to see Ryder's inquisitive eyes watching her, and she squirmed, uncomfortable with someone witnessing a moment of weakness, but instead, she met his gaze, daring him to say something. He smiled at her, only the smallest upturn of his lips, and then looked away.

The sky had begun to lighten, though dawn was still some time away. Aella glanced at Ryder, who nodded in her direction before standing to stretch. They ended up taking watch the whole night, not wanting to wake the others when they were unable to sleep themselves.

Just as Aella was about to rise and rouse the others, a faint rustling sound caught her attention. She stilled, and her hand instinctively reached for her dagger.

"Did you hear that?" she whispered.

Ryder nodded, stepping forward with careful, measured steps. "Stay sharp."

The rustling sound grew louder and closer, breaking the stillness of the early morning. A forest creature would not make that much noise. She rose to her feet, crouching low, her senses on high alert.

From the edge of the trees, a figure appeared. At first, it was just a dark shadow moving between the fog and branches, but as the figure stumbled forward, Aella realized it was a man. He moved slowly, his steps uneven and labored.

Ryder stepped in front of Aella, raising a hand for caution as the man staggered closer. His clothes were torn and dirty, and his face was gaunt, eyes wide with fear.

"Stay where you are," Ryder commanded, his voice low but firm.

The man didn't respond at first. His eyes darted wildly between Aella and Ryder, and his mouth opened, but no words came out—just a dry, rasping breath. Blood trickled out of his nose and into the scruff on his upper lip.

Aella moved closer but stayed a step behind Ryder, her grip tight on her dagger. "What are you doing out here?" she demanded, her voice sharp.

The man's knees buckled, and he collapsed to the ground. "Please...help me..." His voice was barely a whisper, hoarse and broken. He struggled to lift his head, his eyes bloodshot and wild.

Ryder's brow furrowed, but he kept his distance. "What happened?"

The man's hand trembled as he raised it to point toward the direction he had come from—the direction of the lake. "Tumbaco..." he stammered, his voice shaky. "It was attacked...by monsters. They came from the lake."

Aella's breath caught in her throat, her heart quickening as she exchanged a glance with Ryder. The destruction was spreading.

"We need to wake the others," Ryder said, his tone filled with urgency.

Aella moved swiftly back to the camp, shaking Cyra awake with a firm hand. "Wake up. Something's happened."

Cyra stirred, her eyes fluttering open, immediately alert. Ivan sat up beside her, his hand already on the hilt of his sword.

"What is it?" Cyra asked.

"There's a man from a nearby town," Aella explained, glancing back at the figure who still trembled on the ground. "He says they were attacked by monsters"

Cyra shot up, her eyes wide as she exchanged a glance with Ivan. "We need to get to the lake. Today."

CHAPTER 20

A FTER ABOUT AN HOUR of hard travel, where each member of the party rode their horses into a full-on gallop, the trees started to thin, and the slope of the hills smoothed down to a gentle curve. Eventually, they came through the edge of the forest and saw a large body of water in the distance.

At first glance, the water appeared calm and almost serene. Yet the group knew better due to the violence that pursued them and the man from earlier who told them that monsters were at the lake.

Cyra squinted, bringing her hand up to cup the top of her brow as she searched the horizon for anything out of the ordinary. The lake itself spanned for miles with no end in sight, appearing more like a large sea rather than the sweet-water lake it was known for.

Yet something felt off, even from the distance they kept. It was as if time was frozen. Normally lakes of this size had much going on around them from lakeside creatures like turtles and waterfowl to birds in the air and elk, deer, and wolves drinking at spots along the shoreline. There wasn't even any insects buzzing around; no flies, dragonflies, weevils, cicadas chirping, or anything.

It was simply eerily silent. It was as if time was frozen in this spot, not one living thing to be heard or seen.

"We're here," Mikah muttered, his voice barely audible. His gaze fixed on the placid surface, though his posture was tense.

The closer they got to the water, the more was revealed. What seemed like a clear reflection of the sky warped and twisted, distorting the clouds and treetops like an oily black mirror, showing an ugliness that was less a reflection and more of a mockery. Strange ripples spread across the surface, yet there was no breeze to be felt. The group stopped several feet from the edge.

Aella stepped ahead of the others, her body rigid as her violet eyes narrowed. "That's not just water," she said, her voice tight. "It's something else. Something...wrong."

Cyra moved beside her sister, feeling the stillness in the air that had no place in a forest that should be filled with life. She couldn't shake the discomfort crawling up her spine. Ivan was moving past her toward the lake's edge.

"Ivan," she said, reaching out to stop him.

He glanced back at her briefly, a reassuring smile on his lips before he crouched beside the shoreline. "I'm just checking it out," he said softly, but there was something in his tone—something almost daring. Without waiting for a response, he reached out and dipped his fingers into the dark water.

"Idiot," Aella muttered under her breath, her hand instinctively resting on the hilt of her dagger.

Ivan jerked his fingers back immediately, his face twisting with discomfort. "It's cold," he said, standing and flexing his fingers. "Too cold." He wiped his hand on his pants, grimacing. "And sticky, like tar." The substance smeared across his khaki pants, the residue still clinging to his fingers.

A ripple spread from the spot he touched, widening in unnatural circles. Beneath the surface, shadows became defined, swirling just beneath the surface.

Aella stepped closer to Cyra, her voice low. "I don't trust him, Cyra. There's something off about this whole situation, and we can't afford to be reckless. Not here."

Cyra's jaw tightened, her gaze flicking between Aella and Ivan, but she remained silent.

Ryder broke the quiet. "The lake isn't natural. A dark magic resides here. You can feel it in the stillness of the earth." His gray eyes were locked on the lake, taking in every detail as though trying to decipher its secrets.

Mikah nodded in agreement. "We should fall back. Those monsters are in there. We might be able to take one at a time, but what if more break the surface?"

Cyra took several steps forward. Her hand hovered over the surface of the lake while her senses tuned into the wrongness that pulsed beneath. She could feel the darkness as if it was a living thing, watching them.

"This lake is the source," Cyra whispered, her voice barely carrying over the stillness of the clearing. "The monsters, the lack of magic... It's all coming from here."

Ryder's voice cut through the air again. "Then we've found what we came for. Now what?"

Cyra didn't answer. Her mind churned, processing the magnitude of what laid before them. The lake pulsed with dark magic, an energy that promised destruction if left unchecked.

Aella took a step closer to her, brushing her hand against Cyra's arm. "We need to be smart about this. There's more going on here than we understand. You can't just—"

"I know," Cyra said, her voice strained as she pulled her arm away, her hands raking through her curls. "But we don't have time to waste. We need answers."

Aella's jaw clenched. "I am aware." She stopped herself, biting back the rest of her thoughts as Mikah and Ryder exchanged looks.

"We need to leave," Mikah declared.

Ryder nodded. "The longer we stay, the more likely something will come out. We know what we need to."

As they all looked back at the water, the surface rippled once more, and for a moment, a shadow too large to be ignored passed beneath, sending a fresh wave of unease through the group.

"Let's go," ordered Cyra.

Without argument, the group turned to flee as the water continued to churn.

CHAPTER 21

PETRA LEANED FORWARD AGAINST the edge of the balcony, letting the cold stones dig against the skin of her forearms as she stared past the garden and out to Reddel and the various streets and buildings. She squinted, squirming against the cushion of the bench as low hums and grumbles escaped her lips the harder she thought.

Rheanna watched both the horizon, and her, and couldn't help but chuckle at her sister. "Nervous about Cyra and Aella, too?"

"Yeah..." Petra admitted, slumping back against the cushion with a loud fluff of cloth beneath her thighs. "They should have been back by now, right? They left two days ago, and the lake isn't that far."

"No, I don't think..." Rheanna admitted, though having lived in Dalmer most of her life, her perception of travel distance was skewed. "But I'm certain they're alright. Aella is pretty strong, and you've seen Cyra in training. She's nowhere near as good as Aella, but she can hold her own pretty well."

Petra smiled gratefully at Rheanna. Slowly, she leaned over to the small stone table and poured herself and Rheanna a cup of sugary tea. Neither of them let their true thoughts be known, however. Petra had her own fears and worries, but Rheanna was full of doubts as well.

Doubts about how the mission in general. She believed that Cyra shouldn't have gone. Alone, Aella was powerful, given her fearsome reputation as the Silver Death. A slayer of many whose deeds almost dipped toward legendary. With Cyra being the future Queen, Rheanna didn't find it smart or safe to send her into direct danger. Also, since Cyra had no children, that would mean the throne would go to Rheanna next should the worst happen.

And that was something Rheanna absolutely did not want since the thought of it scared her. The fear of not only losing a sister but of having to assume responsibility she felt ill-equipped to handle. Despite being the second born, she felt she lagged in every aspect to her younger sisters. She was a schoolteacher who could manage a classroom of children but not a kingdom of people.

She couldn't even tell the man she liked that she had a crush on him or confess her feelings for said man to any of her sisters.

The thought of it all curdled her stomach, but she didn't dare voice her thoughts and instead smiled to keep Petra from worrying.

A slow breeze that billowed out from Reddel carried with it the scent of baked goods, exotic spices, and life. Rheanna drank it all in as she deeply inhaled and turned on the bench to take her turn for a vigilant scan of the roads and castle gate to see if they could see any hint of their sisters. Instead, she found her gaze drifting toward the city and the people within.

Then, a thought came to her to help lessen Petra's quiet worry. Rheanna smiled and lowered her cup as she nonchalantly spoke. "Have you ever been into the city before, Petra?"

The younger girl seemed puzzled by the question, looking back at Rheanna with a dull expression. "What?"

"The city. Reddel. Ever been out there in the streets? Went shopping, stopped at a tavern, or seen a play?" Rheanna giggled, pointing past the castle walls.

"Oh. No. Mother and Father never let me leave the castle," Petra replied, frowning as she looked where Rheanna pointed. Her face turned contemplative. "They said a princess shouldn't be seen walking the streets alone since there are a lot of dangers out there."

Rheanna reached forward to touch Petra's arm, giving it a reassuring squeeze.

"I kind of understand," Rheanna said, pulling back to brush Petra's hair as she settled back to sit. "I've only ever seen the city from afar myself, even when I was a little girl before being sent away. My friend Maude Bushnell, Ivan's sister, was supposed to come and study here. I remember being so jealous at the time because Dalmer was so small and so cold. It was like an enclosed city of ice and slush, so I never got the chance to experience the city."

"That must have been lonely," Petra murmured, pulling her knees onto the chair and hugging them to her chest.

Rheanna hummed, shrugged, and laughed. "At times, yeah. But I had a lot of people. The Bushnells, the village people, the children at the school I taught."

Then, a thought came to her, and she stopped brushing for a second to think it through before carefully speaking. "You know...maybe after Cyra returns and after we do the coronation and she becomes Queen, we should see if we can go into the city together—you, me, and maybe Aella to make her smile. Bring some guards. We can dress as plainly as possible, get some food, and do some shopping. Make it a whole sisters' day out."

Petra's eyes lit up at the suggestion, and she turned where she sat, releasing her knees. The fear and worry that she wore plain as day on her face melted away to reveal the youthful innocence of her nature. "Really? We can do that?"

"Who says we can't?" Rheanna laughed. "We have so many problems going on, why don't we live a little for just one day?"

Then Petra smiled sheepishly as she sipped at her tea excitedly. For a while, Rheanna watched her as she, too, drank and enjoyed the simple pleasure of snacks and relaxing. All the fear and worries of the day disappeared for now with this simple conversation. How she had lived for years without her sisters before this she didn't know, and she doubted she could ever go back to it now. To live alone with a family that treated her like their own but were still separated by a wall of duty. Maude was younger than her, but she felt more like a best friend than a little sister, and with Petra, she felt a growing protectiveness for her. She was glad, at least, that her younger sister had grown up sweet and innocent instead of haughty and demanding.

The breeze was warm and sweet, and the sky above was a gentle azure hue that promised a glorious day. Eventually, things settled down further, and when Rheanna thought about getting up to squirrel away lunch to the library classroom, two servants she had never seen before approached.

One was tall with brown hair and hazel eyes, and another was shorter but sweeter, with soft red hair and a freckled face. Both looked concerned, with dark furrowed brows as they walked conspiratorially together. Anxiety was plain on their faces.

"Oh! Hello there, how can we help you?" Rheanna asked, knowing that, as a princess, it should have been the other way around.

They hesitated for a moment, but the shorter, freckled one stepped forward and bowed respectfully. "We're sorry to disturb you, princesses, but we were wondering if Princess Aella was around? We can't find her."

Rheanna blinked but remembered their mission was one of secrecy. She wondered why Aella, of all people—someone who wasn't exactly a 'people person'—kept a private staff.

"Oh, she's out right now. Doing...princessy things," Rheana lied but laughed. "But I can take a message for her if you want?"

"Apologies Princess, but it is very urgent, and we need to find her as soon as we can," the taller one said, bowing down before she leaned in and made as if to clear the table of cups and whispered, "We're her personal informants. My name is Cora, and my friend is Laney. We have an important message about the Cleansers that she really needs to hear."

Petra froze as Rheanna put two and two together.

"I can very much take the message for Aella now," Rheanna replied, leaning forward to help clean the table as well.

Several bits of laughter and jovial chatter echoed in the hallway behind them. A few servants and a guard walked past the doorframe and away from the group, traveling further into the recesses of the castle. Laney bit her lip and looked back.

"Not here; not out in the open. Too many eyes and ears in the walls. The staff love to gossip."

"We could go into my quarters then. Act as if you're cleaning it and I'm making demands?" Rheanna suggested before Laney shook her head.

"Wouldn't that look improper? If the princesses run off with two maids for some reason, the servants could gossip. There's already gossip about Princess Aella's... tastes...in companions, and I doubt you would want that impropriety following you."

Rheanna was taken aback by the suggestion and blushed, not knowing about Aella's reputation already in the castle. Her face contorted to a grimace. It wouldn't have been any different if she had a man sneaking into her bed chambers each night, even if she had let Ivan in before. She wondered if anyone suspected anything of them, which made her heart quicken just a bit.

"I know a place we can go," Petra stated.

Rheanna looked at her with widening, surprised eyes, but then shook her head and smirked. Of course, Petra would know the castle's secrets. She had lived here all her life and probably had gone searching through every nook and cranny.

"Alright Petra, take us there," She said, standing up and preparing to move.

The hallways of the castle were thankfully not too disorganized, especially in the central keep. The outer walls and towers were defensively made to be confusing to attackers in case of breaching, but the inner sanctum was simple with straight hallways and abrupt turns in a grid layer. It made sense since the castle was a home as well as a fortress. So, Petra led them deeper into the castle's interiors, past the bedrooms, the war room, throne room, dining hall, and library to a larger section in the west wing.

Along the way, they passed several guards, and Rheanna noted one of them as Luca, whose gaze followed the younger princess without shame. Shyly, Petra slightly waved and smiled at Luca, who in turn grinned back before heading off with his superiors. A warm fuzzy feeling swelled in Rheanna's belly, seeing the sight. She couldn't help but smirk at their innocence.

Eventually, they made their way to their destination: a simple storage room with cleaning supplies, brooms, dusting bins, and another doorway leading to the servant hallways, where they traveled through the castle, often unseen. The room was dark but large enough for all four women to squeeze in with plenty of elbow room.

"Is this good enough?" Rheanna asked, looking at the two servant girls.

Cora nodded and visibly relaxed.

"Good. But please tell us what all this secrecy is about and what it is you have to tell Aella."

"As you know, Princess, we report to Princess Aella since she...conscripted us...to be her informants," Laney replied tersely, giving Rheanna the impression that their conscription wasn't exactly voluntary. "She asked us to keep our eyes and ears open in case we hear information about the Cleansers.

She was very adamant—to a terrifying degree—that we dig for information on her behalf."

Petra gasped at that and whispered under her breath, "Just like my stories," before looking back at the other two with wide eyes full of wonderment but also fear and worry.

Fear and worry that manifested in Rheanna as well as she leaned forward closer to the girls. "So, what's the information?"

"They plan to make moves during Princess Cyra's coronation. Word got out that it was going to be happening soon, and they intend to do something to keep her from ascending the throne as Queen. They want to make an example of her in front of all the other royals as well," Laney said in a whisper.

"No, that can't happen," Petra gasped, grabbing hold of Rheanna's sleeve. "Rhe, we have to do something. We must tell Cyra and Aella when they get back!"

"I agree," Rheanna said, her face softening to lessen her sister's worry. "And we will do something the moment they're back. They should be back any day now."

"Thank you, Princess Rheanna," Laney said, bowing down several times before she grabbed at Cora's hands and shuffled away. Her body movements were tense and jittery. "We'll be around the castle if you need us. Our duties tend to have us sweeping and dusting outside of the royal quarters."

They quickly left, leaving Petra and Rheanna to themselves now, who slowly slinked out of the closet room and slid against the door behind them with a deep sigh.

"This is far more serious than I realized. I feel like we're fighting a war already, and our enemies are all around us," Petra said, staring at the ceiling above her. "This is becoming too much like my stories and I'm not too fond of it becoming our reality."

All Rheanna could do was lean over and hug her younger sister close to her.

"We're not going to lose. We won't let them do anything to Cyra. We've got each other," she said.

And she meant it.

CHAPTER 22

T HE CASTLE WALLS CAME into focus as the group trudged
back from their journey, exhaustion and stress weighing
heavily on their shoulders. Aella led the way. Her face was
expressionless, but the tension in her posture was unmistakable.
Behind her, Cyra walked silently, her eyes distant, still processing
the horrors they had witnessed. Mikah and Ryder flanked them,
their faces grim, while Ivan brought up the rear, his expression
unreadable.

As they approached the gilded castle gates, a familiar voice
rang out.

"Aella! Cyra!" Petra shouted, her waves flowing freely
behind her as she ran across the courtyard and to the stables to
meet them. Rheanna followed quickly behind, her eyes scanning
the group with concern.

Once their sisters began to dismount, the two rushed them.

"Oh, thank the goddess!" Petra collided with Cyra,
squeezing her middle tightly while Rheanna threw her arms
around Aella.

"What happened?" Rheanna asked breathlessly, coming to
a halt beside Petra. Her gaze darted anxiously between them, her
heart pounding. Aella looked as cool and collected as always,

but black gunk clung to her clothes. With her hair popping out at all angles and dirt smudged on her cheeks, Cyra was visibly disheveled. Despite herself, Rheanna couldn't help the way her eyes lingered on Ivan. He was covered in dirt and grime but still strong and steady as ever. She quickly averted her gaze before anyone could notice.

"Where's Nahlil?" Petra asked.

Cyra looked away as her eyes filled with tears, unable to answer.

Aella placed a hand on Petra's shoulder. "He didn't make it."

Petra's face fell. "What do you mean? What happened?"

Cyra opened her mouth to speak, but her voice caught in her throat as the image of Nahlil's lifeless body with the bird-like creature hovering over him flashed before her eyes.

It was Ivan who stepped forward. "We were attacked. One of the monsters killed him."

Rheanna's breath hitched, her eyes widening in shock. "A monster? What kind of monster?" Her voice was barely above a whisper.

"Something utterly unnatural. It looked something like a bird," Ivan replied, his gaze meeting hers for a brief moment before turning away. "It came while we were sleeping."

Rheanna wanted to reach out for Ivan, glad he was home given what they had faced, but instead, she focused on Cyra, who looked pale and shaken. "Are you alright?" she asked softly, placing a hand on her sister's arm.

Cyra nodded, though the weariness in her eyes betrayed her true feelings. "We'll explain everything inside. But it's...it's worse than we thought."

Petra grabbed onto Aella's arm, looking up at her older sister with wide, fearful eyes. "Aella, please tell me what's going on."

Aella hesitated, and her normally sharp features softened for a moment as she looked down at Petra. "It wasn't just one monster," she admitted, her voice low. "The Black Lake is full of them."

Petra clung tighter to Aella. "How can this be happening when there is no magic?"

"We don't have all the answers yet," Cyra said, trying to reassure her little sister. "But we will. I promise you, Petra."

Petra gave an appreciative smile, and Rheanna said, "We should get inside. We need to figure out our next steps."

Cyra nodded, her expression hardening as she looked toward the castle. "Yes. We have to debrief the council and figure out what we can do next."

With that, the group began to move toward the castle doors, the weight of what they had experienced settling over them like a heavy cloak. Rheanna fell into step with Aella and Petra, who still held on to her older sister's arm.

Under her breath so no one but the three of them could hear, Rheanna said, "Laney and Cora came to us."

Aella's head tilted toward Rheanna, but that was all the acknowledgment she received, so she continued. "They have information to share with you about the Cleansers."

"Thank you," she said with a dip of her head.

Rheanna held in a sigh, wishing to get just a little more out of her younger sister.

Cyra and Aella entered the war room first with Rheanna and Petra following closely behind, but when the latter went to sit, the other two stayed standing in the front of the oval table. The council was silent, waiting for them to tell them about their harrowing journey. The members looked on in curiosity and anxiety.

"We saw one of the monsters ourselves while we were less than a day away from the Black Lake," Crya said. Gasps filled the room, but she continued, "One of us was killed, but we still completed our mission. What we found was worse than we expected."

A ripple of unease passed through the room. Norton leaned forward; his brows furrowed. "What do you mean?"

"The lake isn't natural," Aella cut in, her violet eyes flashing as she took over the explanation. "The water is producing the monsters that are terrorizing our kingdom and attacked us."

Lola nodded and said, "I can attest that we were close to the lake when attacked as well." A stray tear ran down her cheek. "No one else should have to die."

"What kind of creature was it?" asked Bianca, her usual sneer replaced with worry.

"A bird-like monster about the size of a small child," responded Aella, her arms crossed over her chest.

The room fell silent. A shift in the energy was noticeable: shock mixed with apprehension.

"How did you survive?" questioned Talmadge, his eyebrows raising in his wrinkled face.

"We killed it," explained Cyra, "by chopping off its head."

"At least we know we can defeat them," he said.

The members hummed and nodded in agreement, but their relief was short-lived. "It took all of us, even with our magic, and still one of us died. We cannot underestimate this threat."

"And you didn't think to report this sooner?" Bianca sneered, her voice cutting through the tension like a blade. "If these monsters are real, the council should have been informed immediately."

Aella's eyes narrowed, her hand resting on the hilt of her dagger, though she didn't draw it. The action alone was enough to make her threat real. "We quite literally just got back not even an hour ago. Are you really stupid enough to think we took a day trip after nearly being killed and losing one of our men?"

Bianca looked taken aback by the blatant disrespect and stammered for a reply, but Aella continued to cut her off, leaning menacingly in her chair.

"We also had other priorities. Our whole mission was to go out there and investigate, and we did that. We found where the monsters were spawning from, and we survived to bring this information back to your ungrateful ass."

Bianca opened her mouth to retort, but Norton raised a hand. "Enough," he said firmly. "This is no time for petty arguments. Council member Lola already confirmed the existence of monsters. We needed more."

Cyra nodded her gratitude toward Norton before continuing. "The lake was surrounded and consumed by dark magic. Whatever those creatures are, they're not natural—they're part of something bigger."

"Dark magic?" Marine echoed, her face grim. "You're certain?"

"Absolutely," Cyra said, her voice steady now. "There's no doubt. Whatever's happening in the South, it's tied to something powerful, something ancient. And we need to figure out what it is before it spreads."

Talmadge let out a heavy sigh. "And what do you propose we do about it? You've been gone from the capital for years. Do you even know where to begin?"

Aella's eyes flickered with barely concealed fury, but Cyra spoke before her sister could lash out. "We need to gather more information. We have to figure out why the lake holds magic when the rest of the kingdom has not for a century."

"Do you think these monsters and the unrest are connected?" Norton asked.

"I do," Cyra said, her voice firm. "The timing is too close. The Cleansers, the monsters, the assassinations... They're all tied together somehow. And until we understand how, none of us are safe."

The representatives exchanged uneasy glances. Even Talmadge seemed slightly unsettled by the gravity of the news, though he remained silent.

Marine leaned forward, her blue eyes serious. "If what you're saying is true, then we need to act swiftly. There's unrest festering in every corner of the kingdom, and now we have dark magic to contend with, as well."

"Indeed," Norton agreed, his brow furrowed in thought. "We'll need to strengthen our defenses, but more importantly, we need answers."

"We can deploy some soldiers to investigate and instruct them not to engage. We need them back alive," Aella suggested.

"Very well," Norton said. "We'll send scouts, and the coronation must happen as planned."

"Agreed." Cyra was already turning toward the door when she said, "The kingdom is in danger, and we need to act quickly."

With that, the meeting came to a close. As the sisters exited the room, their hearts heavy with the weight of what they had seen, Aella caught Cyra's arm and whispered, "We need to move fast, Cyra. Whatever's coming...it's already here."

CHAPTER 23

THE NIGHT AIR PRICKLED against Aella's bare arms as she slipped past the castle guards, along the outer walls, and out into the Capital itself.

While she didn't need their permission to leave—since she was a princess and no one would dare stop her anyway—she found it easier to avoid them altogether. If Laney and Cora had information about the Cleansers this quickly without leaving the castle grounds, then that would have meant that some of the guards were either gossiping fools or informants.

She was more liable to believe the latter of the two. Often, fools and informants were the same anyway, if the servant girls were any indication of the caliber she was working with. The girls were older than Petra but younger than Aella, and from what she found out, they enjoyed spending their free time away from cleaning up after messes and dusting royal belongings at certain local ale houses close to the castle gates.

Made sense. It was where the guards rotated out, the prices were often higher to compensate for the servant wages, and the quality of men and women, Aella mused, were much better and refined to parlay and play with—a perfect place to meet, especially for one like her.

With a smirk, the assassin cleared past the defensive walls, scaled down a rocky cliff face, leaped past stone palisades and a few buttresses, fell into an alley, and then out to the crowd of citizens stalking the nightly streets of Reddel. Soon, she found herself standing before the alehouse "The Gilded Pot"—complete with an amusing yellow chamber pot—before she slipped on in.

Inside, it was like every alehouse she had ever been to before. They had a certain charm she liked that you couldn't get in an inn or a tavern. Taverns were for eating and drinking and were respectable establishments. At inns, you would expect a room and board.

Alehouses, though? Cramped, full of tables, and they only sold booze and nothing else. People were packed wall-to-wall as they laughed, cajoled, and told tall tales. The walls were white plaster but yellowed with grime and time. The exposed overhead beams rocked with dust and debris occasionally from partygoers on the second floor, who found the time to sneak off with cheap mugs of ale in hand. The floor was hardwood and smoothed by years of shuffling feet, though those same feet dirtied the floor in a layer of mud, straw, and stray rocks.

The smell of the place hit Aella first. A sort of sour pungency from sweat and overused orifices. A scent she nearly forgot from her time in the castle and was often hidden by the stank of the swamp where the assassin's Guild was based.

Crinkling her nose, Aella pulled up her hood to keep herself hidden as she swam through the crowds, looking for her mark. Eventually, she spotted the two girls; both were at the bar with a cup of ale in their hands, and they were wearing simple dresses.

Laney's was forest-green with a low, plunging collar, while Cora wore a rosy-pink one that accentuated her shoulders and waist.

Laney was busy fluttering her eyelashes at a common, average-looking man, seemingly enticing him to buy her drinks. On the other hand, Cora seemed disinterested and was busy glancing around for something better to occupy her time. The furtive stares she gave to the crowd reflected her flighty nature that reminded Aella of a sparrow.

Aella's mouth tipped up as she smirked and met Cora's eyes on the other end. Cora stared at her like a deer to the hunter, stiffened, and then—finding there was indeed something better to do—turned toward Laney and tugged on her sleeve to end the conversation.

Laney glanced back, saw Aella, and instantly deflated as she turned to the man beside her and pushed him away, though he didn't seem to get the hint.

"Come on, honey. I know you want me to stick around," the man drawled, his speech slurred.

"I don't think she is interested," Aella interjected, coming in between the girl and the man who was much too old for her. She leaned against the bar top and ordered her own drink before her gaze slipped back to the man. He stared stupidly at her.

"That is your invitation to leave. Thanks," she said flatly.

That seemed to stir him as he said, "Would you like to take her place?"

Aella's violet eyes narrowed, and she looked the man up and down slowly. She lifted her head, letting her hood fall back just an inch. "No thanks."

Recognition dawned over his features, a look of horror quickly replacing it. "I'm sorry," he stammered and then backed away, bumping into another man as he fled.

"That was impressive," Cora said with a grin plastered across her freckled face.

"You didn't have to completely scare him away," muttered Laney into her ale cup. She must have consumed quite a bit already.

Aella raised an eyebrow. "I think I was doing you a favor. Besides, I'm here on business. No time for useless men."

Laney sighed but nodded. "You're here about the queen's coronation?"

"What have you heard?"

Cora began, "The Cleansers are planning on making a move on the coronation. They've been painting 'The Unworthy' on every street and trying to recruit everyone to their cause." The girls exchanged a look which caused Aella to pause.

"Have they tried to recruit you?"

"They've been trying to get to everyone within the castle, and we're all loyal to the queen, but..." Laney drifted off.

"Sooner or later, someone is going to crack," Aella finished, taking a large swig of her ale.

"Unless," Cora hesitated, but then continued, "they already have someone." The girl pulled on the edge of her puffed sleeve.

Aella's eyes narrowed. "What do you know?"

"Nothing really, but there have just been so many rumors," Cora said. "It is starting to become scary to work in the castle."

Laney placed a reassuring hand on her friend's arm. Her hazel eyes met Aella's as she said, "The staff has been receiving threats saying if we continue to support the queen and royal family we will suffer."

A shudder ran down Aella's spine, and her fist connected with the bar, making both girls jump. "You should have informed me as soon as either one of you or your families received a threat." It came out more harsh than she meant it to, so she took a deep breath, closing her eyes before continuing, "Next time you're threatened, come to me immediately."

Both girls, wide-eyed, nodded quickly, and Cora spoke, "We didn't want to bother you with such matters when you have your family to protect."

In an almost gentle voice, Aella responded, "You girls are under my protection. No one will harm you." Before they could respond, Aella turned away and stomped out the door, pushing bodies as she went. She had led those girls into danger. She was no better than Creaton. Her body buzzed with unspent energy, her magic aching to be released, but she pushed it down. She would find another way to release her emotions.

Natalie stood at the large basin, washing a pot as Aella came barging into the kitchen. A quick survey of the large space proved no one else was in the room, but even if they were she did not care. Her steps did not falter as Natalie turned, her mouth parting to ask a question, but Aella silenced her with her lips. They spun, and Aella heaved her lover onto the wooden counter, pressing between her legs. The sound of clattering cutlery and moans filled the room.

Aella pushed Natalie to her back, her thighs hanging just over the edge. Aella's mouth left a trail of kisses down her neck, over her bodice, and continued lower.

Aella lowered her head, purring, "Let me feast."

The next few days passed in a blur as they prepared for Cyra's coronation. The castle seemed to be in constant motion as people came and went. After Aella relayed the information, they decided that the coronation would be small with only the council, their families, and the leadership of their allies in attendance. Normally, it would be open to the public, but they thought it unwise. She would do anything to make Reddel safe for Hollin.

After a fitting for her coronation gown, she met with Ivan.

"Why hello, my beautiful queen," Ivan greeted her as she approached him. He was with a few guards in the garden who dispersed quickly to give them space.

"Not queen yet," she laughed.

"But soon enough." He winked and interlaced his arms with hers as they walked through the luscious grove.

It was a pretty place, a small bit of heaven within the already impressive, luxurious castle. Cyra herself hadn't really had time to fully explore it because of everything that went on between the Cleansers, forging her connection to her sisters, dealing with her parent's death, the Black Lake, magic, training, and now the coronation.

But now that she was here, she enjoyed it, especially with Ivan by her side. The garden was full of life, with tall evergreens cut into a pleasing shape, low hedges that ran up to her waistline separating different sections of the garden from one another, bushes carved into animals and figures, and flowers of every type spreading all along the ground in various hues of pastels and bright colors. The nearby apiary provided the constant buzz of bees to flit around, and the smell of pollen and honey filled the air with a sweet, almost heady scent that made her relax.

Green vines of ivy wrapped up around everything as well, from walls to pillars and even the various bird baths and statues of little angelic cherubs, making it all look overgrown, but in a managed, cultivated way that was evocative of an enchanted forest. Cyra guessed they had Petra to thank for that. She often found the girl nestled with a book in her room, or among the flowers wherever they bloomed, coaxing them into growing for her.

"I must admit that I'm quite nervous about all of this," Cyra sighed. "What if the Cleansers make it in?"

"Then I will protect you."

"I don't think you can defend me from them all."

He halted, turning to her and placing his hands on her cheeks. "No one will even get close to you if I'm around."

Heat spread to Cyra's cheeks, and she moved away from his touch, continuing their walk. She didn't particularly like the idea of him thinking she needed his protection. She had fire magic and was the soon-to-be queen of Linnosa, but instead of making him feel inferior, she stayed silent.

"Do you remember when we were children?" Ivan asked. "I swore I would marry you someday."

Cyra laughed. "Of course. I swore I would marry you, as well."

"That could still happen. Couldn't it?"

"I suppose, but we were just children then. So much has changed."

Ivan stopped once again to face her. "My feelings have not changed."

"You barely know me anymore. Fourteen years have passed since those promises, Ivan." Cyra didn't know why she was fighting this, but something about it felt off. She still had too many secrets to keep, too many things she couldn't share with him. Would he still want to marry her if he knew it all? She felt like all she did was battle with secrets when it came to Ivan.

"I've gotten to know you all over again over the last few weeks," Ivan pleaded, his hands intertwining with hers.

"You don't know everything. You can't possibly tie your life to mine without knowing."

"Then tell me."

Cyra hesitated. She didn't distrust Ivan, but she hadn't even told her sisters about Hollin, so she couldn't tell him. Her daughter was too precious to her. But there was something she could tell him. After the trip to the Black Lake and their conversation, she owed him just a bit of truth.

"There's a prophecy about my sisters and I," Cyra blurted.

His eyebrows pulled together. "What does it say?"

"Four shall emerge, but only one will rise," Cyra said then continued, "We believe it means all but one of us must die to restore magic to the kingdom."

Ivan's brown eyes widened in surprise, but he pulled Cyra into his chest, and the smell of cedar enveloped her.

"Thank you for telling me," he whispered into her hair.

"I would like us to grow closer. There is just so much going on," Cyra explained.

He pressed a finger to her plump lips. "No need. I want you, Cyra. That is all that matters."

Ivan lifted her chin, his hand sliding into her fiery hair as his lips meant hers. He tasted like the sun on a winter's day, minty and warm. Cyra froze for a moment but then reacted, kissing him back slowly. The kiss was gentle and soft. The two pulled away, and Cyra stared up at Ivan, whose hand was still wrapped in her curly tendrils.

"You are mine," he said with such certainty that Cyra almost believed him. A pit grew in her stomach.

"Maybe," she responded.

"I'll help you figure out this prophecy. You will not be harmed."

Cyra nodded. She was usually more assertive with her romantic advances, but something held her back. The kiss left her feeling lacking, like something was missing.

"Does the prophecy have to do with why you all left Reddel?" Ivan asked.

"Yes. The Oracle apparently saw it once Petra was born and ordered our parents to separate us."

"Isn't it dangerous for you all to be together now?"

"We would have to face this prophecy eventually no matter what, I believe."

Ivan hesitated and then asked, "Are all of your sisters aware of it?"

"Of course."

"Aren't you worried? You barely know them. Especially Aella. She is Silver Death, the most infamous assassin in the kingdom."

Cyra's jaw slackened as she faced him. "How could you say that? She's my sister."

"I don't mean to offend you, but you should consider her background. Not even just her. Do you think any of your sisters want to die?" Ivan's words came out quickly, attempting to persuade her.

"Well, I am offended. Don't ever say anything like that again," Cyra commanded, looking every bit a queen as she glared at Ivan.

"I'm sorry. I'm being foolish." Ivan hung his head, and a bit of Cyra felt guilty for a minute, but then realized she had nothing to feel guilty for. He was the one who spoke out of turn.

Before they could say anything else, the sound of giggling interrupted them. Aella and Natalie came into view, tripping over each other with Aella's arm wrapped around Natalie's waist. Once they saw the other couple, their laughs ceased, and Aella removed herself from the other girl. Natalie smoothed out the skirt of her cook's uniform and adjusted her apron as all amusement fled from Aella's face. Her sharp features homed in on Ivan, her dislike of him evident every time they came into contact.

"Don't let us stop your fun," Cyra said, winking a golden eye, but Aella's glare didn't soften.

"I have to get back to the kitchens anyway, Princess." Natalie curtsied to Cyra then squeezed Aella's hand before running off.

"I wish to speak with my sister," Aella stated.

"Go ahead," responded Ivan cockily.

Aella's mouth clenched. Cyra watched her struggle to hold herself back when she said, "Alone."

When Ivan didn't move to leave, Cyra turned to him. "Leave me with my sister. I'll see you later."

He bent and placed a kiss on her forehead but left without another word.

"How can you stand that man?" Aella asked, violet eyes rolling. Cyra wondered if her eyes would one day get stuck in the back of her head by how often she saw her rolling them.

"Relax, Aella," Cyra sighed.

"I don't trust him. There's just something about him that is off."

"I know you don't. But trust me."

Aella crossed her arms and said, "You're lucky I do."

Cyra shook her head. "I'm worried about my coronation."

"I know. I've been in contact with the guards and coordinating security. Every person who enters this castle will be verified before they enter," Aella informed her confidently.

"It is not just that." Cyra struggled to find the words. "After it is over, I will be queen. I will have the whole country to look after. What if I am not ready?"

Aella shook her head. "I have never met anyone as ready as you are. You've already been making all the decisions since we came back."

Cyra's eyes grew pleading. "But it'll be official."

"You were born for this," Aella reassured her. She hesitated for a moment and then placed her hand on her older sister's back, rubbing gingerly.

Cyra smiled, leaning into her sister when an idea entered her mind. "Once I'm crowned, I'll name you Head of the Queen's Guard. You will command the army."

Aella paused and thought about Cyra's words for a moment. Cyra bit her lip; maybe she should've formed this as a request instead of something Aella had to do. She didn't want to force her sisters to do anything.

"I appreciate the offer. May I think it over? I'm not sure what I will do after all of this," Aella asked.

"Of course. You've been amazing with organizing everything. I really appreciate it."

"I don't want to see any of you harmed," Aella admitted. "At first, I didn't know why I was even coming here, but you've all grown on me."

"I love you too, Aella," Cyra said, wrapping her arms around her younger sister and placing her chin on top of her silver head.

"Let's not get ahead of ourselves now." Aella laughed but hugged her sister back.

CHAPTER 24

"*M*ommy!"

Hollin's voice sent Cyra sprinting into the darkness. *"Hollin! Where are you?"*

Cyra frantically turned and twisted, but she could see nothing. She could only hear her daughter's pleas.

"Help me, Mommy!"

A choked sob worked its way up Cyra's throat as she clawed at the dark air, searching for her daughter, fighting for her.

Her daughter, her fae ears exposed, appeared in front of her. Cyra attempted to cover them, but Hollin stepped out of her reach.

"You promised you would protect me, Mommy," she said *sadly and then collapsed to her knees, releasing an ear-splitting scream. Cyra lunged for her, but only darkness met her.*

Sweat covered her skin despite the cold air as she shot up in bed. Cyra twisted out of her bed sheets, panting, and ran her hands through her tangle of red hair. The longer she was away from Hollin, the more frequent the dreams had become. Anxiety climbed its way into her chest and wouldn't let go.

A quiet knock sounded at her bedroom door, and a brunette head poked around the corner. Emerald eyes that reminded her so much of Hollin surveyed her worriedly. "I heard you scream." Petra waited a moment before adding, "I have nightmares, too."

Cyra gestured to her sister. "Come on, then."

Smiling, Petra climbed into the bed with Cyra, snuggling in close. They drifted off, holding one another.

Petra stood on the dais in the gilded ballroom. While the throne room was perhaps the most opulent section of the castle—and the library a second most beautiful room to her—the ballroom showed off the full majesty of Linnosa.

Over the centuries, it had hosted hundreds of kings, queens, princes, princesses, and dignitaries from close to far away. When the relationships with the fae were better before the magic went away, those who were honored among the fae often were here as well, and displays of magic, music, and more echoed in the halls. Not only was it a place of politics and networking but a space of extravagant fun.

Ornate paintings done in pastels, oils, and watercolors covered the walls. They depicted scenes of the Gods in various poses, portraits of Linnosa's past royals, and breathtaking landscapes from all corners of the kingdom. A few outliers—rare collections acquired over the years—were also on display. The baroque frames were hand carved and varnished darkly to contrast with the marble white they stood against. Pure gold trim decorated the molding that ran from the floor, ceiling, and around the thick stained-glass windows.

Above, a large dome nearly encircled the entire room, and curved colorful glass glittered light down in a shower of ruby, emerald, and more when the sun was high. The chandelier had ten rows of glistening diamonds that reflected the candlelight within them during the night, sending orbits of light and shadow down to the floor when people danced into the twilight. Carved out of square stones of granite, marble, and slate, the floor had shaved silver between each crevice to keep the stones in place while people danced and romped around.

Guards in gleaming armor lined every wall and along the dais, prepared for any hint of the Cleansers. Armed with swords, halberds, and shields, they stood as an intimidating force for the unprepared. At least a hundred people of various colors from all over the world were in attendance, patiently waiting for the new Queen of Linnosa to be crowned. No one was dancing yet but instead sat on small, simple, cushioned thrones placed around the dais to watch while the food was shared and soft orchestral music weaved through the room.

Petra wore a mint green dress with silver detailing of various flowers along the bottom, her hair piled on top of her head in a braided crown. She stood next to her sisters, Rheanna and Aella. Rheanna was in a shimmering, cerulean gown with a sweetheart neckline, and her black hair fell in loose waves around her shoulder. Aella dressed in a silver strapless, skin-tight dress that fanned around her feet slightly. Her hair was pin straight, both sides braided into a half up/half down style. Petra was so delighted when she saw Aella for the first time ever in a dress she squealed until her sister threw a dagger at her. She stifled a laugh at the memory as she waited for her oldest sister.

"Presenting Princess Cyra Noelle Voelbel, the heir to the throne of Linnosa," boomed the announcer as the heavy doors of the ballroom creaked open and revealed Cyra. The once whispering crowd now seemed to hold their breath as they took in the beautiful queen. She was decorated in a golden dress, the waist tight and the sparkling skirt puffing out until it hit the ground. The neckline plunged low, accentuating her already ample cleavage. Her ears were adorned with long diamond earrings that almost reached her shoulders, and her scarlet hair artfully placed into a low bun at the nape of her neck, saving room for the crown that would soon be on the top of her head. Six guards marched with her to the dais, three on each side, their golden armor complimenting her dress, their hands placed on their swords.

A soft smile graced Cyra's face as she made her way up the stairs and to the center of the dais, making eye contact with each of her sisters before she stood forward to face the crowd. Petra gave her a reassuring smile while Rheanna's looked more like a grimace, and Aella sent her a wink. The Oracle seemed to appear out of nowhere, her wrinkled body covered in a pure white gown and cape. She hobbled up to Cyra's side with the crown every ancestor has always been crowned with in her grasp. Four gems of red, blue, green, and clear were placed at the center of the crown where the highest point met.

"We are here today to crown the rightful heir of Linnosa, Princess Cyra Noelle Voelbel," the Oracle croaked, "Do you acknowledge yourself as the rightful heir?"

Cyra glanced among the crowd of onlookers, all patiently waiting for her answer, and caught the eye of Ivan, who nodded slightly. "I do," she responded.

"Will you always act within the best interest of Linnosa?"

"I will."

"Do you promise to love and protect Linnosa?"

"I do."

"Then with the power invested in me by the goddess, I announce you as the Queen of Linnosa."

Cyra bent, and the Oracle placed the crown upon her head. Once she stood back up, the crowd began to chant, "Long live the Queen." The room was alive with energy, the people alight with hope and the orchestra picking up pace, playing a waltz.

The Queen descended the steps and called out to the crowd, "Now, let the ball commence."

As soon as the words were said, the guards along the wall stepped forward and aside and let the servants do their jobs. Out from the walls in hidden service doorways came the ones specifically chosen for this day. Men and women dressed in simple navy and gold—dresses for the women, pants for the men—came out to await the rising of the gathered. As soon as they stood, the servants grabbed the simple cushioned thrones, picked them up, and carried them to line the walls to clear the floor for dancing and merry making.

The soft orchestral music picked up, and trays of food, wines, teas, sweets, and more were pulled to one section of the ballroom to be picked and eaten by whoever was hungry. Several hoverers were already making a straight line for either cheese or wine as voices began to echo within the opulent room.

Petra turned to her other sisters to find tears streaming down Rheanna's face and laughed.

"I can't help it. I'm just so proud of her," she blubbered. Proud was one word to describe it, but she was perhaps a bit envious. She noticed the way Rheanna's eyes bore into Cyra.

Petra rubbed her back as Aella said, "Such a short ceremony."

"And now you all must survive your first royal ball," Petra muttered as she led them down the stairs and into the crowd where Luca stood, staring hopefully at Petra. She had to admit he looked exceptionally handsome in his armor and curly blond locks arranged neatly.

Rheanna squeezed her hand. "Go get your man."

Before Petra could object to them leaving, Rheanna had swept Aella away, leaving her face to face with Luca.

"Would you do me the honor of dancing with me?" he asked shyly.

Petra no longer wanted to be angry; it was exhausting so she said, "Yes."

His eyes widened, a bit shocked by her acceptance, but he quickly recovered, taking her hand gently in his and leading her to the dance floor. They began to waltz, and it reminded Petra of all the previous balls they danced together.

"I've missed you," she whispered.

He sighed deeply. "I've missed you as well."

"I'm not saying I'm past everything that happened, but I would like to mend it."

"That is all I could ask for."

He spun her around then pulled her tight to his chest. She lay her head against it and listened to the familiar sound of his heartbeat as they swayed to the music.

On the opposite side of the room, Aella and Rheanna came to a halt as Aella gaped at the handsome figure who leaned lazily against the ballroom doors. She marched over to him, Rheanna following close behind.

"What are you doing here, Karif?" she hissed when she got close enough.

"Who's this?" Rheanna asked, looking warily between her sister and her employer.

Karif looked Rheanna up and down, his eyes raking up her slender figure, and pulled her hand to his mouth, planting a gentle kiss before saying, "I am Karif Lin, Princess."

"Oh." Her mouth dropped in realization, her hand still in Karif's. His storm cloud gray eyes were a bit more mesmerizing than she'd like to admit. Karif Lin was a well-known name in this kingdom as he was the leader of the Guild of Assassins. He was known to be as cruel as the Silver Death.

"Let go of my sister, you ass." Aella pulled Rheanna's hand out of his grasp.

"Oh, relax. I am not here to harm any of you, but I do have some information," his eyes cut to Aella. "We have gotten quite a few offers to get rid of our new queen."

His gaze found Cyra, who was talking to the Hefguard royals and their sons. It was as if all the air was snuffed out of the room at the sudden threat to their sister. Both Rheanna and Aella stiffened as they reached for the weapons hidden within their dresses. Rheanna's hand hovered along the hem at her waist where a dagger was concealed and readied her mind in case she needed her magic. Her head swiveled from side to side trying to search for a possible threat.

"You better explain yourself this instant, or I will gut you like a fish." Aella's dagger was already in her hand, her teeth bared.

"I just said I mean you no harm. Come on, Aella. You know me better than that." Karif huffed and shook his head.

"Then why are you here?" Aella questioned, her stance still stiff and knife ready.

"To warn you. You have more enemies than you'd think, and they now know you are a royal. I wanted to offer my help," Karif explained quickly.

Rheanna began to question the type of relationship these two had. Given her relationship with Natalie, Rheanna doubted it was romantic, but there was definitely something there. His concern for Aella was palpable.

"How would you like to help?" One of Aella's silver eyebrows arched.

"Well, not only will I be your eyes and ears in our world, but I brought a friend." He gestured to someone, and seconds later, a tall man with auburn hair approached wearing a lopsided grin on his face.

"Ripley," exclaimed Aella, a grin forming on her face.

"My favorite little silver-haired murderer!" Ripley replied as he joined their little group. "And this must be one of your beautiful sisters."

Rheanna blushed at his words and said, "I'm Rheanna. Nice to meet you." She shook his hand, a bit dizzy from the now two gorgeous men whose attention was directed toward her.

"Ripley will be staying with you. Just a little extra protection," began Karif, and when he saw Aella about to object, he continued, "Don't start with me. He can go around this castle and the capital in general unnoticed. You cannot."

"I suppose you're right about that," Aella begrudgingly agreed.

"May I dance with your stunning sister?" Ripley asked, his hazel eyes still pinned on Rheanna.

Aella's eyes rolled. "Ask her, not me."

"May I?" He extended his hand toward her, and just as she was about to take it, the ballroom erupted in screams.

CHAPTER 25

C YRA FLEW TO THE side, her crown hitting the ground as several of the windows shattered, spewing glass everywhere. She looked up to see one of the princes of Hefguard, Atlas, covering her, his black hair flopping into his green eyes.

"Are you alright?" he asked urgently, several small cuts peppering his handsome face.

She had no time to respond as a creature that resembled a large wolf—but with black scales instead of fur—roared, preparing to pounce atop of them.

Just as the beast reared and lifted, Cyra raised her newly manicured hand without hesitation and called upon her flame. Instantly, a wall of flames erupted around them in a protective circle, catching the wolf almost immediately as it fell into the fire, screamed like a man, and rolled away to put the flames out along its mane.

This gave Cyra and Prince Atlas a chance to scramble away as Atlas pulled Cyra to her feet. Cyra searched the frantic crowd for any of her sisters, unable to locate them in the chaos.

Malcolm—Atlas' brother and another prince of Hefguard— rushed by them with their parents in tow, directing the guards to where the monster was among the layer of broken glass.

"Get out of here and to safety," Cyra shouted at the princes as she started toward the beast.

"I'll help you," Atlas responded.

"Your magic doesn't work here. You would just get in the way – Go!"

She couldn't waste another moment on the Hefguard royals and hoped they would heed her warning. The beast roared again as a guard jumped in front of Cyra. The creature opened its jaws and tore his head from his body. Blood spewed across the marble floor and the queen. Cyra stared in horror for a moment before shooting into action. Both hands up, she began to send bolts of fire. The beast roared again as fire bounced off its scales. Its monstrous head turned toward her, red eyes homing in as it leaped. Her back hit the floor. Tiny shards of glass dug into her skin. The weight of the beast's paws pressed in on her chest. Its rotten breath caused her to gag as she struggled beneath it. Suddenly, the weight eased, and the creature yelped. Rheanna stood bewildered with a sword of pure water shimmering in her palm. Sticky black goo dripped off the edge of the blade.

Aella appeared beside her, twin daggers in her hands. "It's time to try that blade of fire, Cy."

Cyra heaved and conjured the sword in her mind. She didn't hesitate when it appeared in front of her, clamping her hand around the fiery blade. It didn't burn her, though if it had, she wouldn't have noticed. The beast charged for her sisters. Cyra leaped toward it, cursing the skirts of her dress as she sunk her blade into its side. It cried out in pain and slashed its claws toward

Cyra, narrowly missing her torso, but instead ripping the side of her skirts. Rheanna and Aella took the moment to drive their own blades into the creature. It turned on them. A black paw collided with Rheanna, sending her skidding across the dance floor. The sickening smack of her skull on the edge of a piano echoed throughout the ballroom.

"Rheanna!" Cyra gasped.

Cyra shot Rheanna a pained look. None of them would be saved as long as the creature lived.

Petra leapt into the fight with Luca at her side. Vines enveloped the creature as she called to her power. "Hurry!" she yelled. "I can't hold it for long!"

"Go for its brain," Aella commanded as they both took running steps toward the beast.

Cyra let out a battle cry and jumped onto the creature, plunging the sword of fire through its brain and out its neck. Aella dug her dagger into its chest. The beast sagged and hit the ground. Cyra rolled off its back, chest heaving. Her sword vanished as her control of her magic fell.

"What did I miss?" asked Rheanna dizzily, her hand clenching the back of her head. The girls all made their way to their sister as she attempted to stand but stumbled.

"Whoa, girl. Be careful. You definitely have a concussion," Aella said as she grabbed her waist to stabilize her.

"That was impressive," said Atlas, eyes wide with appreciation.

"I thought I told you to leave," Cyra responded.

"Well, I got my parents out, but I couldn't leave a Queen alone with a monster."

"She wasn't alone," said Aella.

"She has us," chimed Petra, both hands on her hips.

"And I saw that. You four are insanely impressive." The Hefguard prince cast them each an appraising glance. The queen and her sisters were a force to be reckoned with.

"They are aware," added Luca. "They are the princesses and Queen of Linnosa. Even without their powers, they are exceptional."

Petra looked at Luca with such love in her deep green eyes that it was clear that any issues they had previously must have been forgiven. Guards and soldiers began to pour back into the ballroom.

"We need to get Rheanna to a healer," declared Aella, already pulling her toward the door.

Cyra nodded. "You take care of her. I'm going to deal with all of this." She gestured to the chaos of the room.

"I'll stay with Cyra," stated Petra.

The girls began to instruct the soldiers on what to do as well as meeting with guests to make sure they were alright. Thankfully, none of their guests were fatally wounded; a few cuts and bruises, but their guard had taken the brunt of it. Twelve soldiers in all were killed from inside the gates, and no one had seen the creature enter Reddel. If it spawned from the lake as they believed, how did it get within the gates with no one noticing? Why didn't it kill any citizens? Why did it seem mostly focused on the girls? So many questions they didn't have answers to. Cyra would have to ask the Oracle her opinion on it all.

"Queen Cyra!" called a guard.

"What's wrong?"

"The Oracle is gone."

CHAPTER 26

AELLA'S MIND REELED FROM the adrenaline of the night as she fell into her room. The silver straight jacket of a dress she was in begged to be ripped off, but she halted at the man who sat on her bed.

Her dagger was out and pressed against his throat in two steps. "You knew this was going to happen," she seethed.

"If I knew all that was going to happen, I would not have come tonight, and I definitely wouldn't risk my life by coming to your rooms." Karif laughed, causing the blade to slightly slice into his neck, a thin stream of blood appearing.

Aella grunted in frustration and ripped the dagger away. "I know. How could this have happened?"

Karif tilted his head. "You really care for them."

"That's not important," Aella dismissed his words. In their industry, loved ones were a weakness, and despite their history, she did not feel comfortable exposing hers.

"But it is. You are Silver Death. You cannot care for them," Karif challenged.

"I know that. I cannot control it."

"It is a good thing I came here. I will help you protect them. That blue-haired one is quite beautiful."

"Don't you dare," Aella warned. She couldn't imagine pure, innocent Rheanna dealing with a person like him.

"Well, I'm not the one you have to worry about. I'm not staying." He sounded a bit disappointed by that statement. Aella was already aware of the way Ripley also looked at Rheanna. He was one of the best of them, but at the end of the day, he was still an assassin, a cold-blooded murderer. She would stop that from ever happening as well.

"I'll handle it," she murmured.

"I don't think I've ever seen you in a dress." His eyes sparkled with mischief.

"Out," she commanded, grabbing his arm and pushing him toward the door.

"You look quite beautiful. I mean I would even—"

"Don't you dare finish that sentence," growled Aella, cutting him off. He chuckled as she opened the door and threw him out.

Natalie was standing in the hall, causing Karif to bump into her. "Oh, I didn't mean to interrupt anything." She went to turn away, but Aella stopped her.

"Natalie, I was just throwing him out. Come in."

"Oh, is this your lady friend?" A grin was plastered onto his handsome face as he looked between the two girls.

"Natalie, let's go." She dragged the girl inside, then shut and locked the door. She could swear she heard his laughter as he walked down the hall.

"Who was that?" Natalie asked hesitantly.

"Just an old friend."

"Did you two..." She trailed off awkwardly.

Aella stared at her. "I do not swing both ways. Girls only for me."

Natalie let out a breath. "Oh, thank the goddess."

"Were you jealous?" Aella teased her, wrapping her arms around the woman's waist and pulling her closer in. She watched as Natalie's face flushed.

"Of course not. He is just a very attractive man and was in your room, so I don't..."

"Well, he's a man, so definitely not for me, but besides that, he is more like a brother than anything," Aella reassured her.

Natalee hummed and pressed a kiss to Aella's collarbone. "I'm happy to see you're safe."

"Don't worry about me. I can handle myself."

"But I do enjoy handling you," Natalie purred with a wink, "Let's get you out of this dress."

Their bodies were intertwined and in the bed before they had time to discuss anything else.

"Cyra!" Ivan's voice sent Cyra spinning toward him and falling into his arms. He hugged her tightly before pulling back, assessing her for injuries. "Are you alright?"

Relief washed over her at seeing Ivan, safe and sound. "Yes, but Rheanna was injured." His gaze grew panicked for a moment for a moment before she reassured him. "She'll be okay."

"Is she in her rooms? I'll go to her," asked Ivan.

Cyra nodded then pushed up on her tiptoes to kiss him. His hands circled her face as he leaned into it, making it more passionate. She loved how much he cared for her sister.

The clearing of a throat pulled them apart, and Cyra blushed as she forgot their audience. They were in the hallway, just outside the now-destroyed ballroom. Both Hefguard princes watched with uncomfortable expressions.

Atlas offered his hand. His black waves fell into his green eyes while he nodded at Ivan. "Hello, I am Atlas Nicola."

Ivan stared at his hand, and Cyra thought for a moment he would not shake it, but eventually, he grasped it and said, "I'm Ivan."

"Nice to meet you. I'm Malcolm." Malcolm also held his hand out to shake, which Ivan was much more willing to take.

Ivan's dark eyes watched Atlas as he turned to Cyra. "Let us know if you need anything at all."

She smiled appreciatively, her gold eyes glowing. "Thank you."

Before Atlas and Malcolm left, Ivan wrapped his arm around her waist, pulling her closer. Cyra unwrapped herself from him, not liking the possessive way he touched her. No one owned her.

"What was that all about?" Cyra asked, arms folding over her chest.

"I just wanted those royal pricks to know you're mine," Ivan stated. His words rubbed her the wrong way.

"I'm a queen. I am no one's property. And besides that, they are allies that Linnosa greatly needs." She shook her head slightly.

He moved toward her and laid a dark palm on her cheek. "You're right. I'm sorry. That was inappropriate of me."

Her heart softened at his touch, and she gave him a small peck. "I forgive you."

CHAPTER 27

T HE CASTLE HAD BEEN breached, the Oracle was missing, and everything was spinning out of control.

"What are we going to do?" asked Petra, her eyes searching her oldest sister's eyes.

"You and I are going to comb through that woman's quarters and figure out what she knows." Cyra launched forward, still covered in blood and in her tattered dress, her crown not in sight. It must have tumbled off in the battle.

"Something must be wrong," Petra said manically as she followed after her. "I've known the Oracle my whole life. She wouldn't just leave us."

"Either way, we need to get to the bottom of it."

Petra agreed but stayed silent, wondering what they could possibly find. The Oracle's chambers were in the basement, close to the dungeons, so Petra never found herself venturing there. The idea of the dungeons in general barely crossed her mind; it was not something she liked to think about. They descended the spiraling staircase that led to the basement level of the castle. Petra attempted to envision what the old woman's space would look like, but her usually overactive imagination could not conjure anything.

A shiver rippled down her spine at the sounds of groaning. The drop in temperature from the castle's isolated walls to the basement's cold stone and brick only worsened her unease. She kept her gaze pinned to Cyra's back, watching the sway of her knotted curls, refusing to look down the hall she knew led to the dungeons. At the far wall, opposite the dungeons, was a black, metal door with serpent shaped doorknobs that spiraled up the center. The darkness of the lowest level contrasted with the vibrancy of the rest of the gilded castle and set Petra further on edge.

Cyra hesitated for a brief moment before pushing the door open, straining against its weight. It was hard to believe that the Oracle would have opened it several times a day. A musky smell that Petra couldn't place greeted them. The stone walls that covered the hallway extended into the Oracle's chambers. There were no windows or natural light given they were at basement level, but a variety of candles floated around the room without even one hint of electricity from what she could tell. With a flick of her hand Cyra lit the candles, the tiny fires burning bright and filling the room. Shelves covered every inch of the walls. Petra moved closer to inspect their contents when she gasped in horror and stumbled back. A jar with an underdeveloped fetus stole her attention, but she quickly realized there was a variety of alarming items such as limbs, organs, and unknown creatures floating nearby. In the space between, someone had scattered herbs, crystals, and other small knick-knacks.

"Why would the Oracle need all this?" Petra asked as she stepped farther away from the shelves.

"We know she can see the future," Cyra's eyebrows scrunched together in thought. "What if she has access to other magics?"

Goosebumps prickled along Petra's flesh, a feeling of dread washing over her. "I suppose I didn't really know her at all."

Cyra hummed in response as she began to finger through a pile of scattered papers on a black, wooden desk, the surface nicked and carved in multiple locations. As Petra looked around the room, she noticed all the furniture bore similar marks. The bed frame, side tables, and chairs all seemed as if they had been clawed into. Petra was struck by the complete and utter oddity of it all. She had never seen the Oracle's abilities of prophecy as magic, but what else would it be? They believed that magic had not been seen within Linnosa for over a century until the girls, but the Oracle and her magic made that untrue. The more Petra learned of the woman, the more she didn't want to know anything else.

Petra joined her sister at the desk and sat in the matching chair; it was extremely uncomfortable, which didn't come as a surprise. She reached for one of the drawers and began to rummage through it. An old, tarnished silver brush with a few scraggly hairs caught her attention. She lifted it and ran her hand over the engraving along the handle. *Selmana Hormanick.* She ran through her memory, looking for recognition of the name, but it ran blank. It was another strange thing, something that seemed so sentimental among the experiments and oddities of the chambers.

"Have you ever heard of her?" Petra asked as she passed the hairbrush to her sister.

Cyra paused, examining the item before swiftly handing it back.

"No, but I doubt it's important."

Petra shrugged, but something made her slip the brush into her skirts.

"I knew it!" Cyra shouted, her freckled cheeks red with anger as she stomped her foot.

"What?" Petra moved to her sister and peered around her to look at the aged leather book she held.

On the page was an illustration of the creature that attacked them. *The Jaquil.* A description sat below the drawing, a feather bookmarking the page.

"She brought it here," Cyra yelped. "It's all here. How to lure it and set it on a target. Everything she would need to bring it here." She stared wide-eyed at her younger sister, terror and triumph at the discovery reflected in her golden gaze.

"But why would she do that?" Petra wondered out loud, but her mind began to connect the dots before her sister even spoke.

"I'm not sure, but she is the one who separated us. What if she's the one who brought us back?"

Petra began to contemplate it. How did they know whether her prophecies were real? Why did their parents trust her? Now that she thought about it, she couldn't even recall where the Oracle was from, who her family was, or her origin story whatsoever. Her brain felt scrambled as one thought stood out among the rest.

"You think she killed our parents." It was not a question, but a statement.

Cyra's eyes fill with hot tears. "I think she may be behind it all."

Light knocking awoke Rheanna, and pain throbbed in her head as her eyelids fluttered, fighting against the heaviness of sleep and a concussion. She found herself in her pale blue sheets, snuggled in a mountain of pillows and blankets. The knock sounded again, pulling Rheanna a little more out of her daze. The night prior came back in pieces. Cyra's coronation, the creature attacking them, everything until her loss of consciousness. She attempted to heave herself off the bed and stumbled, her palm stabilizing her on the night table. Once she felt sturdy enough, she made her way to the door and threw it open.

"Thank the goddess you are okay," exclaimed Ivan, wrapping his burly arms around her. His embrace instantly relaxed her, his familiar scent enveloping her as she let out a small sigh. It took a moment for her to respond, but she wrapped her arms around his middle.

"My sisters?" she croaked out, her throat dry with sleep.

He stepped back, his hands going to her shoulders as he looked into her eyes. She could have sworn a sort of jealousy passed over his features before he said, "They're fine."

A sigh escaped her as overwhelming relief washed over her. The small burst of energy that got her out of bed left her suddenly, and her knees buckled. Before she could hit the ground, Ivan heaved her up by her armpits.

"Of course. Your slimy ass has to harass my sister the moment she is awake." Aella pushed past Ivan, putting a tray of food and water on the sitting table before taking Rheanna from his arms.

"You're a real piece of work," Ivan scoffed.

"Please no fighting," Rheanna muttered sleepily as her sister gently guided her back to bed. "Just go, Ivan."

"Seriously?" His face contoured in anger, his head shaking. When no one answered him, he stormed out, slamming the door behind him.

Rheanna groaned as she settled between the pillows once again. Aella began to pull the blanket over her sister, brushing her fingertips across her forehead.

"Rest for a bit more. We have a lot to do," she whispered as her sister fell back into oblivion.

CHAPTER 28

WITH THE CORONATION OVER, despite the chaos that ensued after it, Cyra was now the queen, and it was her responsibility to protect the kingdom and its citizens. She should have called a council meeting immediately after the attack last night, but she didn't want to do it before Rheanna was able to attend. That left Cyra sitting at the head of the council table, one of her sparkling crowns atop her unruly hair, waiting for the last member to join them so the meeting could commence.

Jasper Talmadge hobbled into the well-lit room, a black cane assisting him. He wore a slight grimace, presumably from pain, as he walked. Cyra hadn't noticed it before, and she wondered if he always used it or if she was just oblivious. The second he was in his seat Bianca opened her mouth to criticize. "Why wasn't a meeting called directly after the incident?"

"There were more important matters to attend to," Cyra said coolly. She could already see Aella's hands clenching into fists from the corner of her eye. The assassin and Southern representative were like oil and vinegar, and it gave Cyra a headache.

Bianca scoffed. "I think a monster invading the castle is pretty important, especially since the entirety of the council and the heirs live here now."

"You did not even believe monsters existed a week ago. Do not pretend to be all worried now," Rheanna snapped. Cyra glanced at her, a little surprised, but also proud of her sister's out of character comment.

Bianca turned her narrowed gaze onto Rheanna. "From what I hear you barely survived the attack. Don't act all tough now."

Rheanna's face turned pink, and she slid down in her seat.

"I didn't see you risking your life. We handled it, didn't we?" Aella said through gritted teeth.

"Well, that should be discussed—"

Levine Alvarez, one of the West representatives, cut off Bianca. "As you so kindly pointed out, the queen and princesses risked their lives last night. Why don't we show them a little grace?"

Sidney, the other West member, nodded along to his words.

"We need to focus on how to secure the castle and the kingdom in general," Norton said, cutting a glance at Bianca, "Not on attacking each other."

"I would be lying if I didn't say I was concerned. I brought my children here. After Nell..." Lola took a deep breath and continued, "We were supposed to be safe here." There was a bit of accusation behind her words, but Cyra could sympathize with her fear. She looked as if she had not slept in days. Dark circles of purple plagued her eyes, and her usual sleek and styled hair was frizzy and unkept around her face.

"I know, Mrs. Donovan. My sisters and I were able to handle the threat and will continue to do so. We have also learned some troubling information," Cyra said gently. If she was not seated so far from the woman, she would have placed a hand on her shoulder.

When no one else spoke, Petra took it as an invitation to share what they had found within the Oracle's chambers and her involvement with the Jaquil attack.

"I never liked that old hag," muttered Aella. She folded her arms across her chest and leaned her chair back on its two hind legs.

"The Oracle has always acted in the best interest of the kingdom," Norton said. "Are you sure she is involved?"

Cyra nodded. "The evidence is all over her rooms."

"What would she gain?'" questioned Marine. The older woman massaged her temples slowly as she processed the information.

"Does it matter? She is involved, and now she's missing." Aella turned to Cyra and continued, "I could hunt her down and kill her." An excited and ruthless smile transformed her features as she waited for her sister's reply.

Cyra hesitated. "We need to stay together. I think that will be the safest option right now."

If there was an attack, all four of them would need to be in the castle to defend it. Regardless, she would never send her little sister to kill anyone. She refused to use her the same way so many have before.

"I should eliminate the threat. The wench tried to kill us," the assassin argued.

Before Cyra could respond, Talmadge spoke, "Disgusting behavior. Utterly disgusting. You should not even be permitted—"

"Don't you utter another word," Norton said, his tone commanding and face hard. Talmadge looked as if his eyes would pop out of his wrinkly face as he stared, red faced at Norton.

"You have no right to speak to me—"

"But I do," Cyra silenced him as she stood from her chair, and the scraping caused everyone's gaze to snap to her. "I am exhausted and embarrassed from the lack of loyalty on this council. We can disagree without belittling. You are all adults; act like it."

After a few seconds of silence, Cyra sat down and said, "I think it is time we ask for aid."

A few gasps sounded around the room, and Sidney Tapia murmured, "We haven't called for aid since the banishment of the fae and other magic born."

"I am aware, but this calls for it. Honestly, if we were smart, we would try to make amends with the fae as well. They could—"

"That is preposterous," Lola exclaimed. "They are killing machines. We cannot fix monsters with more monsters."

Cyra fought to control her temper, her fists clenching and unclenching on her dress. These fools would rather die than ally with the fae. She thought of her sweet and gentle daughter, about the male who sired her, and was astonished by the fear Linnosa held for their species.

"Do not interrupt your queen," Aella seethed. She was ready for a fight, but Cyra had had enough for the day. They would not be fighting each other when there were bigger threats on the outside.

She took a steadying breath. "I am only saying we should consider it."

"Absolutely not," Bianca dared to speak.

"I have to agree," Petra said weakly, playing with a strand of her brown hair nervously. She attempted to make herself smaller, sliding in her chair, as if Aella would attack her simply for agreeing with Bianca. Cyra couldn't blame the child, given the horror stories they were told growing up about the fae, but her heart squeezed at the thought of Hollin's aunt being afraid of her.

"Understood. Disregard the fae for now, but we do have the Hefguard royals here now. I can talk to them before they leave." Cyra decided not to argue with their arrogance, but she made a silent promise to herself and her daughter to educate them all one day.

"I hate to be blunt, but I don't believe Hefguard would agree to help us without something in return, and given our current troubles, we don't have much to offer them," Marine said.

"This is why I brought it in front of the council. Does anyone have any ideas?" Cyra asked, one eyebrow arching.

Marine went to open her mouth but closed it as if weary of what she had to say. Talmadge had no such qualms as he spoke, "We can offer your hand in marriage to one of their sons." A smirk formed on the old man's thin lips as he sat back in his wooden chair. For the first time this entire meeting, he seemed momentarily satisfied.

Cyra's jaw fell open, but she closed it quickly. This was the obvious solution. She was queen, after all. It would be silly of her to think she could marry for love. Ivan's big brown eyes crossed her mind, and she knew it would crush him.

"She is not cattle to be sold," Aella said, a dagger already in her hand. Cyra met her purple gaze and shook her head slightly. Reluctantly, the younger girl put the dagger back in its sheath on her thigh.

"No, but she is our queen and will do what is best for the kingdom," responded Talmadge. "Won't you?" He directed that question straight at Cyra, a full-on grin across his wrinkled face.

"Of course, I will do what is needed." Cyra kept her expression neutral.

"But what about Ivan?" Rheanna wondered aloud, her blue eyes growing large.

"Who is Ivan?" Bianca said with a flick of her pale blonde hair. "If I were Cyra, I would be more than happy to marry Atlas or Malcolm." She sat forward on the wood table, her chin in her palm.

Cyra shook her head and palmed her forehead.

"We could offer one of the princesses, if they are more willing?" Norton suggested hesitantly.

"Hell no," Aella declared, her arms crossing her chest.

"Petra is much too young," Rheanna protested, causing Petra's face to go red, but she still smiled at her sister in appreciation. Nothing would be separating the youngest sister and her guard.

"Then what about you?" Marine said.

Rheanna's face blanched for a moment before she composed herself. Her gaze flicked between her sisters and the counsel members.

"I...I suppose," Rheanna struggled to get out. She was the only one without a significant other, and she was of the proper age.

"Rheanna and I will both meet with the royals and discuss it with them. We will do what is necessary." Cyra smiled at Rheanna encouragingly and concluded the meeting swiftly. Her head swam as she thought about how she would break the news to Ivan.

Aella admired Natalie while she gathered the ingredients for oatmeal berry cookies. She perched herself on the edge of the stone counter. Natalie moved with familiar ease within the kitchen, her raven hair in a loose braid down her back, a few dark strands framing her face. The light from the open window over the sink cast the room in a glow, and the sun reflected off the gold accents.

"You know, you could help instead of staring," Natalie scolded as she placed a basket of red berries next to Aella.

She smirked. "But you look so good doing it all."

Natalie shook her head at her lover. "Get your ass off the counter."

Aella chucked and hopped off, turning to face the ingredients and said, "This is your domain, so what do we do first?"

"In two separate bowls, we have to combine the dry and wet ingredients." She gestured toward the bowls and two piles of items.

"Sounds easy enough," said Aella, but she stood staring until Natalie pushed a bowl toward her and pointed at the dry ingredients.

"Mix them in this bowl. I premeasured them, so don't worry about that."

Aella began, adding flour, sugar, and baking soda when an excited voice filled the room.

"Whatever you're making, I want some!" declared Petra, rushing into the space with Cyra and Rheanna following after her.

"If you want to eat any cookies, you have to help make them," Natalie said sternly, one hand on her hip.

"Okay!" Petra replied enthusiastically, bouncing to Natalie's side and doing as she was told.

Cyra leaned against the counter across from Aella, a grin plastered on her face. "I see now why you forgot about our training."

Natalie noticed the exchange and said, "I'm sorry, I can be quite the distraction."

Smirking, she said, "I can see that." Cyra winked at Aella, who blushed slightly.

"Well, put us to work! I want cookies too," demanded Rheanna, a smile on her full lips.

Natalie gave each of the sisters a job until the dough was prepared. They then rolled it into small balls to place in the oven. Rheanna went to put away the bag of flour that was left out by the sink, when she tripped, causing it to explode up into her face and land like a powdering snow fall on the rest of them.

"Stars help me. I am so sorry. I'm such a klutz," stammered Rheanna, who stood up, blue eyes stark against the white powder covering her face.

Natalie exploded in laughter, which infected the rest of the girls, all of them doubling over and clenching their stomachs, even Rheanna joined in. While all the sisters were distracted, Natalie grabbed two eggs, spiriting one right into Aella's face and other at Petra's stomach. Both sisters made shocked noises, and Natalie darted to the other side of the kitchen.

"Oh! It is on!" giggled Petra, grabbing a handful of berries and smearing them on Cyra's cheek.

Baking ingredients flew around the kitchen, most of them finding their marks, but the strays still hitting the floor and furnishings. Aella chased after Natalie with an egg in hand. She caught her, twisting her around. Planting a kiss on her lips to distract her, she smashed the egg into her hair. They both fell into a fit of giggles when the timer of the oven went off.

"Perfect timing!" called Natalie as she dashed to remove the cookies.

"Finally! I'm starved," exclaimed Petra, leaning against the messy counter. The rest of the girls snickered. "What! Making this mess builds up quite the appetite."

"She has a point," said Rheanna, and they all erupted into laughter once again.

They spent the rest of the morning eating cookies and sharing jokes.

CHAPTER 29

T HE MORNING LIGHT STREAMED into the room through the wispy golden curtains. As the light tickled her face, Aella stirred, rolling away from it and toward her lover. Natalie lay peacefully with her chestnut hair fanned out around her. Aella reached forward to drag the tip of her finger down her sharp jaw. Never had Aella felt like this in all her eighteen years. Natalie was so pure, so sweet, while a monster lurked silently beneath her own skin. Somehow, Natalie cared for her, but only because she had not seen that side of her yet.

Natalie's chocolate brown eyes fluttered open and reached her hand up to hold Aella's to her face. Her skin was soft and flawless, unlike Aella's calloused palm.

"Good morning, love," Natalie purred, pulling Aella's arm around her.

"Hello," she whispered into Natalie's ear.

"Oh, if only we could stay like this forever."

"Can't we?"

Natalie huffed. "I have breakfast to make for your sisters."

"But you are already being of service to one of the princesses." Aella lazily dragged her fingertips down the length of Natalie's exposed upper leg, tangled within the white sheets.

Natalie shuddered, her eyes closing before she began to push the blankets away.

"If only we were all princesses," she said with a roll of her eyes. She pulled her cook's uniform over her naked frame, the material catching on every delicate curve. Aella couldn't help but stare, heat building in her core

"You could be," she whispered.

Natalie froze for a moment, her dark eyebrows furrowing, but shook her head. "Don't say things you don't mean."

Aella's heart sank at the cloudy look that overcame Natalie's features. She jumped out of the bed, not bothering to put anything on. She placed both palms on the side of Natalie's face, making her look down at her.

"I mean it."

"I am a cook in the castle, in *your* castle," Natalee exclaimed exasperated.

"And what of it? Cyra is the queen. I'm third in line. The crown will never fall to me, and I wouldn't take it even if it did." Aella poured out her reasoning, gripping Natalie's face tighter but still so gently.

"I can't." Natalie pulled away from her as she bent down to put on her shoes.

"No. You mean you won't," Aella clarified. Bitterness washed over her as she thought about the way Natalie made them hide their relationship. She had to be embarrassed of Aella, of the rumors that surrounded her. Everyone knew she was a monster in sheep's clothing. The only reason the council even let her step foot into the castle is because they knew she would never be queen. The ruthless, heartless, cold wench of a princess. The killer. Her sisters were meant for this life, but Aella was created for an entirely different one.

"We were having such a nice morning. Must we really ruin it?" Natalie pleaded.

"You're just like the rest," Aella spit out.

"What do you mean?"

"I am nothing but a monster to you."

Natalie stepped closer, her arms reaching out to embrace her, but Aella quickly stepped back. "You aren't. I just can't..." She trailed off, looking down before she reached for Aella again, this time able to wrap her arms around her.

"I have to get to the kitchen. I'm sorry," Natalie said as she pulled away.

Aella didn't respond but nodded her head. Tears began to well in her violet eyes, but she fiercely blinked them away. Instead of letting emotion overcome her, Aella strapped on her fighting leathers and speared for the training yard.

Cyra hit the ground hard as Aella's fist connected with her chest, knocking the wind straight out of her. She laid gasping as she attempted to regulate her breathing.

"Get up," Aella demanded, fury clear on her face. She had been relentless during this entire training session, constantly laying the girls out without any corrections. It was like she was out for blood.

"What's going on with you?" asked Petra as she helped Cyra from the ground.

"I thought you all wanted to be strong. I thought you didn't want me to go easy on you," Aella ranted, beginning to pace the arena.

"We want you to train us, not just beat us up. This doesn't help anyone," Cyra stated.

"It's not my fault you're all weak," Aella spat at them. "Maybe Mommy and Daddy dearest should have sent you all to be tortured your whole childhood, then you could be just like me."

Cyra knew her childhood was not easy, but this was the most Aella had ever spoken about it. She could only imagine how brutal it was to have created the Silver Death. She constantly had to remind herself that she knew Aella the princess, not the assassin. There was a whole other side of her they were not familiar with.

"Is that what's wrong? Are you angry with our parents?" Cyra questioned hesitantly.

Aella turned on her, getting in her face. "Your parents. Those bloody idiots were not mine."

"Aella..." Petra said.

"Don't you bloody start. You've been coddled your entire life. I don't want to hear one word come from your privileged mouth," Aella practically roared at her little sister. Petra shrunk away, tears pricking her eyes.

"We don't speak to each other like that," Rheanna interjected, shaking from the confrontation.

"Now I am being shamed by the weakest of them all?" Aella laughed bitterly. Cyra had never seen her like this, and she would be lying if she said it wasn't scary. She had seen Aella get angry with others, but never one of them.

"Take a breath. This isn't about us, is it?" Cyra asked, reaching her hand to rest on Aella's shoulder.

Aella shrugged it off and stomped from the training yard without another word. The three girls stared after her in pity and a little bit of fear.

"One of us needs to go after her," Cyra said.

"If not, some random guard or servant might be killed," Rheanna muttered.

"That's not fair," responded Cyra. She was worried for Aella and wondered if maybe something had happened with Natalie. They seemed to be getting along so well, and their relationship softened Aella.

"I'll go," murmured Petra. "I know she doesn't mean to hurt us. Something has to be wrong."

The other two looked at Petra, and for a moment, she thought that Cyra might tell her no being as overprotective as she was. Instead, she smiled and nodded.

"Alright but be careful. She's in a mood, and I don't know what made her so mad today."

"I know, but we all know she doesn't mean it," Petra replied, shaking her head and smoothing her hair out.

"No, she doesn't, but she still doesn't need to lash out," Rheanna added with a sigh before she slumped back against a bench and hugged a knee.

Petra turned to scurry after their sister before she got too far. Cyra and Rheanna exchanged worried looks but trusted their youngest sister to handle the situation.

It didn't take long to find her. Aella ambled away at a slow pace, prowling like a panther stalking prey, but once she saw Petra, she picked up her pace.

"Aella!" Petra called. Even at her brisk pace, she struggled to keep up with her sister. "Don't ignore me!"

The silver-haired assassin didn't falter or even look back as she stomped her way through the castle, heading toward her rooms, Petra guessed. Petra's breaths came out in heaving pants as her eyes narrowed to slits. If Aella wanted to play dirty, so would she. She raised her hand and twisted, a single vine shooting up from between the marble tiles in front of Aella and grabbing hold of her ankle. The girl fell backward, cursing as she brought out one of her daggers to cut at the vine, but with one thought, it grew thicker and encapsulated both her legs.

"You bloody brat! Let me go!" Aella screeched, her hands slicing at the vines that only grew stronger.

"Tell me what's wrong," Petra said calmly.

"You are. You and those self-righteous, judgmental wenches. All of you with your nice lives," she spat at Petra, looking up with her with such malice, for a moment, Petra was almost hurt. "You all look at me and see a monster. Everyone looks at me and sees a monster."

Petra kneeled in front of her angry sister and stared into her violet eyes. "You are not a monster. You are my sister, and I love you." She brought a hand to her scarred cheek and whispered, "We love you."

It was like something exploded in the older sister as a sob erupted from her chest, startling Petra. She stared in shock at the tears that flowed down Aella's face before banishing the vines and pulling her sister to her chest. Over her shoulder, she made eye contact with Luca, his crystal eyes wide. Ever so slightly, she shook her head and mouthed, "Go." With a dip of his blond head, he was gone. Petra's hand rubbed soothing circles into her sister's back as the tears soaked the front of her training leathers.

"I don't want to be a monster," Aella choked out.

Petra smoothed the silver hair around the assassin's face back as she continued to reassure her softly. "You did what you needed to do to survive. Do not be ashamed of that. You are Silver Death. You are Princess Aella Leigh Voelbel. You are my sister, and I love every version of you there is and ever will be."

Instead of responding, Aella cried even harder, her entire body shaking, the last fourteen years coming out at this moment. Petra had known from the second she met her that Aella had not had an easy life, being eighteen and one of the most notorious assassins of the Linnosa.

"How did you end up in the Guild?" Petra asked softly.

Aella blinked away her tears, wiping her sleeve across her cheeks before answering. "The king and queen gave four-year-old me to Creaton Lin—the previous esteemed war general and secretly the owner and creator of the Guild. They gave me to the most vile and dangerous man they could, and in turn, Silver Death was created."

Petra didn't know what to say. The parents she knew would never give their child to such a man, but the parents she thought she knew would also never hide the existence of three of their children.

"I'm sorry. On behalf of our parents, I am sorry."

"I appreciate it, but it's not your responsibility," Aella said. "And the people I truly want the apology from can no longer give it."

"You will have to learn to live with that."

"Stars, I may have been killing at your age, but you are wiser." Aella smiled half-heartedly.

Petra teased, "Well, it's quite clear I am the smart sister."

Aella, with tears still pooling in her eyes, playfully hit her sister on the arm and began to pick herself off the floor, reaching out a hand to help the younger girl up. "Don't think this means I'll be nicer."

"I wouldn't dream of it."

CHAPTER 30

"READY?" CYRA ASKED, STANDING in the doorway of Rheanna's room, looking extravagant in a navy blue off-the-shoulder gown with a low decolletage. It shimmered with tiny crystal stars sewn around the bouffant skirts. Rheanna matched hers in color, both the sisters representing the color of the royal family, but with a skirt that flowed around her with sleeves that reached just below her elbow. The entire gown was overlaid with a shimmering silver fabric.

Rheanna took a deep breath, feeling it deeply in her chest, and then nodded, looping her arm through her sisters for support, and then led them out the door, down the hall, and toward the grand dining room.

They were hosting dinner for the Hefguard Royals: King Leonard and Queen Elspeth Nicola, as well as their two sons, Atlas and Malcolm. Rheanna had done a bit of research on these nobles, partly out of her own curiosity for how other royals lived and governed their kingdoms, but also out of the necessity of this alliance. They needed to know who and what they were dealing with, as well as how best to approach them. If they were to succeed in prevailing over the Black Lake, the Oracle, and anyone else who threatened the safety of Linnosa, they needed Hefguard.

From what she read, King Leonard shocked the entire Hefguard court when he married not only a commoner but one who came from a long line of witches. A line where the family had magical powers that were manifested throughout their lives, not unlike Rheanna and her sisters. It seemed to work in their favor. While no one knew what the queen's abilities were—as she kept them pretty close to her chest and rarely used them—their sons were fortunate to inherit magical abilities. As an earth witch, Atlas was able to create spells at a whim that could be charged or strengthened by crystals he carried around. These crystals could even be configured into jewelry and accessories, making it easier for him to manipulate them. Malcolm, by contrast, was a healer. He was known for alchemy and creating potions and elixirs with magical elements. He was often the head of any medicinal efforts by Hefguard.

Unfortunately, they were under the same magical malaise that affected Linnosa whenever they stepped into the kingdom's border. Any magical effects they had on them became nullified, just like any other magical species or artifact. Aside from the Oracle and monsters, apparently.

Once they got to the grand dining hall, Luca opened the doors for them, giving them each a sweet smile as they walked in. The Nicolas were already seated around the gilded table, but they all stood as the two girls walked in. Both of the sons greedily took in the stunning sisters as they made their way to their seats.

Cyra allowed King Leonard to sit at the head of the oversized, rectangular table, which was a place of honor and normally where the King or Queen of Linnosa sat for meals. Gracefully, his wife took the spot beside her husband, being easily within arm's reach of him while Rheanna sat next to her, Malcolm next, and Cyra and Atlas on the other side of the table.

Once they all sat, servants began to file into the dining hall, carrying with them silver trays full of roasted pig, green beans, and various dishes both savory and sweet. The sweet smell of the candied yams in particular made Rheanna's mouth water, and she tried to stymie her hunger since this meal was not one of familiarity but diplomatic formality.

"Thank you for inviting us to this private dinner, Queen Cyra and Princess Rheanna," Queen Elspeth's dainty voice filled the silence of the room.

"Please, call us Cyra and Rheanna," Cyra said warmly, "We feel privileged to host your family."

"You may refer to us without titles as well. I prefer Leo," the king responded, but then continued, "While we are flattered, we imagine this has to do with the unrest in Linnosa?"

"We thought the monsters were just rumors, but we saw firsthand how real they really are," Elspeth said.

Rheanna shifted ever so slightly in her seat as she began to serve herself food, only the sound of cutlery against glass filling the room for a few seconds.

"Yes. Well, I guess we will skip the pleasantries then. We are hoping that Hefguard will supply us with aid as our army is not as strong as yours." Cyra appeared confident in her words, but Rheanna could detect the slight tremor in her voice.

Leo nodded. "We imagined it as such. While we would love to send aid, we can't just give away soldiers freely."

Cyra remained silent, waiting to hear what he wanted, but Elspeth was the one who continued. "Both of our sons are unmarried. A marriage between Linnosa and Hefguard would benefit us both, making our alliance even stronger, and fortifying our kingdoms."

"We have discussed this. Princess Rheanna is—"

"Nothing against the princess; she is quite beautiful, but she doesn't have the command of the kingdom." Leo paused looking between Cyra and his two sons. "We are willing to have a marriage, as long as it's you, Cyra. You can choose which son as a courtesy."

Rheanna was relieved, but also a bit rejected that they didn't want her, though she felt guilty for it. Both Hefguard princes were quite entrancing, but the idea of an arranged marriage took away any hope of romance. Ivan would be available if Cyra married one of the princes, and maybe her sister truly would fall madly in love with whichever one and wouldn't mind if Rheanna and Ivan had their own happily ever after.

"I... Well, I... What about your sons? Do they have no say?" Cyra said, a bit flustered and blushing.

Atlas grinned and leaned toward her. "Oh, I can assure you, my brother and I would be honored to marry you."

"I have no objections," Malcolm added, a sly smirk on his face.

Rheanna's heart almost skipped a beat at the way they both stared at Cyra. Now, she wished she was the one who was stuck choosing between them. Her older sister did have a knack for getting everything she wanted. Why couldn't she be the one to make men fall over themselves?

"I will do what is best for my kingdom, and I would be honored to marry one of your sons." Somehow Cyra was able to compose herself and look as sure as ever once again.

"Wonderful." Elspeth's face broke out into a joyful smile with a small clap of excitement. "My husband and I will head back to Hefguard tomorrow morning and will arrange aid to be sent to you in two weeks. We expect you to make a decision by then. The other son will notify us of your choice when he returns."

"Thank you for your candidature," Cyra responded, taking a bite of her green beans.

"We expect you to really get to know them, Cyra. We've heard of your, uh, relationship and hope you will end it in respect for our sons," King Leo said with a grimace, shifting in his seat.

Cyra's cheeks pinkened, which only added to her beauty, but she nodded. "Of course. I look forward to getting to know both of you." Her golden gaze pinned each brother, who each dipped their head in return.

"We all know she will choose me, the more charming brother," Malcolm said with a cheeky wink.

Atlas huffed. "She'll choose you, alright. Only if she wants to be stuck with a delusional prick for the rest of her life."

Despite herself, a giggle escaped Rheanna, and she quickly clamped her hand over her mouth. Cyra's eyes were full of amusement as she took in their brotherly teasing.

"Act like gentlemen, or she may just send you both packing," Elspeth said with an eye roll.

Cyra laughed, but they were all aware there was no way she would. They needed the reinforcements that Hefguard could provide, and Cyra wouldn't turn it away, no matter what she needed to do. But right now, it didn't seem all that much of a sacrifice. Rheanna didn't want to be around when Cyra told Ivan the news though. He would be devastated.

The rest of the dinner passed by in a blur, and Rheanna quickly found herself consumed by daydreams. It was not like any of the Hefguard royals were interested in her, anyway. They all swooned over Cyra's beauty and eloquence. If only they saw her when they sparred, then they would realize she was not always so ladylike.

Her mind focused on one fantasy in particular. One she used to hyper-fixate on while in Dalmer whenever she had a free moment. She and Ivan would consummate their love, get married, and then grow old together in that wonderful frozen village with three children. Two boys and a girl—or even the other way around with two girls and a boy. She wouldn't be picky about that.

She could envision it perfectly. A little cottage nestled in a grove of evergreen trees with a small garden for the warmer months she could enjoy growing with their little ones as she, in turn, watched them grow. The inside of their home would smell just like Ivan—earthy with cinnamon and cedar—and she'd eventually become the headmistress of her little school. People from all over Linnosa would speak of her academics with pride.

Even now she sort of daydreamed of having Ivan to herself instead of Cyra. To be a princess with Ivan as her personal guard. To have him defend and protect her like Luca with Petra. Stand guard at her door but sneak in for kisses and cuddles, and eventually, she could marry him and make it all happen. Maybe she could even leave the castle when they married and live in that small rustic cabin next to his parents, all built by his hands as was Dalmer's custom. Even Maude could live next door or even come to the capital in her place.

It just wasn't fair sometimes.

Rheanna loved her sister, but a small part of her resented her because of Ivan. Why did Cyra get everything she wanted, and with practically no effort on her part, while Rheanna had to work so hard for even a portion of what her sister had? Not just Cyra, but Aella and Petra, too.

With a sigh, Rheanna excused herself from the dinner after having only touched a portion of her food and slipped out of her seat to leave. She found herself wandering through the castle, deep in a melancholic funk, feeling sorry for herself. The hallways were dark and silent. Not even the servants were out this late.

The balcony was as Petra and Rheanna had left it. The small stone table and benches were still covered with cushions, and the awning above dappled with flowers and vines. Rheanna wandered out, kneeling slightly atop one of the benches as she pressed down to her elbows over the balcony's edge and stared up to the sky above where twinkling stars awaited her. The constellations—some of which she knew—gazed back, welcoming her to the infinity above.

"Wow." The sound of an unfamiliar voice caused Rheanna to freeze, her hands clenching the railing of the balcony she stood at, watching the sleeping city of Reddel. The owner of the voice moved beside her; his own large hands placed against it as she looked over at him. She recognized him as Ripley, Aella's handsome friend she met the night of Cyra's coronation. His gaze was turned down at her as he was several inches taller, his auburn hair, a deep red against the backdrop of the night sky.

"You aren't supposed to sneak up on a lady," Rheanna chided, a bit breathless from his attention.

"I have a feeling you are not quite the lady you let on to be." The lanterns hanging along the balcony caught in his mischievous eyes, looking greener in this lighting.

Rheanna gasped, truly shocked by his boldness, even though she was aware of his profession and the way Aella handled herself. "I am a princess."

"And I am an assassin. Seems like we make an unlikely pair."

"We aren't a pair at all."

"Oh, sassy. I like it."

Rheanna rolled her eyes, sighing and asked, "Was Aella always so…"

"So murderous? Cold? Dead inside? I would say so," Ripley chuckled.

"I wouldn't say that." Rheanna searched his eyes. "It's just that she's so hot and cold. I feel like right when she starts to let her walls down, they are back up the next second."

"I have never seen her walls down, so consider yourself lucky."

Rheanna pondered that for a moment and decided to change the subject, feeling a bit romantic on a balcony with a handsome man. "You owe me a dance."

"Believe me, I haven't forgotten." His eyes roamed over her body. "I will collect."

CHAPTER 31

D READ POOLED IN CYRA'S gut as she searched for Ivan and found him in the guard's training area, dueling one of the men who came to the Eye of the Storm Inn to retrieve her all those weeks ago. Cyra watched them dance around each other, weaving, ducking, and swiping as they tried to best the other. Ivan's white blouse, hung loosely, sweat pooling along the chest and back area. Every inch of his body glistened with it, his hair damp.

They stopped when Ivan disarmed the other man, both laughing and clapping each other on the backs. Ivan made eye contact with Cyra, and his face broke into a smile. He jogged over to her, and she smiled weakly at him as he lifted her off the ground by the waist and spun her.

"How's my fiery sprite?" he asked fondly, nuzzling his face into her hair. She inhaled the scent of his sweat and aftershave mingling together, creating a musky cedar.

"We need to talk." She attempted to keep her voice stable, but his dark eyebrows pulled together.

"Okay." He nodded, wrapping his dark hand around hers, and pulled her into a private game room down the hall. The gaudy room had two yellow striped couches, a bookcase that covered the back wall, and an assortment of game tables for chess and other activities.

Cyra's breathing picked up as she looked at Ivan and attempted to get her thoughts in order. How was she going to tell him that they couldn't be together right when they had just found each other? She knew they really could be something, if they tried, but it was impossible. Making Linnosa safe was imperative to protecting her family and bringing her daughter home.

"We had a meeting with Hefguard regarding them providing aid to help with the riots and monsters," Cyra managed to get out.

"And what did they say? Will they provide aid?" Ivan's brows were still bunched in concern and confusion.

"Yes, but..." Her eyes dropped to her feet.

"But what?" He reached out and tilted her chin up to look at him.

Tears welled in her eyes. "I am betrothed."

"What? To whom? I'll kill them," he seethed as he dropped his hand and began to pace.

"This is to protect the kingdom, to protect my family. I need to do this. I'm sorry."

"What about me?" he questioned. His fist balled at his sides.

Cyra's mouth fell open. "This is not about you."

"Of course not. Who gives a damn about the peasant boy?" His words cut like blades, and Cyra stepped backward, bewildered by his response. He watched the movement and laughed darkly. "Oh, okay. You are afraid of me, but not that sister of yours? Makes perfect sense."

"How dare you—"

"How dare I? You're throwing me away like garbage."

Cyra's heart began to hammer, her throat burning as she reached out for him, but he shoved her off. "Please, Ivan. Please understand. I have to do this."

"I will fix this," he said defiantly.

"What do you mean? This isn't something to be fixed. We need Hefguard," Cyra pleaded.

"Don't you need me?"

She shook her head in disbelief. They may have had the start of a great relationship, but this was bigger than them.

"I need Hefguard," she simply repeated.

"Then have them." He brushed past her and out the door, slamming it so hard the floor vibrated beneath her feet.

All she could do was stare, opened mouth, at the door he disappeared through.

A part of her felt as if she should be crying, the part of her that just lost her childhood love and a silly promise of marriage between two children. Ivan was, in a way, something her fae-lover had never been all those years ago.

There. At the end of the day, that was all she wanted. Someone who was there. Strong arms, a strong body to protect her even when she knew she didn't need it. Someone she could rely on.

Yet relief washed over her after she saw his reaction to what she had to do. She understood his anger, but if he couldn't understand Linnosa would always come first, then he wouldn't make a good partner or king.

And what of Hollin? How would he react to know that Cyra had a daughter by another man and she was part fae? A shiver raised down her spine at that thought. Hollin would come even before the kingdom.

"Did that son of a wench touch you?" Aella shouted as she and Petra exploded through the door to the game room.

"What? No," Cyra exclaimed.

Aella did a sweep of Cyra as if she didn't trust her to tell the truth. "I guess the betrothal is on?" she asked.

Cyra nodded numbly as Petra went to her side to rub her back and pulled her to the couch. "Why don't you sit down?"

"Which one do they want you to marry?" Aella asked, eyebrows raised.

"I get to choose." She answered blandly, still unable to wrap her mind around the way Ivan reacted and how he spoke to her.

Petra let out a gasp and giggled a bit. "Well, they are very handsome at least, Cy. Which will you choose? Atlas is so charming, but, oh, Malcolm is so stoic and mysterious."

Aella rolled her eyes at her little sister's giddiness. "I doubt Cyra cares about that right now."

"Oh right, sorry. Ivan's nice too," Petra said as she attempted to give a supportive smile.

"I wasn't saying that. I definitely think Cyra dodged a bullet. There's something wrong with that man." Aella glared at the door as if he was standing there.

Cyra shook her head, dragging her hands down her face. Maybe Aella had a point about dodging a bullet. The kingdom didn't need a king who didn't even respect their queen.

"I'm tired," complained Cyra. "Exhausted, really."

"Well, I've decided to take you up on the job offer. I will become Head of the Royal Guard," Aella said nonchalantly, but Petra's stunned gaze snapped to her.

All thoughts of Ivan left Cyra's mind, and she gasped, staring at Aella as she gaped and asked, "Really? You mean it?"

"Yeah, of course. Didn't need a whole lot of convincing...or I guess maybe just the right convincing," Aella replied, looking at Petra with a mischievous smirk.

"Oh, Aella! That means you'll stay here with us!" Cyra said, popping off the couch as she rushed toward her sister and quickly wrapped her up in a tight, squeezing hug.

"Don't make a big deal about it. I know with the Oracle missing you need all the help you can get," muttered Aella, but Cyra crushed her to her chest.

"Oh, I love you, Silver Death," Cyra declared and motioned for Petra. "And I love you little flower girl."

Petra squealed as Cyra pulled her into the mix.

A small smile graced the youngest princess' lips as she floated down the hall. She was truly happy for the first time since her parents' murder. Not only did she no longer feel alone, but she had a family, had sisters, who loved her and who she loved.

Nothing was impossible now that they were together. Even with the monsters and riots, she knew her sisters would conquer it all together. Her confidence in each of them made her feel secure.

Her blond-haired guard leaned against her bedroom door with a grin plastered across his boyish face. Her smile grew as she took him in. She would never get over the way his blue eyes tracked and admired her. Her steps grew faster, and he matched them, meeting her halfway and catching her in a hug.

"It's amazing to see you smiling again," Luca whispered into her brown hair.

"Everything is going to be okay," she responded, her hand running through the curls at the nape of his neck.

"I think it just might be."

His breath tickled her cheek as he pulled back an inch, both entranced in the other's gaze. His hand caressed the side of her face and landed on her neck. Her eyes drifted to his lips for a moment. He closed the distance, pulling her toward him with the hand laid on her neck. Their lips met, soft and innocent.

When they pulled back, they were both flushed, chests heaving. He laid his forehead against hers, whispering, "You are extraordinary."

CHAPTER 32

FOR THE LAST TWO days, the sisters scoured the castle looking for information on the Oracle and her origin, but they couldn't find anything. Petra suggested they try their parents' private library in their quarters, a room none of them had entered since the oldest three arrived at the castle which left Rheanna and Cyra standing at the entrance waiting for their younger sisters twenty minutes past the agreed time.

"Should we just go in?" Rheanna asked impatiently, tapping her foot on the ground.

"Might as well. I have my first date with one of the princes in an hour," Cyra responded as she moved toward the door.

"Oh, that's nice. Which one?"

"The oldest, Atlas."

Rheanna went to open her mouth to ask another question but halted as they stood in front of their parents' room. She saved her many questions about the royals for later.

Instead, she focused on the door leading to the room. It was a large and made from a thick, heavy wood and carved immaculately with designs reminiscent of Linnosa's past. Magic ran deep in the carvings, depicting great heroes and kings and queens of the past amid several striking landmarks found within the kingdom.

The door slid open with a creak of its hinges, and the smell of the room wafted out: thick, heady, and perfumed. It smelled much like Rheanna remembered when she was a girl, assaulting her with nostalgic memories from their time together. Of how she, Cyra, and Aella would sneak into the room late at night and try to crawl into their parents' bed where their mother would tell them stories and their father would tickle them into a fit of giggles.

Heavily decorated with memorabilia of their parents' lives, it had a homey feeling even though it was clearly styled for royals. The large marble hearth was filled with sweet smelling cherry logs. A small love seat sat before it, perfect for taking meals and warming by the fire after a long day. Armoires and boudoirs full of clothing lined one end of the walls, with a full-length mirror. A chandelier with unused candles hung overhead, and tall windows of thick glass looked toward the horizon where the sun filtered through in the morning. Complete with a smaller door in the back.

The biggest difference that Rheanna saw compared to her memories was the thin layer of dust atop everything.

Pangs of guilt raced through Rheanna's mind. A sadness at how everything happened so suddenly. She didn't really have the time to think about it until now, and she tried to conjure their faces in her mind. She even tried to think of the color of her father's eyes, but realized she couldn't remember the exact shade. All she knew was they were brown—as she saw in the paintings—but couldn't recall if they were dark like Ivan's or more of a golden honey like Cyra's.

Next to her, her sister seemed to be having the same thoughts and memories running through her head. Cyra stood frozen in the doorway, scanning the entire bedroom with a blank look on her face, almost as if she was fearful of entering.

Rheanna reached out to her and took her palm into her own with a squeeze as Cyra closed her eyes and sighed.

"You know, it's funny. I hadn't thought about their death till now. I was sad when I got the news, but with everything that happened so suddenly I didn't have the time to sit and process it. Seeing their bedroom sort of makes it feel more real than before."

"I know what you mean," murmured Rheanna as she squeezed her palm again. "Without them it just feels like it had been for the last fourteen years. But now all I can think about is what could have been if the Oracle didn't give her prophecy."

"Yeah..." Cyra said, opening her eyes. Then she shook her head, released her sister's grip, and stepped in.

Rheanna followed her toward the closed door in the back that led to the personal library. Compared to the door of the bedroom, this second door was far too simple. It wasn't engraved but was richly varnished to the point of being a darker brown, edging onto black even, and contrasted with the white stone, silver, and gold that surrounded it.

Books of all shapes and sizes filled the room, most of them centuries old as only the most prized of their possessions graced these shelves. There was only one space for sitting, a dark oak desk where Rheanna had flickers of memories of hiding beneath while her father worked, Cyra pressing a small finger to her lips to hush Rheanna's giggling so that he would not find them. They were not permitted in this room as children.

Candles half burnt, quills and inkwells that have long since dried up, and sheafs of papers decorated the desk and a small, simple candelabra stood in the center of the room as the only light sources that Cyra lit with a flick of her fingers. There were no windows. If the door was ever covered up, no one would ever know this room existed.

"Why don't we start at separate sides and work our way to the middle?" Cyra suggested and they both set off to work.

They were used to this routine by now, knowing how to read the title, skim a few pages, and tell whether it was what they were looking for. These books had a thick layer of dust accumulated on them as if they had not been used in a long time, most of them old tomes about faraway lands and creatures.

"Anything?" Cyra called out.

"Not yet."

Rheanna moved to the next bookcase but paused when she saw something peeking out from behind one of them against the wall. She shuffled against it, pushing the heavy shelf aside as it slid against the cold, stone floor until it was fully visible.

A mural of the family tree on their mother's side. The royal family—the Linwoods, one of the oldest families in Linnosa—was displayed in front of her, reaching back for at least a dozen generations. Each of their ancestors had a tiny picture, inscribed with names, dates of birth, and even dates of deaths beneath it.

Rheanna traced her fingers near the bottom where her parents were to trace Sienna Linwood, who married Edgar

Voelbel, her mother and father. Yet, their deaths were not filled in. Probably a direct result of no one in the castle even knowing it existed.

Directly beneath them—as her fingers traced to where it ended—she saw each of her sisters, starting with Cyra. None of them had a portrait.

"Look at this," Rheanna called to Cyra.

"Wow. There are ten generations of Linwoods depicted here." Cyra's gaze wandered over the mural. Her face grew pale as her eyes froze on a single portrait, one of a beautiful girl with raven curls and a cunning smile. The name read *Lewellyn Hormanick*, their great, great grandmother.

"Cyra..." Rheanna began to speak, but the sound of an explosion stopped her. The castles shook. Books flew off the shelves. One hit Rheanna in the shoulder.

"Let's go," she shrieked and sprinted toward the door. Once they were in the hallway, Rheanna peered out the window to see smoke at the front gate and guards scurrying around as they fought people in all black.

Footsteps pounded down the hall, and Ivan came into view with blood splattered across his chest and a sword dripping in grasp. "The castle has been invaded. You both need to get to safety now."

"Princess Aella," the red-headed maid, Laney, screeched.

Aella, who lost track of time sparring with Petra, was headed toward her other sisters to help them search the royal library when she came to a halt. She turned quickly. "What's wrong? Where's Cora?" She surveyed the girl quickly to identify any injuries but couldn't see anything.

Laney shook her head rapidly. Her face was almost as red as her hair. "The Cleansers are within the castle. I sent Cora to warn the other servants."

Aella didn't take even a moment to process the information before she began moving. "Thank you. Now, get to safety. Don't you try to be a hero," she instructed, already running toward her little sister's bedroom. After confiding in Aella that she wasn't ready to go into their parents' chambers yet, Petra went back to her own to clean up.

An explosion shook the building, causing Aella to lose her footing and hit the wall. The smell of smoke burned her nose and made her eyes water. She silently hoped that Laney and Cora would be safe. Her breaths came out in tiny gasps as she sprinted down the gilded hall. Thoughts of her sisters propelled her faster, her feet barely touching the ground at the speed she was going. They thought they were safe in this castle, but they were being attacked in their own home.

Before she could make it to Petra's chambers, three figures in all black blocked her path, masks adorning their faces. The killing calm settled over her, daggers out as they charged her. The first swung a sword and the other carried a silver whip. It lashed out, aiming toward Aella's left thigh, but she quickly darted to the side as the sword wielder swung toward her. The blades sang as they connected. Aella's daggers caught the sword and pushed it down as she spun. The sword clattered to the ground. With a swift kick to the abdomen, Aella had the swordsmen on the ground, gasping for breath.

Pain lanced through Aella's wrist, causing her to drop a dagger as the whip wrapped around it, yanking her toward the second Cleanser. They spun Aella around, slamming her into a gold-embellished wall as their forearm pressed into her throat. Her hand swiped up, slicing across her opponent's stomach as she brought her leg up and kicked out. Their grip faltered as they gasped in pain from the wound now leaking with blood.

The first Cleanser was now on their feet. "You are Unclean," they cried.

They raced toward Aella, but she stepped out of the way at the last second. Her blade stabbed into their windpipe before she yanked it out. The person gasped as they choked on their own blood, falling to the floor.

The second Cleanser looked at their companion then quickly back at Aella, their arm still clutching the leaking wound. Aella started toward them. The masked person quickly shook their head, backing up and stumbling over themselves.

"What? No more fight?" she snarled.

"Don't," a breathless voice gasped from under the mask. There was something familiar in the voice. Aella paused for a moment before she continued her attack forward.

The Cleanser now had their back against the wall, their body visibly shaking. Aella twirled her dagger between her fingers. She yanked the Cleanser from the wall, the blade now pressed to their neck. In one movement, Aella had the mask off, a feeling of triumph quickly overshadowed by dread. A strangled gasp escaped her as she watched Natalie's deep brown eyes flutter with emotion.

Natalie. Her Natalie. She was a Cleanser.

Her palms grew sweaty, but her grip on the dagger held true, never moving an inch away from her lover's throat. The throat she had kissed so many times. Aella had let her into her bed, her family, whilst Natalie plotted the deaths of her sisters, of her.

"I'm sorry," Natalie whispered.

"You're one of them," Aella responded, pulling the blade from her throat and slamming her fists into her chest.

Natalie's eyes brimmed with tears. "I tried to stop it. It wasn't supposed to happen like this."

Aella's fist connected with Natalie's jaw, sending her sprawling on her back. A scream filled the air as Aella stomped on Natalie's wound, pressing the heel of her boot deep.

"You murderous wench." The words hung in the air; violence promised within them.

"Aella!" A terrified voice called, but Aella was too stuck in her rage to respond. Now on her knees with her hands wrapped around Natalie's neck, someone yanked on her shoulders, begging her to let go.

"Aella, please, we need you," Rheanna pleaded. At her sister's cries, Aella looked up. Rheanna and Cyra stood over her, stark fear on their faces. For a moment, she thought it was because of her, but then Cyra said, "Let the guards take her. We haven't seen Petra yet."

Aella's violet eyes flickered to Natalie's red face for less than a moment, disgust and betrayal pooling low in her stomach. The guards moved forward to seize Natalie as Aella turned her back, already moving toward Petra's quarters once again.

CHAPTER 33

A S ONE, THE THREE sisters bounded down the hall with a small army of guards not far behind them, their armor and footfalls the only sounds. Cyra's heart stung with the aftershock of the initial hit. Something had happened, and she was afraid it was something that couldn't be reversed. Her labored breath echoed in her ears as she came to a halt in front of Petra's bedroom door. Luca lay at the threshold, his blue eyes unseeing as he stared blankly at the ceiling.

Aella didn't break stride as her body collided with the door, and a gust of air sent it flying off its hinges and across the room. Rheanna gripped onto Cyra's arm as they followed quickly behind, careful not to disrupt the brave boy's body.

Petra was sitting on her old recliner, her feet pulled up and tucked beneath her. A book laid cradled in her lap as if she fell asleep while reading, except her head was tilted back in an unnatural angle. Dark red spilled from her neck, the once white pages now scarlet.

Aella's pale hands wrapped around her sister's neck attempting to repair what was already lost as Rheanna doubled over, retching. The putrid smell of vomit filled Cyra's nose as she fell to her knees, silent tears spilling over her cheeks. Petra was still so beautiful, even now, even in death. For a moment, Cyra imagined Hollin in that chair instead, their eyes so similar, so alike. A scream filled the air, and only when she felt the burn of it in her own throat did she realize it came from her. Their baby sister was gone. Aella turned to them, Petra's blood dripping down her arms, her eyes red-rimmed with tears and wide with shock.

"This cannot be happening," Rheanna cried. "She was the best of us." Her voice shook with the words.

Aella stood abruptly, calmly, and she said, "They will all pay."

Cyra instantly understood and nodded. "Stay with Petra, Rhe. We will handle this."

Rheanna didn't even try to argue as she fell to the ground next to Petra, running her hand shakily through the girl's hair.

"Don't you dare touch her," Cyra ordered the guards, who stood unmoving around the room, "Guard them. Kill anyone who dares to enter."

They came to attention at her words and silently nodded, saluted, and took up a defensive position by the door. Their shields and swords raised, prepared to strike anyone who dared enter within the chamber of death on the queen's orders now.

Cyra dashed after Aella as fast as she could, fueled by a rage that burned deep within her. Aella was already down the hall, leaving Cyra to see just the flickering steel against smoke, the grunt of several masked enemies, the spray of blood, and silence that soon followed as Aella led the murderous path forward.

The Cleansers who appeared were lithely built, with masks and dark clothing tightly fitting over their bodies. Their identities were unknown.

Cyra was without a weapon, but she called to her fire. The magic flared up inside of her, molten and thick, racing until she conjured a wicked blade of fire in her hand. The searing touch wisped off quivering lines, and the tip dripped sparks upon the floor that hissed and burned yet the fire did not harm her.

The first of the Cleansers attacked her, rushing at her with an axe already bloodied from some unknown victim. Cyra blocked it beneath the metal, sliced through the wooden handle, and embedded the molten blade through their shoulder as they screamed horrifically. Their blood steamed in their veins before Cyra kicked them off her sword and sent them sprawling to the ground.

All it took was one slice, and her opponent was incapacitated. The other two flinched but rushed her now to cut her off, and she weaved past another who had a dagger in their hand, stabbing upward and into their stomach. She swung to slice through the leg of another as they kicked out, only to cut across their knee.

They begged, and a dark thought crossed her mind: she quite liked the sound. It made it easier that their faces were covered, that the image of Petra's bright green eyes forever closed was imprinted into her brain and removed any empathy she might have for them. They were no longer human beings to her.

The two sisters slaughtered the Cleansers. Cyra felt others fighting alongside her, but sorrow blurred her vision as she stabbed and sliced. When they were informed there were no more invaders in the castle, Cyra let her weapon of fire dissolve, and she slumped to the ground as her knees instantly gave out. Strong arms caught her, heaving her up and propping her against the wall as a male voice spoke gently to her. "Cyra, are you hurt?"

She blinked dumbly at the oldest prince of Hefguard, Atlas, his green eyes filled with concern. His brother stood next to him, concern written all over his expression as well, both covered in blood. She wondered how much of it belonged to them and how much to the Cleansers.

"Take me to my sisters," she demanded.

Each brother took a side and helped her walk. Luca's body was now cleared from the threshold, but his blood still stained the white marble as if someone tried to clean it quickly. Inside the room, Rheanna still knelt next to their sister, the bottom of her pale pink dress now soaked in dark red. She looked up as they entered, and Cyra separated from the brothers to sit next to her. A gleam caught her eye, and under the recliner, halfway drenched in Petra's blood, was the brush they found in the Oracle's chambers. Cyra reached for it, but Rheanna followed her gaze and picked it up first, her eyes widening at the engraving. *Selmana Hormanick.*

Cyra slumped over, her vision blurring and the exhaustion taking over.

"Can you please bring her to her rooms?" Rheanna asked softly.

Without hesitation, Atlas wrapped Cyra in his arms and began to walk, his brother only steps behind. Her head lolled into his shoulder, obscuring her view.

"Is she going to be okay?" she heard Malcolm ask quietly.

"She should be. I think she's close to burnout. Do you have any elixirs that could help her here?"

There was a brief pause before Malcolm answered, "They told us not to use our—"

"Damn them. This might be your future wife. You will help her." Atlas' chest rumbled with his words.

Cyra fought to keep her mind alert, but the blackness devoured her.

"Watch over them," Aella demanded.

"You have my word," Ripley nodded and disappeared without another word.

Aella thought about going back and ending the one who betrayed her, but she knew the queen would take care of it. After seeing how ruthless her sister could be today, she had no doubt the wench would be dead by the time the assassin returned. For now, she had one thought and one goal alone. Kill every last person responsible for the youngest princess' death. Every threat to her family would be eliminated by the time she was done.

CHAPTER 34

R HEANNA CONTINUED TO SIT on the floor, soaked in her sister's blood, long after they took her body. The blood was starting to dry, crusting in between her fingers and along the hem of her dress. She couldn't find the strength to stand up as she reflected on it all. Petra was dead, and Rheanna had been too consumed by her own selfishness and jealousy of Cyra to really get to know her. Her body shivered as the moon hung high in the sky, and the fire was not lit within this room. It would likely not be lit again, at least not for a while.

"Princess." Ripley's voice broke through her thoughts and silence. She looked at him with such sadness in her eyes that for a moment he didn't know what else to say.

"Why don't we clean you up?" he said gently.

Rheanna nodded but remained on the floor. He glided over to her, offering a hand, and aided in her standing. Her legs quivered, not from weakness, but from numbness due to the lack of movement for so long.

"Lean on me." He adjusted them so he carried most of her weight as he guided her to her own chambers.

Once they were inside the room, he paused, not knowing what to do next. When he made up his mind, he dropped her on the lounge closest to the bathroom door. He disappeared, and when he returned, he had a rag and a bowl of hot water and soap. Gently, he worked on her forearms and hands first, rubbing away the dark brown. Next, he moved to her legs and feet.

"I think that is the best we are going to get for right now." At this point, he was speaking more for himself than Rheanna, who stared blankly ahead.

The auburn-haired man grabbed the first nightgown he saw from her dresser, a light-blue one, and handed it to her. "You have to do this part."

She took the nightgown and began to work at her dress. The assassin turned to give her privacy while she undressed.

"I'm done," she said, her voice hoarse from the sobs that wracked her body earlier.

Ripley guided her to her bed and tucked her into the blue haven, kissing her forehead. "Sleep," he commanded gently.

"Thank you," she muttered.

Rheanna was sleeping before he even crossed the threshold of her door to leave.

There was so much blood in the air that Cyra could smell it. She was back at the Eye of the Storm Inn. Back, and far away from Reddel and the castle. Far away from her sisters.

The Inn was in total disarray. Bodies lay all along the ground, and blood stained the floors. She wandered deeper into the darkness of the inn. The dead lined up in their seats with hands still grasping at mugs and food. Ron himself was impaled on a spear, embedded in the wall as he looked toward the door as if waiting for Cyra to return.

Her eyes went wide, a silent scream crawled up the throat. Her body took control as she sprinted to the basement. The steps, which normally took her four full strides to clear, took over five dozen running leaps and all the while her heart pounded in her chest. All she could think of was her daughter. Hollin.

"Mommy!"

Quickly she dashed into their little bedroom. There, atop the bed, was Hollin. Her little body tilted to the side as Petra was. Head at an odd angle, with large emerald eyes staring at the door.

"Mommy!"

"Hollin!" Cyra called as she awoke from a nightmare. Her body screamed in protest at her sudden movement, and she gasped in pain. It felt as if she was on fire.

"Cyra?" a worried voice asked. Atlas' face appeared; his eyebrows scrunched in concern.

"Do not move," ordered Malcolm, brown eyes concentrated as he came into view as well. He pressed something into her forearm that cooled her veins, which were threatening to burst.

Cyra knew she was in her room with all the gold and red hues that surrounded her, but for a moment, she couldn't remember what had happened.

It all came back at once. Petra. Her eyes grew wide as she searched the gazes of the two princes in front of her. A sob worked up her throat, and the burning in her veins began again.

"Cyra, I know you've been through a lot, but you need to keep still, or the pain will only get worse." Atlas attempted to calm her by rubbing her arm.

"Petra! Petra is dead," she screamed through her sobs. If Petra could be killed, what would stop them from going after Hollin? What if they killed all of them? Who would protect her daughter? The pain became unbearable now, her vision blackening as she began to seize.

Malcolm spoke urgently, "We need to calm her down immediately."

Atlas straddled her, pinning her arms down as she continued to thrash. There was the sound of a cork popping, and then Malcolm was forcing a liquid into her mouth. Cyra went to spit it out, revolted by the poignant taste, but Malcolm covered her mouth with his hand and forced her jaw closed. "I'm sorry, but I'm trying to save your life."

The liquid slid down her throat, sticky and thick, but she finally swallowed, and her thrashing stopped almost instantly. The pain dulled as the burning subsided. Atlas slowly crawled off her, muttering an apology.

Instead of being relieved with the lack of physical pain, the loss of Petra hit her square in the chest. Tears welled in her eyes and rolled into her knotted red hair.

"Where is Aella? Rheanna?" she asked. There was no way to gauge how long she had been out.

The brothers swapped a glance before Malcolm said, "You promise us you will stay calm?"

Panic squeezed at her heart, but she forced herself to nod and keep the rest of her body still.

Atlas took a deep breath and said, "Rheanna is fine. She has checked-in multiple times but is currently planning the funeral."

Funeral. The funeral for their dead baby sister. A sob burned at her throat, threatening to burst out, but she swallowed it back. "And Aella?"

"She hasn't been seen since the invasion."

Cyra took a deep breath to clear her head. She knew Aella wouldn't just leave them. She must've had a plan. For now, Cyra would have to trust that plan. She shook her head, refusing to dwell on the possibilities about what could happen to her younger sister. Aella had survived all these years without anyone protecting her. She was strong.

In an attempt to distract her thoughts, Cyra shifted to what Malcolm had done to ease her pain. "How are you able to heal me? And what exactly is going on with me?"

Malcolm lifted a small amethyst crystal and twirled it between his fingers. "I'm a healer," he dragged out the words like he was speaking to a toddler, "Therefore, I can heal you."

Cyra's eyes narrowed in annoyance, and she shook her head. "You aren't supposed to be able to wield magic in Linnosa."

"I wasn't. These are crystals I charged and potions I brewed before I came here, just in case. If I wanted to make something new, I wouldn't be able to," Malcolm explained.

"We would appreciate it if you didn't tell your council, though. Our parents do not wish for this to be known," Atlas said.

Cyra could understand why. If other countries knew Malcolm could create potions and charms that could heal or even kill, it would make him a target. Cyra didn't know much about healers, but she had never heard of one who could store and save potions. The magic was always described as something that had to be called upon in the moment.

"Of course." Cyra nodded. She thought of Hollin and how Malcolm was in a similar position to her. She would be a target if she was discovered as well; she wouldn't endanger someone else's child.

The princes both smiled appreciatively, and Malcolm said, "And to answer what happened to you, well, we call it the burnout."

Noting Cyra's confused expression, Atlas took over. "It is when you use too much of your power at once. You basically drained yourself of all the magic you had. If you had pushed yourself any harder..."

"You would have died," Malcolm said, his boyish face serious.

Cyra attempted to sit up in the lush bed, but the second she moved her arms to push herself up, pain exploded through her forearms, and she quickly slumped back down.

Atlas rushed toward the edge of the bed, his green eyes full of concern as he said, "You need to relax. Your body is replenishing your magic. With normal use, your magic continues to rise, but when you drain it, there is a cost."

Malcolm reached out with a clear quartz this time, placing it on her forehead, an instant cooling effect coming over her, but this time drowsiness pulled at her as well. "Rest now, Queen."

Cyra blinked rapidly, trying to keep her eyelids from shutting. "But...what... about...Petra's funeral?"

"We will wake you when it is time," Atlas whispered.

This time, when Cyra drifted to sleep there were no nightmares, only darkness.

CHAPTER 35

"WE NEED TO HAVE a council meeting," Bianca said as she followed after Rheanna in the gilded hall. Rheanna took a quick glance at the girl. She wore a pale blue dress that matched her eyes, and her almost white, blonde hair was in a braid framing her face then pulled into a bun at the nape of her neck. Rheanna would never understand how such a beautiful girl could be so cruel.

"We will not be having a meeting until after the queen is well enough," Rheanna stated coolly, continuing her quick pace as she made her way toward the guards training quarters to confront Ivan.

"But the council needs to discuss what happened to Petra and figure out a course of action," Bianca pushed.

Rheanna swirled toward her, her own blue eyes glaciers. "I am in the midst of planning my baby sister's funeral. I don't have time for you or politics. Once we honor Petra and Cyra is ready, we will meet."

Bianca's lips parted and closed several times before she simply nodded and turned away. Without another thought, Rheanna was back in motion. Her taupe dress swished between her legs. Ivan had been avoiding her since the attack. He had not even visited Cyra while the Hefguard princes never left her side. She wondered if he was ashamed of how they left things. He couldn't possibly still be angry after everything that had happened.

Just as she had feared, she found him in the training yard laughing with a few of the other guards. For a moment, she watched him, expecting him to turn her way or even show a bit of remorse or sadness for what had happened.

Yet he didn't. The sound of his voice was light and airy as if nothing had even happened. Why he never visited Cyra, she didn't understand. Not only had Petra died, but Cyra was physically drained. If he claimed he loved her as he said he did, he should be there for her.

Rheanna was closest to the Bushnells, or so she thought. Maude was her best friend and only family until her sisters returned to her life. She had been there with Ivan when he suffered personal loss, heartbreak, and more. Comforted him in times of weakness, held his hand, and hugged him when he needed it. Right now, she and Cyra needed him, and what was he doing?

Seeing him just laugh and enjoy himself instead of being there for the people he professed to care about only angered her, and Rheanna had no qualms about marching right up to castigate him appropriately.

"Where have you been?" she harshly demanded.

Ivan's eyes suddenly widened in surprise, and the other guards stopped and stood, saluting their princess. For a moment, Ivan didn't know how to respond but soon found himself as he glanced at the guards, placed a hand against Rheanna's back, and spoke in a light voice as he guided her away from the others.

"Why don't we talk privately?" he suggested.

Her eyes hotly narrowed at him, and she stiffened to his touch. Had he touched her like that before, she would have melted into his hand and imagined herself being swept off her feet like some fairytale. Now, her anger was such that she wanted nothing more than to flinch away and show her disdain for him, but she allowed him to guide her away toward the edge of the yard and away from the exercise equipment. The guards he was goofing around with dispersed, not wanting to be caught in the crosshairs of her anger or test the limits of what was supposed to be the sweetest of the four.

He led her beneath an awning that was covered in drying uniforms. The smell of laundry hung in the air, sweet against the sourness of sweat and training. It was close enough to the castle's interior that they could have dipped into its shadows, but it almost seemed as if Ivan wanted to be seen conversing with her. A fact that didn't go unnoticed by her in the least.

Finally, when he faced her, she cut him off from anything he wanted to say.

"Why haven't you gone to check on Cyra?" she asked, harsher than she intended, feeling the accusatory breath spill out with her grievances.

"I didn't know what to say after what happened between us and to Petra..." He drifted off, shifting his feet.

Rheanna crossed her arms. "My sister died, and you didn't say anything to me." That hurt worst of all. Ivan was supposed to be her protector, or at least her friend.

He rubbed the dark stubble on his chin and refused to make eye contact with her. He began to shake his head. "Rhe, I'm not good with this stuff."

"That is no excuse. I'm going through this all alone." Her voice broke at the last word, tears springing into her eyes.

He looked up suddenly, and seeing the anguish on her face, he crushed her to his chest. The smell of wood and cinnamon engulfed her, relaxing her in its familiarity. A sob exploded from her chest, resulting in a few guards looking over to them in alarm.

"I didn't think you needed me anymore. You have your sisters," he said gruffly, his face pressed into the top of her hair.

"Cyra has been ill, and Aella isn't here. Besides that, I will always need you." She sniffled and pulled out of his embrace, rubbing her runny nose.

His eyebrow quirked. "Where is she?"

Her throat tightened at the total disregard of her second statement, so instead of answering, she spun away, her long braid swinging with her.

"Wait!" he called, but she refused to look back.

"I have to plan my sister's funeral."

He didn't follow after her.

The sun was high in the sky as the caravan made its way to the river that ran through Reddel. Cyra sat comfortably in an open carriage, Rheanna, and the princes riding with her. Though she was barely able to walk, she was well enough to travel, especially with Malcolm and his elixirs on hand. They said it should only be a few days until she was back to her full capacity.

The carriage rocked as they drifted down the stony path, meadows of grass and dandelions flanking each side. Rheanna had picked the perfect location to send Petra off in. The carriage in front of them carried her and Luca's bodies, which were covered with an embroidered sheet with the royal crest and laid upon a flat boat made out of driftwood. In between the pieces of wood, Rheanna had weaved wildflowers of every color.

They made it to the alcove where the land created a small beach of brown and black pebbles. Rheanna climbed out of the carriage, instructing the guards, one of which was Ivan, to position Petra and Luca right at the edge of the river.

"Take this," Malcolm said, handing Cyra a vial with an amber liquid.

She did as she was instructed, making a face at the taste she was unable to get used to. On shaky legs, she began to stand, but Atlas jumped to his feet and lifted her gently out of the carriage by her waist. "Lean on us," he whispered to her. Each prince took a side, holding up most of her weight and she sighed in relief.

Ivan caught her eye then, and something like guilt and pity mixed in his eyes. She didn't have the patience for him and looked away. The three of them stopped at the edge of the water, next to Rheanna. Luca's mother, a cook within the castle, stood on Rheanna's other side. Her blue eyes, the same shade as her son's, were bloodshot and wet. They all wore simple black clothing to honor the two young lovers. Cyra could hear others behind them but couldn't take her eyes off the small boat that held her sister.

"We're here today to honor a brave boy and our beloved princess," Norton began, walking around to the front of the group. His expression reflected sorrow as he continued, "Luca Maxon died serving his kingdom and protecting Princess Petra. His sacrifice will not be easily forgotten."

A piercing wail filled the air as Luca's mother hit the ground, clutching her heart. "My son. My only son."

Cyra's heart broke at the sound, and Rheanna knelt to the woman, grasping her hand and squeezing her palm.

"I am with you," Rheanna said soothingly. The woman looked up at Rheanna, cheeks red and tear stained. She nodded, and they stood together, the woman leaning heavily onto Rheanna, but the younger girl stayed steady.

Norton's eyes filled with tears, his lined face displaying every emotion. "Princess Petra Noelle Voelbel was a lively and sweet girl. Her absence will hang heavy within the castle."

Cyra wanted to cry out, her throat burning, her chest aching. Petra was so much more than that, but how could she ever convey the magnitude at which her death would affect them all?

"We wish peace for our fallen," Norton finished. He nodded, and two guards stepped forward, pushing the driftwood deeper into the waters. Two other guards with sticks of fire came forward, lighting the boat. Cyra's magic should have been the one to send them off; shame filled her due to her inability. She watched as they drifted off, tears spilling from her eyes.

Luca's mother and Rheanna clung to each other, sobbing. Cyra would not attend another funeral of someone she loved; she swore it to herself.

CHAPTER 36

HEALING FROM THE BURNOUT, as the Nicola brothers called it, was unpleasant, but what was even worse was sitting in this war room with her insufferable council. They all talked over one another, panicked and filled with fear as they tried to get her to listen as if Cyra didn't understand. They had just said goodbye to her baby sister. One sister dead. One sister missing. Only Rheanna was safe.

"Enough," the Queen shouted. Her fists hit the table, startling the room into silence. "I understand you are all afraid, but I need you all to shut the hell up."

The room exchanged glances, silent. It had been a week since the castle had been breached, but Cyra had not been able to stand on her own until just this morning. She could feel her magic already sizzling just beneath her skin, waiting to be used again.

"There isn't much I can tell you as you all know what happened," Cyra spoke with a sort of detachment in her voice. "I have decided I will marry the oldest Hefguard prince as soon as possible. I have already sent Malcolm Nicola back to his parents, hoping they will send their promised aid sooner as everyday counts."

"I am sorry for your loss, truly, but why would the Cleansers kill the princess? They were in support of her," Bianca questioned. Her face didn't carry her usual snarky expression.

"We don't know," Rheanna responded with defeat in her voice. Cyra already heard the sob that was threatening to come out.

"But what if—"

Cyra interrupted the girl before she could continue. "I'm not listening to you today, Bianca." Her hand flew up to signal the girl to be silent.

To her surprise, the girl didn't speak further, but Marine did. "We are all deeply sorry for the loss of Petra. She was such a kind girl." Her expression genuinely held sympathy and loss.

"She was more than just kind," Cyra snapped. Rheanna placed her hand on top of her sister's, and Cyra relaxed just an inch.

"Of course, we just mean to extend our condolences," Norton said carefully. "Do you know where Aella has gone?"

"That is none of your concern," Cyra said coolly. She wanted to go after Aella but could not with everything else going on. She had to trust that her sister knew what she was doing and would come back safely.

"You don't seem to be giving us much of anything," Talmadge grunted, crossing his arms over his wrinkled chest.

Heat flared in Cyra's body; her flames ready to be called forth. "What do you suppose I do?" Her nails dug into her palms, drawing blood.

"Questioning that rebel we have in the dungeons would be a good start," Talmadge said.

"I have full intentions of doing so but have been recovering."

Talmadge leaned forward in his chair. "This is why the girl should have been crowned. She had proper control of her gifts. She would not be dead if it weren't for you."

The revelation hit Cyra straight in the chest, even though she had already thought it. Petra would be alive if Cyra was not queen. The council members gasped collectively, and flames filled the room at his words.

"How dare you," she hissed. Her flames grew brighter, inching ever so slightly toward Talmadge.

"Go ahead, girl. Show us how *unworthy* you are." Talmadge stood slowly, both palms supporting his weight on the table.

Cyra's gaze hardened, but Rheanna called for her water, creating a barrier between the council members and her flames.

"Cy..." she warned gently.

Taking a deep breath, Cyra withdrew her magic, and so did Rheanna. The group sat silent, both Cyra and Talmadge's chest heaving.

"That is all for today," Rheanna said, dismissing the room. The members all exchanged somber looks again but left without any argument.

Rheanna sighed. "You have to remain calm. I know Talmadge—"

"Do not tell me what I need to do."

"I don't want to fight, but you are the queen. I will be here to help you through it. We need to lean on one another." Rheanna tried not to sound hurt.

Cyra's eyes softened. "You're right. I'm not mad at you. I'm just..."

"I know. You don't have to explain." She reached out and touched her older sister's arm.

"I'll feel much better once we get some answers about this prophecy. I will not lose you or Aella." Cyra added Hollin's name to the list in her head.

"Back to the library?" questioned Rheanna. Cyra nodded, and they headed toward their parents' quarters where Rheanna had been searching the past week while Cyra recovered. She had been trying to find anything about Selmana Hormanick, but all she learned was that Lewellyn was their great, great grandmother and that she died during childbirth with their great grandmother.

After a few hours of combing through the shelves, Cyra fell into their father's desk chair in frustration when a padlock caught her attention.

"Rhe, did you ever get this drawer open with the lock?" Cyra questioned as she eyed it.

"No, I tried looking for a key but gave up," Rheanna answered, shrugging her shoulders.

Cyra raised her hand as she focused on the metal of the lock. It glowed red with the heat then dropped to the ground. As Cyra opened the drawer, Rheanna came closer. In it, there was one singular piece of paper with a note. *You will pay for what you did. September 13, 889.* It was signed by the initials S.H.

"Wait, wasn't that the day of Lewellyn's death?" asked Cyra.

"Isn't that also the day magic vanished from Linnosa?" Rheanna's eyes went wide with realization.

They both sprinted to the Linwood family tree and searched for Lewellyn Hormanick. *March 24, 867 - September 13, 889.* How had they not noticed it before? Lewellyn died on the same night magic ceased to exist in their kingdom, and Selmana, whoever she was, left a threat to the crown.

"We need to go back to the Oracle's rooms," Cyra declared, already running out of the room.

Rheanna's mind raced with all the possibilities, but one thought kept coming to the front of her mind. She refused to voice it or give it power until it was confirmed.

The girls sped past the dungeons, not even bothering to turn when they heard someone call out their names. Together, they pulled on the serpent's handles and entered the quarters. There was nothing routine or calculated about this search. They ripped the room apart. Furniture was toppled over, clothing and books thrown, even the mattress was flipped over. Rheanna was on her hands and knees, looking beneath the bed frame, when a crack in the floors under a side table caught her attention. Placed in between two tiles was a journal. Rheanna crawled on her belly and grabbed it with her fingertips.

September 13, 889

This cursed royal family forced my sister into a marriage with their vile son, and in turn my sister, my twin, is dead. The cunning and lovely Lewellyn took my place as his bride because she didn't believe I could survive him. And now she is dead. The screaming brat that killed her lays healthy in her bassinet, and it takes everything in me not to gut it.

I am keeping this journal to remind myself of my mission and document what I am doing. Mother always warned us about what would happen if we appealed to the Unknown. It would change us forever. As Oracles, the spirits will worm their way into our souls, but I don't care as long as I get my revenge. I have nothing else. Lewellyn was my everything, my other half.

No matter what, Selmana, remember why you are doing this. You are taking the change to get revenge on the family who wronged you: The Linwoods.

Rheanna stopped reading, stopped breathing, as what she feared solidified within her mind, and she dared to say it aloud. "Selmana Hormanick is the Oracle."

Cyra dropped whatever was in her hands and took the journal from Rheanna's hands, her face growing paler as she read the passage. Her mouth opened and closed several times before she lowered the journal.

"I knew she was behind it all," was all she could get out.

"The prophecy is most likely a fallacy," Rheanna declared. "She did it to destroy our family once and for all."

Cyra nodded. "She killed our parents, started the unrest with the Cleansers too, I would guess."

"She brought us all back here so we would be easy pickings, so the monsters or the riots would kill us," Rheanna agreed.

Cyra paused, contemplating, before she spoke. "But why would she leave before watching it all crumble?"

Rheanna shook her head and shrugged. "That, I have no answer to."

They sat in silence for a few moments as they deliberated, but neither seemed to come up with an answer when a guard ran into the room.

"We need you," the guard stated in between pants.

Both sisters looked at each other and then pocketed the journal for later. The room they left was in disarray, but Rheanna didn't care. Now that they knew who the Oracle was, they'd clear the space out, itemize everything they could into a more proper investigation, and try to deduce where she fled. With luck, they would get their revenge for what happened to Petra. It boiled her blood to think they trusted someone who could be so vile.

As the guard led them off to the dungeons, Rheanna squinted her eyes, adjusting to the darker rooms. The cold, whistling winds scared her as a child, and her parents forbade her from venturing this low in the castle. The floor was bare stone and cold as a grave, with moist air.

Deeper into the dungeon's pits, Rheanna noted how the general section away from the oubliettes looked. Cells the size of a small closet lined up against the walls—ten on each side—and were furnished with damp hay, straw, and a thin mattress and blanket. Chains meant to hold prisoners were clamped into the stone. The stench of despair filled the space, and Rheanna eyed the buckets of human waste in each cell, her stomach twisting.

Her gaze drifted to an open cell where three guards stood, two of them holding Ivan, who was panting heavily, his knuckles cracked and bleeding, and red smeared across his face and chest.

Behind him, a body lay in a heap on the floor, unmoving in a puddle of blood. A thin blanket draped across it, hiding it even though Rheanna automatically knew who it was.

Cyra's eyes flared wide, and that familiar heat of rage and surprise filled her heart as she looked from the body to Ivan.

He stared back, catching his breath as he looked away, unable to meet Cyra's gaze. "I just wanted to help. I thought I could control myself, but..."

"We were scheduled to interrogate her tomorrow after your recovery, my queen," the guard who brought the sisters to the dungeon said, bowing respectfully.

Cyra growled, stepping forward toward Ivan as a desire to grab him and wring him like a rag overcame her, though her better judgment stayed in her hands. "You had no right," she growled at him.

Ivan hung his head in shame. "I am so sorry, Cy,"

Cyra angrily shook her head and looked at the other guards. "Remove him. Not from the dungeon, but the castle. I don't want to look at him, I don't want to see him, and I don't want him to return unless I command otherwise," she said then turned to Ivan, her eyes downcast in anger and disappointment. "If I ever decide you can."

Then, she turned away from him.

Rheanna went cold beside her. A part of her wanted to defend the man that she loved, but she knew that Cyra was not herself. She wasn't her sister, but the queen in this moment. She needed to do what was right for the kingdom and set an example.

Ivan stared at her, mouth agape and eyes widened in shock. "You don't mean that," he pleaded.

Cyra didn't answer him. Instead, she demanded that the guards bring the Hefguard prince to her immediately.

"What can he do?" questioned Rheanna, shivering as the cold of the place began to penetrate her.

Cyra didn't answer but instead knelt and grabbed Natalie's mangled face. The woman groaned as the queen turned her head to look into her eyes. "You better live. You owe us that much."

CHAPTER 37

THE HEFGUARD PRINCE SURVEYED Natalie's bloodied and broken face. Atlas' hands softly examined it as she groaned, the woman unable to open either one of her eyes from how swollen her cheeks were. She was beaten beyond recognition.

"She will live, will be in a lot of pain, but will heal," Atlas confirmed as he stood.

"Good. Will she be able to talk?" Cyra asked.

"In a few days. Once the swelling goes down a bit. If Malcolm was here, he could expedite it, but unfortunately, I am not capable."

Cyra nodded while Rheanna observed the way the prince's green eyes followed every movement her sister made. He seemed to revel in her presence, just like every other man. A pit of jealousy dug into her stomach.

Rheanna was unable to contain her next thought. "Will you really banish Ivan?"

Her sister's eyes narrowed into a glare. "I did, didn't I?"

The younger sister willed herself not to balk at her older sister's tone. "Well, I—"

"Stop right there. I am not in the mood to defend my actions. Ivan almost killed the only connection we have to Petra's murder. That should be reason enough." Her eyes glowed with unspent power, daring Rheanna to argue.

All hope Rheanna had of Ivan falling in love with her and forgetting about Cyra disintegrated without him being able to return to the castle. It was not like she didn't understand her sister's anger and frustration, but Rheanna found it hard not to envy her older sister. They had both been dealt the same cards, and yet the fates gave Cyra Ivan, a prince, and the crown. It was shameful to feel that way, Rheanna knew.

Cyra commanded the guards to call a healer to clean Natalie up then marched out of the room, the prince following after her like a puppy. For a few moments, Rheanna simply stared at Natalie's beaten face, wishing she was the one to cause the damage but knowing she was incapable. She knew she would not be the one to avenge Petra, that it would be left to Cyra and Aella. Even after finding their sister brutally murdered, all Rheanna could do was crumble on the ground while her sisters defended their home. If only she had an ounce of their strength, she would be grateful. Instead, she was the pathetic sister, the sister always in the background, unable to control her powers and with less than proficient combat skills. She was determined to find the strength her sisters so easily called upon.

Instead of wallowing in her self-pity, she decided she would do something about it. Cyra was spiraling, Aella was gone, and she had to hold it all together. Petra's death could break them all, if they let it. Without breaking pace, she made her way to the sisters' training yard, the night sky a blanket above it.

Her breath hitched as she took in the reminders of Petra that covered the arena. Wisteria grew everywhere; along the pillars, in between the cracks of the stone of every surface, and along the outer-perimeter. A few stray tears made their way down her cheeks as she surveyed the chunks of rock that were left behind from their last training session. Never again would Petra spirit pieces of earth at them or teach Rheanna how to focus and call her magic. She had to get better for her—had to get stronger.

Standing in the middle of the yard, Rheanna closed her eyes and felt for her power, for the water that could be so easily called if she only dared. The magic hummed through her as pure, warm energy as if it was a living thing inside of her. Her fingertips tingled as she conjured it. She opened her eyes and saw a ball of moving, shimmering water that hovered right above her palm. A smile lit up her face as she shifted her hand, watching as the water flowed and moved with it. The water lengthened as she manipulated it.

"Magnificent," a male voice startled her, but she didn't drop her water. Instead, it sharpened, almost resembling a blade.

Ripley stood, resting against a pillar, his signature smirk on his face and his eyes full of admiration. "What else can you do?"

"Not much, if I'm honest," Rheanna replied, shrugging her shoulders but releasing her magic.

"Don't stop." Ripley raised an eyebrow. "I like to watch."

Rheanna's cheeks heated, but she rolled her eyes. "If you are here to just make fun—"

"Don't be ridiculous. Is there anything I can do to help?" he asked.

"Actually," Rheanna paused thinking it through, "will you help with my training? Aella was helping me before everything, and well, I am pathetic."

It might be hard for her to admit to her sisters, but she was ashamed of herself. The idea of someone else helping her wasn't so bad though.

He pushed off the pillar and said, "I would be more than happy to aid the pretty lady."

She attempted to keep herself from going red again, but she knew it was no use with her pale complexion. "Let's get started then."

He flashed a grin before throwing his jacket off and onto the stone bench at the front of the yard. His outfit was all black and form-fitting as if he was constantly ready for a fight, concealing everything but his hands and face. Rheanna brought her arms up, like Aella taught her as he circled around her. Auburn strands of hair blew in the night air, his hazel eyes tracking her every move. He stayed a bit crouched, ready to leap forward. Before she knew it, he was striking, his hands barely grazing her cheek.

"If I had been a real opponent, you would be knocked out," he stated without judgment.

"What should I do?" Rheanna asked.

"You wouldn't be able to overpower me, and with your lack of combat skills, you need to lean on your magic a bit more."

"It's hard for me. It doesn't come as easily to me as my sisters," she admitted. Her mind drifted to Cyra and Petra and how quickly they were able to conjure their magic. The only time she saw Aella use even a drop of hers is when Petra died, but she shut down that line of thought immediately. She needed to focus.

"I have never seen Aella wield an ounce of magic, but she is capable of kicking my ass. You created a blade in a second when you thought you were in danger." His hazel eyes blazed into her. "This time, try to create a shield when I go after you."

Rheanna wasn't sure if she was capable of it, but she nodded anyway. This was not the time to doubt herself. Instead, she readied herself. She lowered her fists and took a deep breath, focusing less on him and more on the magic that thrummed through her. Ripley lunged forward, striking out with his first as Rheanna closed her eyes. Her blood heated, her power seeming to pour from her fingers once again.

"Damn the goddess!" shouted Ripley, causing Rheanna's eyes to snap open. A barrier of water extended above her head, all the way down to her feet. Ripley was bent over, clutching his right hand, a wild grin on his face and his eyes alight with excitement. The water spilled to the ground, soaking the stone when she realized what she had done.

"Oh my! I'm so sorry." Her hands covered her mouth as she gasped, her eyes wide with alarm.

"Don't be sorry. That was bloody amazing," he exclaimed.

Despite his words, Rheanna took his hand and inspected it, slowly turning it in her pale fingers. The beginning of a bruise covered his knuckles, a red and blue haze. Lightly, without thinking, she brushed her lips over the wound. Her ocean gaze flicked to his face; his eyes were already trained on her. A stirring feeling bubbled in her stomach, heat pulsing through her body from his gaze and the way it seemed to be devouring her.

"Thank you," she whispered.

He glanced down at her lips and murmured, "Shall we go again?"

Next time her family was threatened, she would be prepared.

Reluctantly, she released his hand, a smile forming on her lips. "Let's go."

CHAPTER 38

"**S**HE'S READY," STATED ATLAS grimly.

Cyra started, hopping from her desk chair and to her feet quickly. After waiting days, Natalie was healed enough to talk and ready to be questioned about Petra and the Cleansers. Atlas had been checking on her every day, learning that Cyra didn't have much patience. With her already halfway out the door, Atlas called, "Shouldn't you wait for your sister?"

"I've waited long enough," she threw over her shoulder, not breaking her stride. She hated that this interrogation had been delayed by Ivan already. There had been no word from him since she banished him, but she would eventually allow him back. Right now, he needed to be taught a lesson. They may have had an intimate relationship, but she was his queen, and she would always be Queen, first and foremost.

Two guards flanked her as she walked into the dungeons, one of them moving to unlock the cell that held Natalie. The woman's usually shining black hair was dull and knotted, matted to the back of her head. Bruises peppered along her face, deep purple fading to a sickly green, mostly concentrated along the left side of her face. Black shrouded her left eye, accentuating her pale skin. With an expression full of despair, she looked behind Cyra, searching for someone that would not come.

"You are truly disgusting," Cyra spat as the door swung open.

Natalie crawled forward on her knees, still wearing the same black suit the Cleansers wore when they invaded the castle. "I tried to stop it from happening," she rasped, her voice rough from disuse.

"You are a traitor." It came out as a snarl, causing Natalie to flinch on the ground.

"Hold her," commanded Cyra to the two guards. They each moved to either side of Natalie in the tight cell, grabbing hold of her arms and hauling her up. Cyra stood just within the doorway.

"Please," whimpered the girl.

"My sister is dead, and you betrayed my other one. You will not find pity or mercy in me."

Natalie's almond eyes widened in shock. "Who is dead? Is Aella alright?"

"Do not pretend you don't know. Petra was just a child." Hot, angry tears threatened to spill from Cyra's liquid gold eyes.

A strangled sob escaped from Natalie. "That poor girl." Teardrops left trails down her muddy and blood-crusted cheeks.

This only fueled Cyra's hate further. "No more pretending." She conjured her power, a glowing crown floated above her scarlet head, casting an eerie shadow upon her face. "Was it your plan all along to seduce Aella?"

"I was just meant to get close to one of you." Natalie's voice broke as she sobbed. "I was not supposed to fall in love with Aella."

Scoffing, Cyra called to her flames, her fingertips lighting up. "To get to me? Why bring Aella or Petra into it?"

Natalie shifted awkwardly, her hands splayed and still held by the two guards. "The Cleansers don't find you worthy. Petra was meant to be our queen, and Aella was my in, but no one else was supposed to get hurt."

"But Petra is dead." Her fire grew hotter, fueled by the pathetic look of dismay on Natalie's face.

"We are not responsible for her death."

"So, it just so happens that she is murdered when your people invade the castle? Quite the coincidence." Cyra's eyes begin to glow.

"I promise—"

"Your promises mean nothing to me." Her power lashed out, striking Natalie's chest and cutting through her suit, burning her bare flesh. The girl howled in pain, her body attempting to double over, but the guards held firm. "Why did you kill Petra?"

Natalie panted. "We didn't."

Another flame shot from Cyra's fingers and sliced her thigh. A scream broke from Natalie's lips as her body shook from the pain. A sick sort of satisfaction crept over Cyra to see the one who hurt her sisters now in pain.

"Why did you kill Petra?"

"Cyra, I swear—" Fire danced along her abdomen, and a cry cut off her words. Sweat began to form across her brow, and she couldn't catch her breath.

"No more lies from you. Tell me now." Cyra's voice was pure command. Power rippled off her, filling the small jail cell. Even the guards seemed to balk from it. Natalie remained silent, her eyes fluttering closed when Rheanna's soft voice stole Cyra's attention.

"It won't help if she ends up dead, Cy."

Cyra turned to her younger sister, her chest heaving. "I need to know."

Rheanna placed a hand on her sister's shoulder, flames licking her, but neither the heat nor pain touched her. "I know."

Taking a breath, Cyra let her magic fall away and said to the guards, "We are done for today."

They each gave a short nod, releasing Natalie's arms and letting her crumble to the dirty floor. She whimpered and crawled to the corner of the cell. Cyra would not be satisfied until the woman was dead.

She walked up to the locked gate, her voice ice cold as she said, "Do not think you will escape this."

Rheanna and Cyra walked out arm in arm. Once they were out of earshot, Cyra paused and looked at Rheanna. "It's my fault that Petra is dead. I must make this right."

"How could you even say that?" Rheanna's eyes were wide with disbelief.

"They didn't want her. They wanted me. I was the problem," Cyra said. Her freckled face was already wet with tears.

Rheanna tugged on her black braid. "They are the ones who killed her. Not you. You only did what you had to. You had to take the crown for all of Linnosa."

"If I had let Petra be—"

"I'm going to stop you right there. Petra was a fourteen-year-old girl. She was not ready to be queen, nor did she want to be. You were born to be queen. Do not feel guilty for things you cannot control," Rheanna stated. Her voice was sure and confident, soothing Cyra's panic.

"I suppose," Cyra conceded. She was not fully convinced, but it would do no one any good if she let herself become consumed by it. Every time she thought of Petra, she thought of Hollin. Her daughter would not suffer due to her position.

"We have too much going on to doubt ourselves." Rheanna continued with a joke, attempting to lightening the mood. "We already have the council for that."

"Speaking of the council. We have a meeting to discuss my marriage to the prince." It was Cyra's turn to play with her hair nervously.

"We will face them together." Rheanna held Cyra's hand in hers firmly.

CHAPTER 39

THE COUNCIL ROOM WAS uncomfortably silent as Prince Atlas sat next to Cyra at the head of the table. The members resented the fact that someone outside the council and royal family was within their sacred room. They all seemed to ignore that he would be their king soon enough. Rheanna glanced around anxiously at each of the members. The Northern representatives, Norton and Marine, and the Western representatives, Sidney and Levine appeared to be the most comfortable with the situation while the Southern representative, Lola, fidgeted nervously in her seat. Since the death of her husband, her uneasiness grew. Rheanna heard rumors of Lola not allowing her children to go to the tutors with the other children in the castle. They must always be in her sight. Bianca and Talmadge, the Eastern representatives, disgruntled and throwing glares at the newly engaged couple were anything but out of the ordinary.

"As Prince Atlas Nicola will soon be your king, I believe you should all grow familiar with one another and get accustomed to his presence," announced Cyra, her gaze landing on each one of her representatives. Rheanna gave her an encouraging smile.

"It is my honor to serve you and be allowed in your council," Atlas said, a polite smile plastered on his perfect face.

"Is your brother up for grabs since you are now off the table?" Bianca asked sweetly, her elbows on the table, pushing her chest forward and providing an ample amount of cleavage. It took everything in Rheanna not to laugh, as if the girl could ever get the prince's attention off her sister.

Atlas barely even glanced at her. "He is not currently interested."

Bianca's cheeks heated with the rejection; her blue eyes downcast as she adjusted herself to her normal seated position.

"It is a pleasure to have you," Sidney spoke, giving him a greeting tip of her head.

He smiled graciously as Talmadge interjected, "Do you truly think it is appropriate to have this boy in our meetings?" He shot a wrinkled glare at the prince.

"This boy will be your king. Treat him with respect," Cyra demanded. Her eyes began to glow, but before it could escalate Rheanna added, "We will be discussing their marriage plans. It seems important that he be privy to that information."

Talmadge huffed but didn't disagree.

"That being said, when do you plan to be married—before or after we settle everything?" Norton asked.

"We don't know how long that may take, so I would prefer before if that is alright with your queen," Atlas said, turning to Cyra, a dark eyebrow raised.

Cyra nodded. "I agree. The sooner the better."

Her words lit up Atlas' face.

Lola spoke up, "Do we really think it is an appropriate time to have such a celebration? With the death of my beloved husband and the young princess, I—"

"We will not be celebrating. It will be a personal and quiet affair," Cyra stated. Her fists clenched on top of the table, but Atlas' hand laid atop the one closest to him.

"The marriage of the queen cannot be a quiet affair," argued Levine, the older man sitting up to join the conversation.

Cyra's eyes narrowed. "It will be what I say it is. As Lola said, this is not a time to celebrate."

"Maybe, once everything settles down, we could create more of a spectacle, but for now, my sister and I believe it would be safest not just for us, but for everyone in the castle if we don't have a party. There is no reason to bring unwanted attention to us," Rheanna said before anyone else could object.

Norton nodded slowly. "We do all remember the coronation."

They all murmured words of agreement. Lola sat with a small smile on her lips, more pleased than the rest at this arrangement. She would not have to worry about the safety of her children within a royal wedding.

"Reinforcements from Hefguard should arrive within a few days. Should we wait until then?" Rheanna asked.

Cyra contemplated for a moment then said, "I guess it can be up to the future king."

Atlas glanced around the room before he looked back at his betrothed. "My brother will be traveling with the reinforcements. I would like to wait until he could be in attendance."

"Understandable," said Cyra. "If that is all—"

"Actually, your majesty, I have been hearing reports of possible magic users throughout the kingdom," Lola said, her eyes flicking between Atlas and Cyra.

"I have as well, but from what we can tell they are simply rumors," Bianca added, pale eyes rolling.

"Remember last time you believed such things were just rumors?" Cyra asked, her thoughts going toward the monsters and the attack on the coronation for the second time this meeting. Rheanna agreed with her sister, thinking it would not be wise to make the mistake of pushing aside rumors as they often prove to be true. If there were magic users again, did that mean the prophecy was true? Did Petra's death have to do with it? Or was the Oracle possibly up to something? Whatever the reason, they needed to figure it out immediately.

Instead of arguing, Bianca sat back in her seat and held her tongue. Rheanna's eyebrow raised, surprised by Bianca's lack of spirit today, but also happy she didn't have to play peacekeeper. When no one responded, Cyra continued, "I will have some guards set out to investigate the rumors, and Atlas and I will be married once the other prince has arrived. You are all dismissed."

With that, Rheanna left and headed back to her chambers. Lifting her mattress, she pulled out the Oracle's diary, snuggled to the pillows among her bed, and dived into the origin of Selmana Hormanick.

September 24, 889

It has been eleven days since Lewellyn was killed. The king is already looking for a new bride. He named the spawn who murdered her Rowan. The thing does not even resemble my dear sister, but instead the Linwoods completely with her blonde hair and green eyes.

The curse has already been at work within the kingdom. Magic users no longer have the means to manipulate their powers. The fae, witches, and every other species besides humans are coming down with a sickness, unable to dwell on Linnosa soil as their very existence is dependent on magic.

I am continuing the change into the Unknown. While my power grows stronger, my body weakens, decomposing further with each spell. I will continue to spread the rot throughout the kingdom. Lewellyn will be avenged.

Rheanna sat up in her bed, struggling to untangle herself from the pillows. The Oracle had cursed Linnosa. She had to tell Cyra immediately, but she knew her sister would be off on a date with the prince soon. Only in her pale blue nightgown, Rheanna spirited down the hall, not even bothering to knock on Cyra's door before bursting through it. The maid working on Cyra's makeup shrieked in horror, her hand clutched over her chest, but she visibly relaxed at the sight of the heaving Rheanna.

"I'm sorry, but I must speak with my sister privately." She held the door open for the maid, who looked at Cyra for confirmation. Once her older sister nodded, the woman scurried out.

"What's the matter?" asked Cyra. Her makeup was a shimmering glaze, highlighting her pretty features.

"The Oracle cursed Linnosa so there would be no magic," she said while thrusting the journal at her sister. Cyra's golden eyes expanded as she read the passage. The journal fell to her side as she sighed.

"We should have known. This is all connected to her," said Cyra, exasperated.

Rheanna shook her head wildly. "And that is not all," she said and took the journal from her sister's grasp. She turned to the next page and read aloud.

November 11, 891

Pretending to have this family's best interest has been exhausting. Rowan continues to grow; she just turned two. She might not look like Lewellyn, but she sure does have our family's defiance and spirit. She seems to loathe her father as much as I do. Every time he comes into a room, she screams, but when I do, she reaches for me. She took her first steps, walking toward me. But she is still a Linwood.

The spell I have cast is holding true. Magic continues to run dormant in Linnosa, and I move around the castle unseen, unnoticed, besides when I wish to be. Not one person has asked where I came from. It is like I was here all this time. They don't see me so clearly plotting against them.

Rheanna stopped reading there, shaking her head once again. Cyra massaged her temples as she paced around the room.

"If she was hidden so well, why did she run?" Cyra asked, stopping and tapping her foot against the ground.

"Because she was no longer hidden," exclaimed Rheanna as she thought back to the time she asked about oracles and how to become one. "We all questioned and doubted her."

Cyra's eyes widened. "Did we break her spell?"

"Or were we somehow immune? With our own magic?"

The sisters stood in silence until the maid gingerly knocked on the door and pushed it open. "I'm sorry, but we need to finish preparing you."

"Of course. Come in," said Cyra, waving the woman back into the room.

"I will keep reading," said Rheanna, leaving, but in the threshold, she paused and winked. "Have fun."

CHAPTER 40

T HE SATIN OF CYRA'S emerald gown fell in a train behind her, the skirts smooth and tight fitting along the waist. The sleeves were off the shoulder and running down to her hand where they came to a point at her middle finger. Adorned in gold jewelry, she shined, a matching crown atop her untamed curly hair that she left unstyled on purpose. A shimmer of glitter was smeared across her eyelids and cheekbones.

Per King Leonard and Queen Elspeth Nicola's request, Cyra was getting to know her future husband and king. They were to have a romantic dinner on the terrace in the garden, or at least Marine, who planned it all, claimed it would be romantic. Cyra was not all too worried about how much romance their marriage would hold but more about the protection it would provide her people and family.

She tucked a curl behind her ear, took a deep breath, and allowed a guard to escort her to the gardens. The beauty of it took her breath away every single time, but tonight, it seemed to be exceptionally magnificent. An array of blossoms from roses to tulips filled the veranda, the scent enticing. Tiny fairy lights were alight, adding to the enchanting ambience. A circular mahogany table filled with cheeses, meats, and fruits sat in the middle of a freshly cut patch of grass, two chairs placed opposite from one another. One was already occupied, Atlas standing as Cyra entered through the glass door.

His appearance was clean and tidy, his usually unruly hair tamed, his waves not in his eyes for once. He was in a black tux, and his bowtie was the same satin emerald of Cyra's dress which played well off his deep green eyes. She could imagine that they looked like quite the pair, like a queen and king. He bowed, offering a hand and led her to her chair. Pulling the chair from the table, he invited her to sit before pushing it in for her.

"Thank you," Cyra said, plastering a smile on her face. Her cheeks already hurt from the fakeness of it all.

"My pleasure," he responded.

Silence filled the courtyard, but instead of attempting to fill it, Cyra picked up her glass of wine and downed it. Atlas followed suit as they both began to pick on the array of food displayed. A servant refilled their glasses, they finished them, and it repeated a few times before Atlas decided to break the silence.

"What was your life like before all of this? Before your parents died and you were brought back to the capitol?"

Cyra was a bit startled by the question. Not once had anyone asked about her life prior, assuming she was glad to be back. It was refreshing to have someone acknowledge she had something perhaps worth going back to.

"It was quite great, actually. I worked as a barmaid at the inn my surrogate father, Ron established after receiving custody of me." Cyra smiled fondly at the memories before continuing, "We didn't have an easy life, but it was a good one." She stopped there even though she yearned to talk to someone, anyone about

Hollin. Her throat burned as she thought of the little mass of strawberry-blonde hair.

"That sounds wonderful," he said, and she truly believed it when he said it.

"What is life like in Hefguard?"

"I have no complaints. I'm surrounded by my family, and the country has been blessed with no upheaval in a while."

Cyra pondered his response before asking, "What is it like to live with magic everywhere?"

"We have fun. Learning from our family how to wield it was second nature. My mother's family comes from a long line of witches. On top of that, there are several other species with different access and forms of magic." He placed an elbow on the table, his chin resting in his palm.

Hollin would be safe in a world like Hefguard. Even though she was a princess here, her own citizens would not accept her. She would likely be called unworthy, just like Cyra.

"I have always imagined what Linnosa was like before the erasure of magic," murmured Cyra, taking another sip from her glass.

"Our citizens are diverse but treated with equality. We can learn from one another. Have you ever met a different species?"

Cyra shifted, not answering the question truthfully. "No. I would like to someday, though."

Once they finished the tray, they stood to walk around the gardens, Cyra swaying a bit before Atlas offered her his arm. She may have drunk more wine than she should have, but she liked the weightless feeling it provided her with. Things have been all too heavy lately.

"I know you aren't thrilled about our arrangement, but I hope I can give you a good marriage," Atlas said, avoiding eye contact as he looked up at the night sky.

Cyra paused, bringing his attention to her. "It's not about you. Honestly, there are very few men I would consider to rule beside me, and you are high up on that list."

His forest-green eyes pierced her. "If I am honest, I have been drawn to you since I met you at your coronation."

Her cheeks heated at the compliment, which she accredited to the wine. "That was probably one of the most nerve-wracking days of my life."

"I couldn't tell. You were so confident." His fingertips trailed up her arm, sending goosebumps across her flesh. The feeling stoked a fire in her core.

Her eyelids drooped lazily, her charm turning on. "You think so?"

The sultry tone in her voice seemed to awaken him as well. He leaned forward, whispering in her ear, "Not just confident, but damn near sexy."

Cyra turned, her face now level with his. "Don't bat those green eyes at me. You might get yourself into trouble."

"I think it will get me exactly where I want to be."

"Prove it." Her voice was bold and assertive with the command.

Atlas didn't need any more encouragement. His hand tangled into Cyra's curls, and his mouth was on hers within a second. They stumbled backward together, Cyra's back pressing into a shrub, branches digging into the low-cut of her dress. The kiss was sloppy, aided by the alcohol in their systems, but it felt good. All that mattered was that it felt good. It all boiled down to this moment, their limbs tangling, and breaths mingling. This engagement might be fun after all. Her crown toppled off her head, ricocheting off the stone and sending a crash throughout the silent night air. A guard ran to them, their armor clanking as they awkwardly asked if everything was alright. The couple didn't balk, continuing their perusal of each other until the guard left on his own without a command.

"Should we go to your room?" Atlas asked breathlessly. His chest heaved, pressing against her breasts, and only stimulating her further.

"No need," she whispered against his ear, nipping it in the process.

Cyra tugged on her own dress clumsily. Atlas didn't miss a beat, shrugging his jacket off while assisting her undress.

"Wow," he exclaimed, pausing as he admired her body.

"Show me what it will be like when we are married," she demanded.

And so, he did.

CHAPTER 41

THE EARLY MORNING LIGHT warmed Rheanna's face while she completed her stretches, waiting for Ripley to appear for the training session they agreed to since he found her earlier that week. Birds chirped overhead, flying above the orange sunrise, as the floral aroma of the blossoms left by Petra wafted through the air. The light breeze soothed Rheanna's soul. She lifted it toward the sky and let it caress the loose strands of her hair.

"Beautiful." Ripley's voice broke the quiet of the morning.

Rheanna met his gaze, a soft grin on her face. "It truly is."

"I wasn't talking about the sky."

Rolling her eyes at the smirk on his face, she got up from her spot on the stone ground and took a moment to appreciate the man in front of her. Today, he wore all black as always, but the shirt was fitted, showing off his toned arms and chest despite his lanky build. He wore loose shorts, and a hint of black ink went down his left thigh and ended just below his knee. She wondered what the tattoo was as she took in the sharp lines of his face. A five o'clock shadow graced his jaw, matching his auburn hair that hung a bit into his hazel eyes.

"Enjoying the show?" he asked. The smirk on his lips only grew as she blinked several times.

"Get over yourself," she quipped.

"Is there something in particular you would like to work on today?" His eyes gleamed with mischief.

"Why don't we just start with our normal drills?"

"As you wish, Princess." He winked before he began to jog around the yard. Rheanna attempted to keep up with him. They did a few laps, Rheanna's breathing significantly more labored while Ripley barely broke a sweat. In silence, they finished the rest of their morning routine consisting of a variety of exercises to work on Rheanna's stamina and overall body strength. They had only been meeting for a few days, and already Rheanna's magic was stronger. She was able to call to her power easier and change its shape, no longer needing to close her eyes to envision it.

"How about we try combat with magic?" suggested Ripley.

Rheanna nodded, preparing with her fighting stance. Growing more confident in her abilities, Rheanna didn't wait for Ripley to make the first move but instead pushed him into defense. Her dominant hand, her left, connected with Ripley's forearm as he blocked her. She took the opportunity to spray him with ice cold water, shocking him and causing him to drop his guard. Her foot cut out, wrapping around his ankle and destabilizing him, leaving his chest open as he struggled for balance. With one quick, strong hit to his chest, he was stumbling backward and falling onto his back. Rheanna didn't think as she straddled his chest, a blade of ice pressed against his throat. He let out a throaty chuckle, his Adam's apple barely missing the blade. A grin of pure triumph lit up her face, letting go of the blade, and placing both her hands on his chest.

"Bad move," said Ripley.

Before she could even process what he said, he grasped her wrists, rolled, and flipped her over until she was on her back and he was on top of her, pinning her down to the ground. Rheanna's chest heaved, trying to push upwardly to escape his grasp, but it was no use. His hands were far too strong, and his weight so much so that all she did was flop uselessly up against his pelvis and stomach until she huffed and gave up.

"Not fair," she mumbled.

"Never said it was, Princess. Never let your guard down in front of your enemy."

"I didn't know you were my enemy."

Ripley's face lowered to hers, dangerously close. She could feel his breath on her lips as he spoke. "I can be anything you want me to be."

Rheanna's heart picked up, and her mind became unfocused as she lifted her head to meet him. Their lips touched softly at first and then heated up. Her hands slid beneath his shirt, exploring those abs she knew were beneath it. He moaned at her touch, the sound setting off a ferocity she didn't know she possessed. Her nails dug into his back, arching as his hands began to explore her. A light pressure wrapped around her throat, his large hand resting against it. Breathy sighs released from Rheanna as his lips trailed down her jaw and onto her throat.

The sound of a throat clearing caused them both to freeze. Rheanna flushed red at the knowledge of someone having caught them.

"Can we help you?" asked Ripley, sharpness filling his tone. His hazel eyes bore into hers, not moving from on top of her. She squeezed his shoulder.

"I am sorry to bother you, but you ordered us to alert you immediately with any news," a young girl with red hair responded shakily.

"I'm sorry, Princess. Work stuff." He jumped up, offering his hand and pulling her up along with him. "We will resume this later." With a wink, he was off with two familiar red-haired and brunette maids, Laney and Cora.

Rheanna stood there dumbfounded at what had just happened, her breathing irregular. She had always thought her first kiss, her first everything, would be with Ivan, but in this moment, she felt that kiss with Ripley could not be topped by anyone. Not even Ivan. As if the thought alone summoned him, he came into the training yard from the door Ripley had left only moments ago. Her cheeks heated, hoping he had not witnessed what had just happened between the two.

"Ivan! I thought you were banished?" exclaimed Rheanna.

His smile twitched, but he said, "She didn't mean it. She loves me."

"She's been really stressed with Petra's death and the pressure of the crown. I wouldn't push her. You should probably go." Rheanna knew her sister was fragile right now. She didn't need anything else.

"Come on, Rhe. We're family. You can't want me to stay away." His brown eyes widened, pleading.

Guilt rushed over Rheanna. "Of course not, Ivan, but..."

"Think about Maude. Would she want you to send me away? Wouldn't she want us to protect each other?"

Rheanna paused. He had a point. The Bushnells were always there for her. How could she send away their son? "You'll definitely be able to come back soon. I just don't want to upset Cyra right now."

"I could hide," Ivan begged. His eyes flickered, and his face began to darken in a way she had never seen before.

Rheanna shook her head. "I will talk to her. I promise."

"I was there for you when your sister wasn't." His face became unreadable, his tone almost threatening.

"How dare you—"

"You are a spoiled little wench like the rest of them," he spat at her, full of venom.

Rheanna stumbled back, shocked by his words and sudden change of attitude. "Ivan, I—"

"Every single one of you royals have looked down upon my family for too long. Cyra won't marry me because I'm not some titled highborn ass." He stomped forward, stopping in front of her, barely an arm's length away.

Never had she been fearful of Ivan before, but now, she found herself readying her magic. He reached out, grabbing Rheanna's arm and attempting to pull her towards him. In defense, water sprayed him in the face, clumsy and unfocused by her fear and shock.

"Bloody wench."

A blade settled against her throat, a cool metal biting in her flesh, cutting Rheanna's cry short. Horrified, she attempted to call to her magic, but nothing came. Instead, a burning feeling filled her veins, and she thrashed, screaming.

"Iron," he hissed in her ear.

CHAPTER 42

C YRA WAS MAKING HER way down the hall when the
   sound of a short, high-pitched scream stopped her in
her tracks. She had a visceral reaction to it, instantly knowing
it was from someone she loved. Quickly, she moved toward
the sound, following the sound of scuffing feet and smothered
whimpers, leading her to just outside the royal training yard.

Her golden gaze scanned the scene quickly, assessing as
fire burst from her fingertips.

"Let her go!" A snarl ripped from her throat, her magic
growing hotter in response to Rheanna's whimpers.

The man who held her sister spun around, causing Cyra's
flame to flicker just for a moment before it grew stronger.
Ivan's dark eyes were lit up from her fire, and a silver dagger
pressed against Rheanna's throat flickered with the reflected
light. She instantly recognized it as an iron blade, capable
of blocking magic, which explained why Rheanna was not
using her powers to get free. Cyra's eyes flicked between Ivan's
shocked expression to her sister's tear-filled one.

"What are you doing?" Cyra demanded, slowly stepping
toward them.

Ivan recovered from his initial shock, pulling the blade closer to Rheanna's pale throat.

"I'm fixing it." His gaze glanced down at his captive before he continued, "You have to be the one who survives the prophecy."

"If you think I would let my sisters die in my stead, you don't know me at all."

"But we could be together. You wouldn't have to marry that prince."

"And my sisters would be dead," Cyra snapped, her eyes molten lava with anguish and disgust.

"I thought..." His dark eyes searched hers, but her fire grew even darker in her palm, almost a scarlet hue now.

"You thought wrong. Let her go." Each word was accentuated, a command, but instead of obeying, he brought Rheanna tighter to his chest as a small squeal came from the shaking woman.

"Don't you love me?" His voice was a plea.

"I love her more."

Rheanna's lips twitched as if she were going to smile before Ivan jerked back like he was physically hit by the words. A thin river of red ran down Rheanna's neck causing Cyra's eyes to widen in panic and her flames to roar around her, becoming a halo around her form.

"Choose me," he begged.

"I will always choose them."

Before the words were fully out of her mouth, his body was aflame, and the dagger clattered from his hands onto the tile as he writhed in pain beside it. Screams of agony ripped through the room as Rheanna untangled herself from her would-be murderer. The flames licked her skin, but didn't harm her nor would they ever as long as Cyra was their summoner. A choked sobbed escaped her chest as she collided with her sister, their arms embraced around one another.

"It's okay. I've got you." Cyra soothingly ran her palms across her sister's back.

"He was actually going to kill me," Rheanna exclaimed in disbelief. "Ivan was going to bloody kill me." She pulled away from the hug and looked frantically at the spot Ivan once stood, now nothing more than a pile of ashes.

"Ivan was going to kill me. He's dead." Her ocean eyes went wide before she continued, "How am I going to tell Maude?"

Maude, Ivan's younger sister, had not even crossed Cyra's mind. For the first time since Petra's death, a feeling of guilt crept up on her, but she had to shake it off for the time being. Cyra embraced her sister once again. "It wasn't your fault. I'm the one who killed him."

The guilt she felt was overshadowed by the overwhelming relief that her sister was still standing, that she was alive.

"But only because he wanted to kill me." Her voice cracked at the last word, tears staining her cheeks.

"Rhe, he wanted you dead, wanted Aella dead. And I think..." She trailed off, her eyes glazing as she let her thoughts put everything together.

Rheanna gasped as she came to the same conclusion. "He killed Petra."

Cyra's stomach turned at the words spoken aloud, realizing she tortured Natalie for Petra's death, but it was her own lover who killed her baby sister. She nearly let that man turn her into a monster.

"I need to do better," Cyra said evenly.

"You're trying your—"

"No more excuses. I am the queen. I must do better. You went through the same things but you held it together."

"Barely."

Pausing, Cyra surveyed her sister, truly looking at her for what felt like the first time. Dark circles laid heavily beneath her blue eyes, anxiety knitted her brows together, and her fingernails were in her mouth, bitten down to their beds. While Cyra was spiraling, so was her sister, but in a more silent way.

"I'm sorry."

Sighing, Rheanna said, "We will both do better."

Cyra needed to be honest with her sister and lay everything out. If something happened to her, she needed Hollin to be protected and safe. She hesitated before saying, "There's something I need to tell you."

"I cannot believe you didn't tell me earlier." Rheanna's voice held a reprimand, but a ghost of a grin graced her lips.

"I had to make sure she was safe, but I should have realized earlier that you are her family." Cyra took a deep breath, steadying herself before finishing, "My one regret is that Hollin will not know her Aunt Petra."

"Well, with everything going on, I understand."

"There's more," Cyra said carefully.

Rheanna rolled her eyes but stayed silent, waiting for her sister to continue.

"Hollin is half-fae."

She blinked several times, wondering aloud how Cyra even managed to find a fae in Linnosa.

"There are more than you think," Cyra answered.

Rheanna shivered a bit at the cryptic response. Her knowledge of the fae didn't portray them well, but if her sister had a child with one, she had to reconsider her beliefs.

"Is he involved with Hollin?"

"We both agreed it would be safer if he stayed away." Cyra's voice was soft and sad, causing Rheanna's heart to clench.

"Will you bring her here?"

Cyra shook her head. "Not yet. It's not safe."

As much as Rheanna yearned to meet her niece, she knew her sister was right. With monsters, prophecies, and enemies coming from all sides, it would be too dangerous, especially with her heritage.

"You need to tell the prince," Rheanna stated.

The sisters called for Atlas. If he was to be a part of their family, he must know all the details, even the ones the council were not privy to.

"But wait, before he comes," said Rheanna, "do not tell him about her heritage."

The sisters agreed that would be something he learned after the wedding since it is one thing for Cyra to have a daughter, but for her to be a fae could get Hollin killed.

They met Atlas in the game room. He began to stand up when Cyra said, "We have more to discuss with you, but before we begin, you must swear to never utter a word of it to anyone else." Her golden gaze pinned him, every bit the confident Queen, but Rheanna could see through it. She saw the way her hand slightly trembled as she placed it on the table and how her chest raised unevenly.

Atlas' face was sincere when he responded, "You have my word."

Rheanna let Cyra take control of the conversation, telling Atlas everything about the prophecy that tore them apart and the information they found out about the Oracle and Selmana Hormanick. She told him about her daughter but left out the details about her father. Rheanna studied Atlas, watching his every facial expression and slight gesture.

He seemed alarmed by the Oracle's involvement in everything, but once Cyra explained her backstory, she could see the cogs turning in his head and the dots connecting. He even took the news of being a stepdad well, asking when he would meet her.

"Not for a while. Not even the council knows of her existence. I want to keep it that way until the castle is safer for her," Cyra responded smoothly.

"Understandable. I can imagine she is quite amazing, just like her mother." Atlas' words almost made Rheanna blush, but Cyra had no reaction.

"She is," she said with a slight nod of her head.

"I will protect her as if she were my own." His fist pounded against his heart with the words, causing Cyra to give him an appreciative smile which he seemed to bask in.

"Thank you."

CHAPTER 43

*F*ROSTY SNOW FELL AND *landed on Rheanna's face as she closed her eyes, holding her face up to the night sky. She heard footsteps land on the soft ground beside her and turned to face her best friend. "Maude," she whispered.*

Maude smiled, the dimple showing on her left cheek. "I've missed you, Rhe."

"I've missed you, too."

"Then why did you do it?" Maude's smile flickered.

Rheanna's eyebrows scrunched together. "Do what?"

"Kill my brother." Suddenly, there was a knife in her hand, the same one Ivan attempted to kill her with.

Rheanna stumbled backward. "I... He... He was going to hurt me."

"Liar." Maude prowled forward and Rheanna walked back until she hit something. Pressure wrapped around her neck as a familiar voice whispered, "You can't escape me that easily."

Panic seized Rheanna as Ivan now held a twin dagger to Maude's. She raised hers, plunging it toward Rheanna's heart.

Rheanna awoke with a gasp. Sweat and goosebumps covered her body. Nausea rolled over her and she turned to the edge of her bed and puked. The scent burned her nostrils. She made her way to the bathroom, brushed her teeth with mint, and walked into the hallway. Her hand rested over the thin mark on her neck that the iron dagger and Ivan had left. Hot tears rolled down her cheeks as the memories crashed over her like tidal waves. Ripley, as stoic as ever, leaned against the gilded wall, arms crossed and prominent bags beneath his eyes as if he hadn't slept in days.

"Rheanna," he said hesitantly.

"He's dead," Rheanna sobbed.

Ripley looked around quickly, pushing off the wall and took her arm, gently guiding her to the balcony by her rooms. "You need some air."

As soon as they stepped outside, the cool air calmed her, and a rush of relief settled over her. The tears stopped, and she said, "Ivan is dead."

"I know," said Ripley.

Rheanna's eyes widened in panic. "How do you know?"

He placed his hands on her shoulders, his hazel eyes peering into hers as he said, "I make it my job to know everything going on around here. No one else knows."

"Did you know he tried to kill me?" Tears filled her ocean eyes again.

His face turned into a scowl, his grip tightening on her shoulder. "If he wasn't already dead, I would kill him myself."

Rheanna fell against his chest, and he wrapped his arms around her. "What am I going to do?"

"Survive. All you can do is survive." His hand rubbed up and down her back soothingly. She pulled away, looking up at him.

"How is it you are here every time I need you?" Rheanna asked, tilting her head.

Instead of answering, his lips found hers in a gentle caress.

"I need to go to my sister," she said quietly.

He nodded. "Go."

Rheanna moved swiftly down the hall until she was in front of Cyra's bedroom door. She hesitated but ultimately knocked. Within seconds, Cyra was at the door. They stared at each other for a few moments, fire and water, unmoving. The older sister sighed and wrapped her arms around Rheanna's middle.

"I can't sleep either," said Cyra, her voice hoarse and cheeks sticky from sobs.

"This can't be real."

Cyra closed the door and led her sister to her bed. "I know. I feel foolish for trusting him."

"I resented you because of him. I was so in love with him, and he tried to kill me." Rheanna's watery eyes held her sister's golden gaze. It was time she was honest and truthful with both herself and her sister.

Cyra opened and closed her mouth before she said, "I didn't know. I'm sorry." She placed her tanned hand over Rheanna's pale one.

"We were both fools, truly." Rheanna squeezed her sister's hand.

"Petra is dead because of him. He deserved worse than what I did," declared Cyra, her face screwing into a scowl.

"I cannot even fathom that. And then Maude..." Her words drifted off.

"We have caused her the same pain we have gone through."

Rheanna nodded, covering her face with her palms and falling back in Cyra's bed. "I wish Aella was here."

"So do I, but we have each other."

"Is it alright if I stay here tonight?"

Cyra smiled sadly. "Always."

CHAPTER 44

B LOOD SPLATTERED, SPRAYING ACROSS Aella's stony
face. Instead of the relief she usually felt after killing a
mark, this death only angered her. She wiped her dagger on her
leather pants, already caked with gore from the past week.

The Cleanser at her feet was dead because she had no
information. Just like the others, she swore her innocence when
it came to Petra's murder. No one would admit to knowing
Natalie. They only prattled on about wanting Petra on the
throne and their dislike for Cyra. Aella was getting nowhere,
and her kill count only continued to climb. With a sigh of
resignation, she sheathed her weapon and started toward the one
place she could seek the kind of aid she needed.

Less than an hour later, she stood outside the Guild, full
of regret for ending up back here, but willing to do anything to
avenge her sister. Walking into the familiar, dark building was
oddly steadying. The scent of mildew hit her harder than usual,
and she found it difficult to train her face into her usual cold
mask. Her chin didn't lower as she marched through the dark
and dingy space. The chatter of the Guild members came to a
hush. Aella only looked forward. She almost made it to the aging
stairs that led to Karif's office when a gruff voice made her pause.

"Look what we have here. The pretty princess graced us with her presence," the voice mocked.

Aella instantly stiffened; every muscle in her body tightened as she slowly pivoted on her heel and turned her violent violet gaze to the speaker, eyes narrowing. It was Lionel—the man who believed he would sit at the head of the Guild when Creaton died instead of Karif, despite him being his son.

Lionel was a man in his mid-thirties with a balding head, blue eyes, and a nasty personality. Growing a beer gut from spending his money on prostitutes and alcohol, his days as an assassin were coming to a close. His stare pierced through Aella, and his contempt echoed on her own face. His resentment of her only grew over the years as he hated her for rapidly climbing the ranks, knocking him off his pedestal, and becoming one of the most notorious assassins in the Guild by the time she was fifteen.

"This pretty princess is still as deadly as ever," she responded, her tone smooth and unwavering.

He chuckled, not taking heed to the danger that laced her words. "I've heard about the little brat in the palace dying. You kill her yourself? Pretty princess didn't want to play nice with her little sissy?"

Before Aella could even process what she was about to do, the weakness she was about to expose about herself, she tackled him. They collided, their bodies tangling as they hit the rotting wood of the floor. Her fist connected with his nose, a sickening crack following.

"You've gone soft," he mocked, blood running into his teeth. He had anticipated her attack.

She went to throw another punch, forgetting her training and how she was more agile and fleet-footed than a powerhouse. Her arm raised back, but before it could hit its mark, a pair of hands wrapped around her throat. Her body went rigid as she was cut off from oxygen. Nails dug into the flesh of her neck as they dragged her off Lionel.

Her feet scrambled to find purchase, and her hands clawed at the one who held her tightly.

She would not die like this. Her vision began to blur, and her instincts took over. With a single thought, the pressure around her throat disappeared as the culprit who attempted to choke her began to gasp for air instead.

He released her, and she crawled backward, hitting the moss-covered wall, her gaze instantly found the goon who attempted to end her life, now struggling to breathe, eyes wide in surprise and confusion. His body convulsed as the sudden lack of oxygen sent him into shock.

Aella didn't recognize him, but it mattered little to her. He would die. Her fingers wrapped into a fist, and all air instantly drained from his body with the movement, killing him in less than a second.

A flurry of chaos erupted as his body hit the floor, unmoving.

"You psychotic witch," Lionel yelled, but his eyes went wide in fear as he struggled to stand, wiping the blood from his face on the back of a fattening hand.

He began to stalk toward her, but she could not move, her breathing coming out in short heavy gasps, unable to stabilize it. Her heart was beating so hard she felt as if it was going to implode in her chest as her vision began to blur and the voices around her became static noise.

"What is going on out here?" Karif's voice broke through the static, authoritative and loud.

Aella's wide eyes automatically found his gray stare, confusion lighting up his face before he controlled it once again.

"The dumb wench—" Lionel tried to explain.

"Get the hell out of here, Lionel. I'm not dealing with you today," Karif commanded. He wrapped an arm around Aella's middle and supported her weight as he brought her to the rickety stairs. Sounds of protest followed them, but she didn't have the strength nor energy to make them out.

Once they were within his office, he sat her down on the desk, closing the door and disallowing even his guards to follow. He planted both hands on either shoulder and said, "Breathe, Aella. Just breathe."

Her head was submerged underwater, silver hair splaying and floating around her as she struggled to breathe. A second before she would lose consciousness, her head was ripped from the iron tub by her hair.

"Use your power," Creaton commanded, his hand still tangled at the back of her small head. She looked up at him, her purple eyes pleading. She would deny him as long as her mind and body would allow her, the only act of defiance she could make. Without a word, he shoved her back into the water. Her throat burned in protest, her arms splaying out around her and fighting against the edge of the tub. She was pulled out again, the water sloshing out and spilling over her nightclothes.

"Use your power."

Aella's eyes pricked, and tears mixed with water as she looked at the six-year-old girl, the same age as her, she was supposed to use her powers to stop from breathing. The girl was shaking, her own face tear-streaked, curled up in the corner of the small bathroom. The cold tile wall could not have been much comfort. Aella never knew where he found these children to torment her with.

"I will not say it again," he warned. Her head was yet again submerged, her lungs struggling for oxygen. This time, when he pulled her out, she did as he commanded. Her fist closed, and the girl writhed in the corner, clutching at her throat until she stopped moving altogether. Aella watched the whole time, her violet eyes unblinking. When it was done, Creaton released her.

"Well done, but next time, it will be faster," he said as he left the room.

Her chest seized, her breathing becoming uneven as if she was underwater yet again. Eleven-year-old Karif slipped into the room, glancing at the unbreathing girl before kneeling in front of Aella.

"Breathe, Aella."

The world came crashing back around her. She took her breaths as Karif instructed, breathing in and out deeply. Her heart calmed its racing and Karif sighed in relief.

"I didn't know you still had those episodes," he said carefully, releasing his hold on her shoulders.

"I don't." And she was telling the truth. As long as she didn't call to her powers, she would not have any episodes. Until Petra's death, she had not used her power since Creaton died over four years ago. She had not even hesitated when she used her air to blow open the door, but since that moment, she lived in fear of it happening again and that this reaction would follow.

"I heard about your sister. I'm so sorry, Aella. I know how attached you had gotten." His gray eyes were soft and understanding, and Aella hated it.

"You know nothing." She turned her face away from him.

"I know you wouldn't come back here unless you needed to. What do you need?"

"I need to find who did this to Petra."

Karif titled his head, his arms crossed. "I've heard about you hunting the Cleansers down, but I don't think they did this."

"What do you mean? Who else would do this?" Aella stood and began to pace in the small space.

"The Cleansers weren't after the little one. If anything, they would have gone after the queen. It is her they didn't want on the throne."

Aella considered his words, agreeing with him. Instead of seeing the truth that was right in front of her, she let herself become reckless. Every time she thought of Petra, about her face so full of life, she wanted to burn the whole world down.

"Who did this?"

Karif shook his head. "I don't know, but I can put some of my men on it."

Aella nodded. "Thank you."

"A thank you? Wow, this princess life really has changed you," he teased.

"It has." Her words dripped with sorrow.

"You can always count on me, Aella. I have your back."

Without responding, she got off the desk and walked out of the office, leaving Karif to stare after her. She couldn't let herself continue to feel for people she was unable to protect. Petra was dead, Natalie betrayed her, and Cyra and Rheanna were in danger. Goddess only knew what the people of Linnosa would now face. The second she accepted the title of Head of Guard, their safety had become her responsibility. She had to keep Karif at arm's length, which was proving difficult to do. Even though a small part of her had always known that he was more to her than she was capable of acknowledging. Despite it all, she would protect her family and all she held dear, one way or another.

CHAPTER 45

ATLAS SAT ACROSS FROM Cyra in the receiving room, his head in his hands as she explained the events that took place leading to Ivan's death and the knowledge of who murdered Petra. Cyra didn't hold back and even explained the nature of her relationship with him and the way she tortured Natalie for his crimes. When she was done, he looked up, green eyes blazing. Cyra tried to hide the guilt from her face, imagining the way he saw her: a monster. She knew he must be ashamed of the other night.

He stood up, kneeling in front of Cyra so they were at eye level while she sat on the couch. He rested his palms in hers, giving her hands a squeeze. "I am sorry that happened to you."

Cyra reared back, at a loss for words.

"You have gone through so much in the last few weeks. It has not been easy but just know you have me now."

Tears welled in her eyes. "Thank you."

Atlas hesitated for a moment. "I have to tell you something. Or rather, show you."

Cyra waited for him to continue speaking, but he stood, pulling a clear crystal from his pant pockets and rubbing it between his hands as he began to speak a guttural, foreign language she didn't recognize. The room buzzed with electricity, a sweet smell filling it. A ball of golden energy formed within his hand, and where there was once only a crystal, now a blade laid. The crystal itself had taken on the shape of a dagger the size of Atlas' forearm as he lifted it for her to get a better view.

Cyra gasped, her hand flying to her mouth. "I thought you couldn't use your magic here."

Atlas' Adam's apple bobbed as he gulped. "I have been able to wield it since Petra's death. As a witch, my magic is tied to the earth."

If what he was saying was true, that means that maybe the rumors of the townspeople displaying Earth magic was true as well. They were not rumors at all. Cyra began to speak, about to voice her suspicions when Rheanna busted into the room. Her hair was in its usual braid, but loose strands framed her face, odd pieces sticking out on the top. Crystal-blue eyes wide and frantic, she held up the old leather journal that belonged to Selmana Hormanik. Between gasps she got out, "I found something."

Cyra jumped from where she was seated. "What's wrong?"

Interrupted yet again, a guard appeared behind Rheanna, a strange look on his face. "Queen Cyra, you have visitors."

Atlas, Rheanna, and Cyra all exchanged perplexed looks. It was too soon for the reinforcements, and Aella would have simply sauntered in. They all hurriedly followed the guard down the long hallway to the front of the castle. It was a particularly beautiful day in Linnosa, the windows all open, curtains fluttering with the early afternoon air. The daylight shined through the windows, casting the gilded walls in light.

Cyra's throat burned as she took in the two familiar figures standing in the entryway. Hollin's strawberry-blonde waves hung down to the small of her back now, and she stood at least two inches taller. Her little girl's emerald eyes lit up as she barreled toward her mother with what looked like white blossoms falling out of her hands.

"Mommy!"

Cyra gaped in horror but instinctively bent down to pick up her daughter.

"What's going on?" Rheanna's voice trembled, but Cyra ignored her. Her gaze was pinned on the old man she considered her father. Ron stood tall in his golden royal guard armor, his hand rested protectively on the sword at his side as he glanced around the hallway.

"Why did you bring her here?" Cyra's eyes were molten lava as they filled with tears.

Before Ron could answer, Hollin's small voice broke out in a cry. "You promised to come back for my fifth birthday."

"I know, baby. I am so sorry." Cyra patted her daughter's strawberry locks soothingly.

"Let's go somewhere more...er...private," Ron said gruffly.

Rheanna grasped Cyra's elbow and motioned for Ron and Atlas, who looked like he was barely even breathing, to follow her. She led them to her own rooms and bolted the door. She turned to face them all, falling against the door.

"Who are they?" Hollin said.

Rheanna's eyes flickered to Hollin then back to Cyra, saying nothing and waiting for her sister to respond to her. Atlas stood motionless beside Ron, a startled look on his face. Cyra took a deep breath, her fingers running through Hollin's hair.

"Rhe, this is my daughter, Hollin. Hollin, this is your Aunt Rheanna." She then turned, motioning toward Atlas. "This is Prince Atlas of Hefguard."

Hollin looked between Rheanna and Atlas, her lightly freckled face lighting up with joy and amazement. Cyra noticed that her ears were ever so carefully hidden away behind a pink colored scarf that matched the plain dress she wore. She silently thanked Ron for protecting her.

"Aunt Rheanna from your stories?" The little girl pushed from her mother's arms and went to stand in front of Rheanna, a look of pure awe on her freckled face. "You're beautiful." Rheanna knelt, eye level with her niece.

"Her eyes." She let out a harsh gasp, and Cyra immediately knew what she was seeing. Hollin possessed the emerald-green eyes of their late sister, Petra.

Before anyone else could respond, Hollin was onto the next stranger. Atlas bent down, and Hollin grabbed his cheeks, smooshing them in her small hands. He chuckled, his face growing red from the interaction. "Well, hello, little Hollin. You are just as pretty as your mom."

"You think my mommy is pretty?"

Atlas glanced at Cyra before responding, "Very."

Hollin's gaze narrowed on him. "Are you her boyfriend?"

Rheanna choked on a laugh and said, "She sure is an observant little thing."

Cyra shot a glare at her sister, but smiled at Atlas, whose eyes had grown as big as saucers. "He and I will be getting married."

Hollin gasped, letting go of his cheeks and turning toward Ron. "Did you know about this?"

Ron's face screwed into confusion while he said, "Of course not lil' Holli. I've been with yer."

The girl hummed and turned back to the prince, her arms crossing. "You are a prince?" Hollin's head tilted in question.

"Yes, I am. And you are a princess," Atlas' words made the little girl twirl toward her mother.

"Mommy! I'm a princess!" she declared and started clapping her hands, the same white flowers from before appearing between her hands and littering the floor with each clap.

Cyra rushed to her daughter, gently twisting her palms toward her. The blossoms continued to appear as if from thin air before falling. Atlas and Rheanna's mouths fell open in unison.

Hollin giggled. "Look at my pretty flowers!"

"It seems she has inherited more than just her eyes from Petra," Atlas exclaimed, a tiny grin on his face as he took in the little girl.

Cyra's mind raced as the pieces all came together. Hollin possessed earth magic. Atlas' earthbound power was working in Linnosa once again. The rumors of the citizens showing evidence of earth magic as well. But all of this, only after Petra, who earth magic alone was tied to, was killed.

Rheanna cleared her throat and then revealed, "The prophecy was not some farce, but truth. That is what I was trying to tell you before. It is all in here." She lifted Selmana Hormanick's journal. "Four shall emerge, but only one will rise, and the magic with her."

September 13, 989

Four shall emerge, but only one will rise, and the magic with her. The fourth babe was born today, on Lewellyn's day of death, and she has my Rowan's eyes.

She completes the four and sets the prophecy into motion. The king and queen didn't want a fourth child, despite the powers I made sure were bestowed on each of them, so I had to feed them a farce. A prophecy of how they would bless Linnosa.

But these sisters will destroy the kingdom. I will see to it.

ABOUT THE AUTHOR

Kayla Cosentino writes new adult and fantasy fiction while juggling college courses and spending her days as a high school English teacher. She is currently working on the sequel to *The Sisters Who Were Promised,* her debut fantasy novel. She received her Master of Fine Arts in Creative Writing and English at Southern New Hampshire University and is currently pursuing her Master of Education. She spends her free time reading, listening to heart-wrenching music, and binging Netflix. She resides in New Jersey with her three cats, Theo, Will, & Buffy, and mini dachshund, Tallulah.

www.kaylacosentino.com

author@kaylacosentino.com

www.ingramcontent.com/pod-product-compliance
Lightning Source LLC
Chambersburg PA
CBHW030242120726
47903CB00005B/1584